At the other end of the room was a workbench...

...with an assortment of woodworking and pottery tools scattered on top. There was a glisten in the corner caused by a small packet of gold leaf and a few bottles of rabbit glue. Neatly stored underneath were boxes of rubber mold sections, lengths of aged wood and, for lack of a better description, the skeletal remains of old frames. The body of the unfortunate man was propped up in the corner opposite the workbench. The bright lights in the room did little to diminish the eerie effect of his presence. The horror of the events that led to his sudden end lingered in his eyes, and his chalky white hand reaching out still sent shivers up their spines, despite the brave faces they put on for each other.

"Buck up, old man," Nigel said soothingly, laying his hand on Ernie's shoulder. "Those who knew this man will mourn him. We'll serve him best by establishing how and why this happened. Now, the inspector will be here soon, so it's important we identify and decipher any clues this room may hold, but be careful not to disturb the crime scene. He has a great respect for our work in antiquity, but he considers us nothing more than bothersome amateurs in ugly business like this."

ALONG CAME A Fifer...

by

R. MICHAEL PHILLIPS

An

Asylett Press
Publication

www.AsylettPress.com

Asylett Press

Edited by: Valerie J. Patterson
Senior Editor: Sandra Dugas
Acquisitions Editor: Fredrick Hunt
Cover Art by: R. Michael Phillips

ALONG CAME A FIFER
Copyright © 2009 by R. Michael Phillips
ISBN 1-934337-62-5

Asylett Press
www.AsylettPress.com

Published in the United States Of America
June 2009

Asylett Press
3616 Devils Three Jump Road
Little Plymouth, VA 23091

DEDICATION

To Janice and Christopher,
whose love and support guide my every word.

To Celeste,

I Hope you Enjoy
the Book.

Best Wishes

One

TEN QUID AND A BUS PASS

Ernie Bisquets. He blamed his lot in life on many things, but never on his name. To the contrary, it rolled off his tongue as if he were the mayor of London. Add to that the confident swagger in his walk and you have a gentleman who fits right in among the swells of Mayfair society. Thin and of medium height, he would greet friend or stranger alike with a wink and a nod. He was always impeccably dressed, with shoes polished and the day's paper tucked neatly under his arm. On a leisurely stroll through Grosvenor Square he might stop you for a light, commenting on the weather or a bit of business he thought you might find of interest. You would share pleasantries, even commend him for seeing your point of view on the latest headline, and then with a wink and a nod he would bid you good day.

Most people walked away feeling good about sharing a pleasant moment of their day with a new acquaintance. I'm sure a few even convinced themselves they had met before over cocktails at the club. Did he mention his name? No matter, you're quite sure you'll see him again on Bond Street or strolling through Berkeley Square. Ernie Bisquets had quite an effect on people, so it's no wonder it would be hours before you realized your wallet was missing.

Common pickpocket? Not Ernie Bisquets. He was anything but common. He spent time every day practicing his moves on a seamstress dummy, while refining his cockney accent into the proper vernacular of a West End gentleman. His skills as a pickpocket were unequaled, but he always sounded as if he was shaken out of the pages of a dime novel. On someone else this might appear a cheap deception, but on Ernie Bisquets it was as natural as a kitten's purr.

In the shadows of London, where others less skilled in his profession could be found, his name was whispered with respect. "Anybody can nick a purse at night in a crowd" they would say, "but it's a true artist what does it midday in Mayfair." And it was midday in Mayfair that Ernie Bisquets earned his reputation. He worked the same streets week after week, always taking the precaution to change his approach and appearance. Unlike others who would slip their hand in any stranger's pocket, he took his time, looking for just the right pigeon. He was against violence of any type, and being "blessed with the hands of a magician" he had no need for a weapon. A good week afforded him a few hundred pounds, and a great week topped a thousand. No matter what the take, he spent a few pounds on pints for his cronies at the pub on Friday night and put the rest away for the lean times.

Ernie waited patiently for the bus to London about a block away from Edmunds Hill Prison in Suffolk. His situation left him somewhat self-conscience, but he still maintained a cheery air about him as he boarded the bus. The trip into London was a brief twenty minutes with only a few stops along the way. Ernie occupied his time with thoughts of a more pleasant time in his life until the bus jerked suddenly to the left to avoid yet another American tourist looking the wrong way and then stepping off the pavement. It was enough to bring Ernie Bisquets back from the memories of his illustrious past and plant him firmly within his present situation as a newly released inmate from Edmunds Hill Prison. Looking out the window, he noticed they had passed Marble Arch and were going down Park Lane. A slight smile came to his haggard face as he brushed the dust from his sleeves and folded his hands back over his valise. It was almost eight months to the day that he last walked the streets of Mayfair and the West End. Had it not been for Lord Coats intervening on his behalf, he would have been obliged by the court to wait at least another ten. It seems fortune, after so long an absence, once again placed her hand upon his shoulder.

Lord Patterson Coats was HM Chief Inspector of Prisons at the time Ernie Bisquets was running the prison laundry in Edmunds Hill. It was a dripping soup ladle at lunch one autumn day that brought the two together.

"Pardon me," the chief inspector said, interrupting a conversation between two inmates in the prison laundry. "Could I bother one of you to remove this stain from my sleeve?"

"Give it here, Guv'nor," Ernie replied, motioning to the other inmate to get back to work. He recognized the older man before him—not by his face but by his uniform—as the chief inspector. "I see you were enjoying the navy bean," he continued taking the jacket from the inspector's hand and placing it on the counter. "That's Geoffrey Bard's specialty. 'E's our cook, you know. Thirteen years aboard one of Her Majesty's battleships, preparing meals for some of the most important people in the world...then 'e kills a man for putting too many carrots in his Shepherd's Pie."

"I remember that case," replied the chief inspector, following Ernie to a steam presser. "When they asked him why he did it he said '...because it spoilt the broth'."

Ernie looked up and laughed. "That's right, 'ere you go." He helped the chief inspector on with his jacket. "A littl' quinine, a quick press and Bob's your uncle."

"So, what's your story...Mr. Bisquets?" asked the chief inspector as he admired Ernie's work.

"Wrong place at the wrong time," he cautiously replied, somewhat surprised that the chief inspector knew him by name. "It was late and I couldn't sleep. I went out for a bit of air when all of a sudden this bloke comes round the corner and knocks me down! When I woke up, there was a blackjack and a billfold on the ground next to me, and three coppers standing over me. It didn't matter I didn't look like the bloke they were chasin', they just figured they didn't have to run anymore. I might have dodged it, but they found a banker's wallet I nicked earlier that day tied to a brick on a table when they searched my flat."

Ernie shook his head and walked over to the table by the door. "I should 'ave tossed that in the Thames when I 'ad the chance." He poked around in one of the drawers, finally pulling out a lint brush. "I'm not saying I don't belong 'ere," he continued, running the brush over the front of the inspector's jacket. "As I said, I've nicked a purse or two in my day, and I'm smart enough to figure one day I'd 'ave to pay the piper. I never used a weapon, and I *never* 'urt no one." Ernie tapped the brush lightly on the inspector's chest. "Sorry," he continued, motioning for the inspector to turn round. "Oh, I knows who knocked me down, but I've seen what 'appens when people cross that bloke. The way I see it, he did me a favor. I'll just do my time, and when I gets out, it's the straight and narrow for me." Stepping back around the front of the chief inspector, he took one last look at his work. "There you go, Guv'nor,' he said with a wink and a nod. "Good as new."

"Yes, I believe it is! Well, Mr. Bisquets, thank you for your assistance with this mess I've made. Maybe one day I'll be able to return the favor."

Ernie looked about the bus very proudly, as if to acknowledge to everyone it was the reason he now found himself on his way into London. A slight rain started to fall as the bus turned on to Curzon Street. It had been an unseasonably mild autumn so the planters adorning the street were still lush with color. Ernie Bisquets was enjoying his first hours of freedom, but becoming quite anxious about making a good impression with his benefactor. A left onto Berkeley Street, and then a quick stop by the square to take on passengers. Stretching out his neck—his head now half out of the window—he could see Bruton Street up ahead. It wasn't far now.

Nestling down into his seat, he drifted back into quiet contemplation. Ernie still couldn't believe his good fortune. Two days ago he'd been called to a review board for consideration of early release. It had been explained to him that after a review of his case, along with his exemplary behavior during his stay at Edmunds Hill, he was to be released to the custody of a local official. It was further understood that this was a work release for a period not to exceed the remainder of his sentence. Any breach of the conditions would find him back within the confines of Edmunds Hill.

"It seems you've acquired a new friend," the prison governor had quietly stated, passing the paperwork across a well-worn table to Ernie. "Chief Inspector Coats himself believes you worthy of a second chance. His term is up next week and it's in his service you'll be. You're a pleasant sort so I'll give you a bit of advice." He waited until Ernie had finished signing the papers, scooped them up and handed them to his file clerk. "Mind yourself and do as you're told and you'll make out just fine. He's an important man and friend to the Royals, so he won't be made a fool."

Ernie nodded and they both stood up. The governor shook his hand, wished him well, and handed him two envelopes. The smaller of the two had a note from Lord Patterson Coats as well as the address where he was to report upon his release. In the other he'd found 10 quid and a bus pass.

As the bus turned on to Bruton Street, he raised himself up from his seat, taking hold of the rail above his head to keep from falling into the woman across the aisle. The woman just smiled, likely thankful he didn't fall head first into what was soon to be that evening's meal.

He looked forward through the windscreen, squinting his

eyes to get a better look at the street ahead. Excusing himself, he worked his way forward, being careful not to bump anyone with his valise. They crossed over Bond Street and pulled over to the bus stop halfway up Conduit Street. The sun once again peeked through the clouds as the rain continued on its way up the street.

Ernie took the note from his pocket as he stepped off the bus. He paid little attention to the fact he was obstructing the flow of pedestrian traffic while he stood on the pavement holding his valise in one hand and fumbling to open the note with the other. After a shake or two, and a little help from the morning breeze, it was open. Though he had read the note over and over since receiving it, he read it one more time just to be sure.

> Mr. Bisquets,
>
> By now you know arrangements have been made for your release. I have volunteered as your sponsor, and will provide you with lodgings, a suitable situation, and a modest stipend to be paid twice monthly. You will stay in my employ for the remainder of your sentence of 10 months. Any breach of conduct befitting this situation will be dealt with immediately and without reprieve.
>
> So as not to taint my staff's opinion, and give you a fair go at it, I have omitted portions of your past, stating only that your background is as a valet. It is to your benefit, and with my approval and suggestion, to refrain from any mention of your incarceration at this time. Your arrival is expected on the morning of 4 October, at #81B Conduit Street, London W1S.
>
> Regards, Lord Patterson Coats

Glancing up, he saw he was in front of number 78 Conduit Street and he needed to get to number 81B. From a conversation he'd had on the bus that morning he knew it was a few doors "... before the shop where The Queen buys her knickers". Just ahead, he saw what looked to be the royal coat of arms above a small shop, so Ernie Bisquets tucked the note back into a pocket and continued up the street.

He stopped in front of a beautiful white limestone building, three stories high, with a stationery shop on the ground floor. A large *81* was painted on the glass in gold and trimmed in black.

This must be it, he thought to himself.

Putting his valise down, he took his lint brush—a small

souvenir of his stay at Edmunds Hill—from his pocket, and ran it over his sleeves. The dark wool suit he'd been furnished with was a bit worn, but the best the local charity shop had to offer in his size. He'd also received a new white shirt and a regimental stripe tie. While incarcerated he'd worn shoes supplied by the prison, so he'd walked out in the same shoes he'd walked in with—brown wingtips, barely broken in. Even though he'd spent his last hours at Edmunds Hill in the prison laundry, cleaning and pressing every thread of his suit, he gave it one last brushing just the same.

He took a deep breath, picked up his valise, and entered the shop. A portly little man who appeared to barely fit down the narrow aisles of the shop approached him. He had a round face with little eyes tucked neatly behind puffy red cheeks. His dark hair was two sizes too small for his head and a black mustache, that looked more like a boot brush, was two sizes too large for his face. "And what, sir," he asked, pulling a small pad and pencil from his waistcoat and leaning forward so as not to miss a single word of the order, "can we get you today?" His upper lip twitched a bit when he smiled as if trying to shake the boot brush loose from under his nose.

"Is this 81B? My name is—"

" No! No! No!" the man snapped back. "One more door up."

"Sorry. It's been a while since—"

"Yeah, yeah, yeah." The man dismissed Ernie with a wave of his hand and squeezed back down the aisle. "A bigger sign…that's what he needs…and you can tell him I said so!"

With a bit of a laugh he found himself on the pavement once again and noticed a doorway recessed slightly from the rest of the facades. It was a small, gothic style door, beautifully carved with a weathered coat of black enamel and polished brass fittings. To the right was an intercom with a small brass plaque above it. #81B was engraved in it and below the number, in smaller type, were the words—Second Floor—ELAC.

He pushed the button on the intercom and—from the windows above—he heard the faint ringing of the bell. With no response, and not giving himself a chance to get nervous, he waited only a moment then pushed the button once again.

"Who's calling, please?" a woman's voice crackled from the speaker.

"Ernie Bisquets."

Two

THE EAST LONDON ADVENTURERS CLUB

THERE WAS A harsh buzz and the door sprang open to a marble vestibule and a wide staircase in front of him, much wider than he'd thought possible compared to the doorway. He entered, closing the door behind him and ventured up the carpeted stairs. At the top, a very friendly, older woman greeted him. She was as round as she was tall, dressed in a gray uniform and white apron.

"I'm Annie Chapman. I'm the housekeeper here."

"Ernie Bisquets, ma'am," he replied, his attention captured by the vibrant colors of the Oriental carpet he stood on. The sunlight poring in from an etched glass dome in the ceiling high above shone on him like a spotlight.

"Well of course you are!" she replied with great enthusiasm, shaking his hand. She stepped aside, allowing him to enter the large foyer. The polished marble floors and gold embroidered silk wall coverings made clear he was no longer in Edmunds Hill. "We've been expecting you, we have. His Lordship was called away, but Nigel is here."

Ernie continued to look around nervously. To his right were two wide doorways—fluted pillars on either side with matching sideboards between them—obviously leading to other rooms. "Nigel?"

"Yes. I believe Lily is here, too."

His eyes continued around the room, surveying the numerous antiques and artwork, before returning to meet her gaze. "Lily?"

"Oh yes, Lily—the American. They'll both want to meet you, they will, but let's get you settled in your rooms first."

The grandeur of the flat was matched only by its size. Not only did it occupy the two floors above the stationery store, but it also appeared to include the two floors above the next store up on

Conduit Street. Still amazed that such an unassuming door below could lead to such a grand flat, he smiled at the woman. "Rooms?"

"Rooms?"

"Yes, rooms," she laughed. "You're a stitch, you are! Come on, grab your case and follow me."

"Sorry. You must think me a right proper fool," Ernie remarked, composing himself enough to utter more than just a single word. "There must be some mistake. I don't know what I was expecting, but this is more than I could 'ave imagined. Are you sure the Guv'nor wants me?"

"Don't be silly. All the arrangements were made, and here you are."

Ernie just scratched his head. "What did you say your name was?"

Mrs. Chapman waved her hand so he picked up his valise and followed her toward the stairs. A remarkably agile woman for her stature, it was all he could do to keep up with her. She stopped short in front of one of the doorways, leading to a very large room lined with bookcases. "Mr. Bisquets has arrived!" she hollered out as if selling fish, startling the two occupants in the room.

With a polite wave to acknowledge his presence in the doorway, they turned back to the table they stood by and the newspaper that apparently had captured their attention.

"We'll get him settled and have him back in time for lunch," she continued, cutting off any attempt of a proper introduction by pushing Ernie along toward the stairs.

"Off you go...oh, it's Mrs. Chapman."

"Mrs. Chapman?" Ernie responded, holding on to his valise for dear life as she pushed him up the stairs.

"My name...you did ask my name...Mrs. Chapman, but you can call me Annie." At the top of the stairs she steered him to the right and down a long hallway. "My rooms are one floor up" — she blushed — "but His Lordship suggested you take these."

"This is for me?" he whispered with great surprise, entering an opened door. This was far from what Ernie expected of servants quarters.

In front of him were marble-topped, walnut nightstands on either side of a matching poster bed. There were two large gothic doors on the wall to his left that opened to a wardrobe, flanked by bookcases filled with leather bound copies of literary classics. At the opposite end, facing a small tiled fireplace, was a seating area furnished with overstuffed chairs and illuminated by three large windows that looked out over Conduit Street. There were four obviously important works of art on the walls, framed and lighted from above.

"Well, of course, it's for you." Mrs. Chapman smiled. "We certainly can't have you sleepin' in the hall now can we? You've earned a right proper bed, you have. Just leave your valise by the wardrobe and I'll take care of putting your things away."

Ernie nodded and placed the case down next to the wardrobe.

Pointing to a small door next to one of the bookcases she quietly continued, "That's your private loo, there. You should clean up and get ready for lunch. His Lordship—and no finer man walks this earth—took the liberty of filling your wardrobe with proper attire." She took his arm, leaned close to his ear and whispered, "Leave this suit on the chair after you've changed and I'll see it gets to the local charity shop. It's a polite and handsome lad you are, so we don't want anything to take away from that."

A bit embarrassed, he nodded in appreciation for the care Mrs. Chapman was taking regarding his appearance. He understood now why she'd rushed him up the stairs.

"Thank you, mum, it's a kind woman you are to look after me like this. I'd like to thank His Lordship, too. Will 'e be back soon?"

"He's on The Queen's business you know…not sure when he'll be back…but he calls in as regular as tea at six. Look at the time!" She put her watch back in her apron pocket and turned towards the door. "I've got to start lunch so you get yourself cleaned up and down to the lounge by twelve," she said, and started off down the hallway. "You'll get a proper introduction then."

Looking at the clock on the mantle, he saw he had a little more than an hour before lunch.

He took off his suit coat and sat down on the bed to relax for a moment and collect his thoughts. It was a lot to absorb, especially compared to where he'd spent the last eight months. Was it a trick? Had they surrounded him with all these expensive trinkets to see if he really was rehabilitated? And what about Lord Patterson Coats not being here? Was he really off on The Queen's business or was he waiting down the street, ready to jump out and grab Ernie as he ran by with a painting under his arm?

Glancing around the room, he scratched his head and continued to question himself about his situation. Why would a man of such wealth and apparent position take an interest in a common reprobate? *What does he possibly have to gain? He can certainly afford the best valet in London, yet he chooses to hire the clerk in a prison laundry.* The more he thought about it, the clearer the vision became of seeing himself in the role of Elisa Doolittle, prancing about Conduit Street with a basket of fresh cut flowers. *Oh, wouldn't that be loverly?*

He resolved that it didn't matter whether or not the circumstances were as innocent as they appeared. He'd made himself the promise to go straight long before he met Lord Patterson Coats, HM Chief Inspector of Prisons, and it was a promise he fully intended to keep—no matter what temptation was placed before him. Giving it one last thought, though, there was something he was absolutely sure of—in a house this elegant, lunch couldn't be anything less than brilliant. With that thought in mind, he set about getting dressed for lunch.

He opened the wardrobe and found an assortment of broadcloth shirts, neatly folded on shelves to the right. There were five suits, one of which—a Harris Tweed—caught his eye and was chosen for the day. The required socks and under garments were in drawers to the left below a mirrored and leather topped shelf where personal items could be kept.

On the shelf, propped up on a hairbrush, was an envelope with his name written in a now familiar hand. Upon opening it he found £200 and a note. He walked over to the window, sat down in one of the chairs and, holding the note out to the light, began to read:

> *Mr. Bisquets,*
>
> *Please allow me to apologize for my absence. Had it been anything but a Royal request, I would certainly have been there for your arrival. Be the circumstances as they are, I have asked Mrs. Chapman to look after you and make the proper introductions to my nephew, Nigel, and our colleague Lily Corbitt.*
>
> *So you know, before my departure I had a discussion with Mrs. Chapman regarding the particulars of your past. She agreed there was no need to entertain that topic at this time, and will allude only to your situation in Suffolk as valet to a gentleman in service to The Crown. His recent marriage and your desire to return to London have brought you to my employ. This should satisfy any curiosity surrounding your past.*
>
> *Under normal circumstances you would be traveling with me, but for now it is best that you acclimate yourself to*

your new surroundings. Nigel will explain your duties and answer any questions you might have regarding the ELAC.

I hope to bring this matter that has my attention to a close within a fortnight, and return soon after. Until then, I leave you in capable hands. You will find £200 enclosed to cover any personal necessities I may have missed.

Regards, Patterson Coats

Rising to his feet Ernie neatly folded the note, placed it back within the envelope and tucked it under the socks in his drawer. What *ELAC* was still puzzled him, but he was sure lunch would bring answers along with the soup.

After cleaning up and dressing he did as Mrs. Chapman asked and left the wool suit folded on a chair by the door. With it he hoped that chapter of his life was also behind him. His dignity restored—and the Harris Tweed fitting as if it were tailored specifically for him—he made his way back down the hall to the main staircase. Taking a deep breath, Ernie paused at the top, preparing himself for whatever was to greet him in the lounge, and then stepped confidently down the stairs.

As he approached the doorway leading to the lounge, he heard voices in animated discussion. The female voice seemed to be dominating the conversation, leaving little room for the male voice to answer.

Peering in, he saw Nigel and Lily standing across the room by an Edwardian sideboard. The lounge was decorated as lavishly as the foyer, but softened by the addition of two comfortable sofas leading to a grand fireplace. The surround was limestone carved in the form of a medieval castle, with each level depicting different aspects of a bloody siege. A fire crackled behind stone lions who guarded the entrance. Ernie stood there silently with his fist raised, poised to knock on the pillar as soon as the opportunity presented itself.

"Well, go on!" whispered Mrs. Chapman from behind him, startling him. "They can go on like that for hours, they can. I'm sure Nigel will be very happy for the interruption."

"Excuse me, Guv'nor," Ernie started, clearing his throat and knocking softly on the pillar. "I'm—"

"Baskets!" Nigel exclaimed, grabbing hold of his interruption in an attempt to escape his current conversation. "And not a moment too soon. Ernie, isn't it?"

He held out his hand and crossed the room to where Ernie

was standing. Nigel was dressed very well in a tan suit and white shirt, but despite the exceptional abilities of his tailor there was something frumpish about his appearance. He was clean-shaven with thick locks of curly black hair. His young face was deceiving, as he was closer to forty than thirty, but he was possessed of a pleasant disposition and boyish charm. Black rimmed glasses, that rested low on the bridge of his nose, framed his deep blue eyes and gave him the appearance of a university professor. Just from the limited conversation he'd overheard, it was clear to Ernie this fellow was incredibly intelligent, if a bit cackhanded.

"Bisquets, squire. Ernie Bisquets."

"Of course, Bisquets." Nigel took his hand and shook it earnestly. "My uncle has spoken very highly of you...please, this way...and mentioned you were arriving today. This is our colleague, Lily Jean Corbitt."

Ernie followed him over to the table where Lily now stood, where he'd seen the two of them studying the newspaper earlier. The stern expression on her face softened to a smile as she put down the paper in order to shake his hand.

"Welcome. It's a pleasure to meet you."

"I'm sorry to interrupt, Miss."

"Oh, you're not interrupting," Lily replied, tossing a smug look in Nigel's direction, "but you did save *someone* from having to admit once again he was wrong."

Nigel grimaced. "I'm not wrong.

"And please don't misunderstand our arguing," Lily ignored his protest. "Nigel and I have been friends since Oxford, despite our differing opinions on just about every subject—"

"Except antiquities," Nigel interjected.

"Agreed, although dear Nigel is content to remain buried in the past whereas I find technology fascinating."

"Often to the extreme," Nigel regained the floor. "And this business at the Musee d'Orsay Monday night is nothing more than the fumbled robbery attempt of an old fool. You're giving this amateur far too much credit."

"Amateur?" Lily snapped back. "I doubt that. This was no old fool. He has us believe he scaled the wall and came down through the glass on the roof. I have to believe he had an intimate knowledge of the museum's alarm system and the routine of the guards because he breaks in when the guards are at the farthest end of the museum. Then he sets off the silent alarm in the central gallery and the motion sensor on the painting. The motion sensor alarm only rings in the Impressionist Gallery and it can't be heard in other parts of the museum. The secondary alarm that is also attached to the painting, and supposed to lock down all the museum doors when tripped, never went off. As a result the guards were unaware of the break in until the police arrived fourteen minutes after the first alarm went off. This was more than enough time to cut the painting from the frame and escape, yet they apprehended him five feet from where the painting was resting as if he was waiting for them. It begs the question, why didn't he run? He's dressed in baggy black nylon with his face blackened, making it impossible to discern his exact features. So, they hang the painting back on the wall and cart this fellow off. Then they arrive at the station and find the back of the police van empty. Your amateur vanished before they even found out his name! You're wrong Nigel, this was no fool's errand."

"Suffolk, wasn't it?" Nigel asked, dismissing Lily's sermon with a wave of his hand and turning his attention back to Ernie.

"Yes, squire, 'round Newmarket."

"Fine area, Newmarket...please, we're not that formal here, Nigel will be fine...but quiet compared to London, wouldn't you say?"

"Yes, very much. It feels very good to be back."

"So, tell us a bit more about your situation up there and..."

"I'll not have you standin' 'round gossiping while my soup gets cold," interrupted Mrs. Chapman. She pushed them along, one at a time, towards the other end of the room where a large table was set for lunch. "I'm sure Mr. Bisquets is famished after that long trip down from Suffolk. Why, I could hear the grumbling in his stomach on my way up the hall. And I'm sure he has lots of questions for you, haven't you, Mr. Bisquets? Now, off you go."

"She keeps our sheets to the wind, she does," Nigel laughed, pointing Ernie to a chair and pulling out another for Lily. "So, Bisquets, what would you like to know?"

"Well, I was wondering..."

"Yes, go on," Nigel eagerly replied, taking his seat at the foot of the table.

"...what's *ELAC*?"

"What! You mean you don't know?" Nigel gasped, making little effort to hide his pretended amazement.

"Pay no attention to him," Lily replied from across the table, rolling her eyes as she placed a napkin in her lap. "It's nothing so dramatic. We're the East London Adventurers Club."

Three

THE SOUP IS SERVED

"EAST LONDON ADVENTURERS Club?" Ernie asked, somewhat confused. He hesitated, and then what should have remained an unexpressed thought burst forth before he could stop himself. "But...this is Mayfair, the West End."

"Right you are, Bisquets," replied Nigel, starting to grin. "Originally, we were on Blackfriars Road, not far from the Southwark tube." Nigel continued, brushing at some invisible crumbs from around his plate. "Brilliant lodgings they were, too, but my uncle thought it best to relocate to a more surreptitious location...what with the threats...and eventual explosion..."

Ernie's eyes opened wide in amazement. He looked from Nigel to Lily and back to Nigel, hoping for some indication that they were having a bit of sport with him, but it never came.

A wonderful aroma had filled the room. They all turned and saw Mrs. Chapman standing at the kitchen door with her tray. "No sense dredging up that old business, now is there?" she said, giving Ernie a reassuring wink. She bustled over to the table and balanced her tray as she ladled out his soup. "It's his first day and you'll have him under the bed, you will. Besides, His Lordship—and no finer man walks this earth—wouldn't let a bit of harm come to any one of you, would he, Miss?" Mrs. Chapman paused before filling Lily's bowl.

"Right you are, Mrs. Chapman," Lily replied briskly, giving her bowl an eager, anticipatory sniff. "Mmm, Colcannon soup," she murmured.

Lily was an American, a little more than five feet tall, with an innocent farm girl smile. Her shoulder length red hair encircled her face, accentuating dreamy green eyes. Where other women would work for hours to make themselves beautiful, Lily's beauty was quite apparently natural. Well-tailored clothes hinted at the soft curves beneath, but Lily was strictly business and not a woman to be crossed. Despite her bickering with him, one could sense a deep fondness in her for Nigel, but it appeared unrequited.

"Yes. Yes. Right you are Mrs. Chapman," agreed Nigel, examining a trail of soup on his tie leading from the bowl to his chin. "Just a bit of bad luck, Bisquets, that's all. Nothing to be concerned about. Now, before we discuss your duties and apprenticeship with the Club, I'll give you a brief history."

Apprenticeship? Ernie raised a finger to interrupt, but noticed Mrs. Chapman shaking her head from across the room, indicating this was not the time to ask questions.

Ernie quickly snatched up a roll and held the basket out to Nigel. With an approving smile and her serving tray in hand Mrs. Chapman bumped open the door with her bum and disappeared back into the kitchen.

"Yes, good show," Nigel continued, taking a roll and passing the basket on to Lily. "It was during the Crimean War, the winter of 1855 I believe, when the seeds of the ELAC were sown. Not long after Balaklava...*Into the valley of death rode the six hundred...* and at the request of Her Majesty Queen Victoria, Lord Ambrose Coats was dispatched in secret to meet with Cavour in Sardinia. A military man himself, Ambrose understood the severity of Britain's position after that devastating battle and the ensuing winter. The *Risorgimento* was...would you like a bit more?"

Suddenly realizing the oration had stopped and the question was directed at him, Ernie looked up to see Nigel and Lily smiling at him—and the now empty bowl on his plate. "Sorry," he quietly sighed, sitting back upright in his chair and wiping the last remnant of soup from his chin. "I had a bit 'o nerves this morning and missed breakfast."

"Quite all right, Bisquets, Mrs. Chapman will be very pleased with your overwhelming approval of her soup. Now, where was I?"

"The *Risorgimento*," Lily whispered as she returned to buttering her roll.

"Yes, thank you." Nigel pushed his chair back from the table. "The *Risorgimento* was forging Italy out of a group of independent Italian States and Cavour was one of the chief proponents of the struggle. The Queen explained to Ambrose the need to protect Britain's identity with regard to Sardinia entering the war, so

Ambrose explained this to Cavour along with the advantage of having Great Britain as an ally in *his* struggle. In January of that year, Sardinia declared war against Russia, and brought much needed supplies and support to the allies."

"I'm sorry," Lily burst forth in laughter. "Every time he tells this story and mentions Sardinia I think of the Marx brothers. You know, that movie where Groucho is the governor of—"

"With additional help from Florence Nightingale," Nigel interrupted, shooting a stern look at Lily, "and not the Marx brothers, by spring the allied armies were bearing down on Sevastopol, and by the end of summer the Russian Bear had been brought to his knees. Ambrose Coats quietly received the Victoria Cross for his service to the crown and the East London Adventurers Club was chartered a year later."

Mrs. Chapman had returned to clear the soup bowls from the table as Nigel rose from his chair and walked over to the breakfront behind him. "For the entire reign of Queen Victoria, Britain was at war somewhere in the world, so the East London Adventurers Club was called on from time to time to handle delicate matters for Her Majesty. For generations now we have assisted the reigning monarch in matters of state when discreet inquiries were the prerequisite." He took out a bottle of sherry and three small glasses from a locked cabinet and brought them back to the table.

"For the most part," he continued, filling each glass and handing one to each of them, "we engage in locating artifacts for the museums in London. It explains our appearance in different parts of the world when we are called on to handle 'delicate matters'." Nigel raised his glass and motioned to Lily to do the same. "Welcome, Ernie Bisquets, to the East London Adventurers Club!"

"Thank you, squire," Ernie replied with a smile, still a bit confused yet feeling more at ease in his new surroundings. "You mentioned duties?"

"Yes, very good." Nigel placed his glass down on the table in front of him. "Your situation as valet is one more of assistant than servant, the details of which I will leave to my uncle upon his return, and to say I believe you will find him less demanding in that regard than your previous employer should suffice."

Ernie nodded to indicate he understood, hesitated, and then asked, "What did you mean by apprenticeship?"

Lily placed her hand on Nigel's sleeve, indicating her desire to answer the question. Pushing her plate forward, she leaned over the table toward Ernie and in a hushed tone began, "Patterson Coats believes you're possessed of certain skills, skills that could prove invaluable in our endeavors." With a wink and a smile she sat back in her chair. "Of course, your participation in our activities is purely voluntary, but something we hope you will give serious consideration to."

"We won't be breakin' the law, will we?"

"Breaking the law?" Nigel exclaimed with a laugh. "I would say not! Our service to The Crown is to assist in upholding the law, at times maybe in unconventional ways, but nonetheless, on the side of the law. Our only caveat is that we operate with discretion when on The Queen's business," he continued, in a more serious tone. "You understand that the information you acquire within these walls must not go any further than our group. There are those who, in an attempt to embarrass The Crown, would deliberately misconstrue the facts and our intentions. Our day-to-day activities with antiquities are the exception, but caution should still be the order of the day."

"So, you're a secret society?" Ernie asked curiously.

"Nothing so mysterious," Lily replied, finishing her sherry and placing the glass near Nigel. "You'll find Nigel has a flair for the dramatic when it comes to the ELAC. Just think of us as private rather than secret."

"Yes, quite," Nigel responded to Lily with a smirk as he refilled her glass. "Well, Bisquets, what do you think so far?"

Before he could answer, the door to the kitchen swung open and Mrs. Chapman appeared once again, this time with a tray of tea and warm scones. "He thinks a bit 'o clotted cream with these scones would be just right, don't you, Mr. Bisquets?"

"Yes, thank you, mum, that would be very nice indeed."

"Mrs. Chapman is right," Lily said, placing a scone on her plate. "We need to give Ernie a chance to catch his breath and digest all this information. I'm sure this is all a bit overwhelming. Maybe as a diversion after lunch we can get his opinion on that article in the newspaper we were discussing about the Musee d'Orsay?"

"Brilliant!" Nigel exclaimed, wringing his hands in anticipation of what he seemed to think would be support for his conclusions on the matter. "You'll see, Lily Jean Corbitt, that was nothing more than a buggered attempt at robbery."

Ernie smiled, continued to enjoy his scone and listened politely as Nigel and Lily bickered back and fourth over whose deductive skills rivaled that of Holmes himself. He found it more than interesting as they bandied about details of previous matters the ELAC was involved with. Some he remembered reading about in the newspaper at the time, others were so sensational he was astonished he hadn't read anything at all about them. But they all had one thing in common, never was there a mention of the East London Adventurers Club in any public statement of the matters.

"Beggin' your pardon, sir," Mrs. Chapman interrupted, surprising all of them with her sudden presence at the table. "There's a Lady Constance Beckett in the foyer. Says her uncle's missing." She leaned close to Nigel and in a concerned voice continued, "The poor lass seems very upset about it. Been cryin', she has, from the look of those eyes. Should I show her in?"

"Yes, yes, by all means," Nigel said, rising from his chair and indicating they would retire to the sofas by the fireplace.

"Maybe I should leave you to your work," Ernie said, excusing himself from the table.

"*Our* work." Nigel replied. "You're in it now Bisquets." Nigel smiled, slapped Ernie on the shoulder and continued in a lower tone so as not to be overheard, "And I can tell by the look on your face you sense something is amiss here, too. We're not a detective agency, poking about in the shadows, peeping through keyholes and such. So, why would this troubled woman ring the bell at 81B Conduit Street? Is her presence here just happenstance? Even that irritating little man in the stationery shop below has no idea who we are or what we do. It seems that nonsense about the Musee d'Orsay will just have to wait until we find out who Lady Constance Beckett is and why a missing uncle would bring her to the East London Adventurers Club. Ah, here she is now."

Four

A LADY AT THE DOOR

M Y DEAR WOMAN," Nigel began with a start, stumbling across the room, "you're trembling." He took her hand and escorted the woman to one of the sofas. Nigel's efforts assisting her to the sofa, albeit noble, were superfluous, as she moved with a determined gait. It was difficult to discern who was leading whom, and for that matter, with what intention.

Still clutching her hand, Nigel sat down on the edge of the cushion next to her. "Please, Mrs. Chapman, a drink of water for our guest. A deep breath now, you're amongst friends here. Mrs. Chapman will be back in an instant, so take a moment to compose yourself."

Ernie seated himself on the sofa across from them and pushed the box of tissues on the coffee table toward the woman. She nodded in appreciation, taking one and dabbing at the corners of her eyes.

Lily returned a soft, reassuring look each time the woman glanced over at her, but she gave no indication if she'd quite made up her mind about the intentions of their guest. She quietly sipped at her sherry as she stood behind the sofa where Ernie was seated.

"Please forgive me for interrupting your meal," she said considerately, struggling to hold back more tears. "My name is Constance Beckett and I must speak to Patterson Coats."

Lady Constance Beckett was a tall, striking woman with aquiline features. She wore a broad-brimmed, black straw hat with a white silk band that covered most of her short, black hair. An ermine trimmed coat, partially concealing a white silk blouse, protected her from the weather, and a long black skirt hinted at the black leather boots beneath. Her dark eyes twinkled from the tears. There was a hint of pink in Lady Beckett's high cheeks, but the red of her lips was the only other trace of color to be found. Her commanding presence notwithstanding, she was remarkably soft spoken.

One could sense an unexpected event was the cause of her sorrow and abrupt arrival, yet her countenance nagged at an agenda. Whatever the reason, she succeeded in capturing their complete attention as they eagerly anticipated the details surrounding Lady Constance Beckett's appearance on the sofa, by the fireplace at 81B Conduit Street.

Mrs. Chapman had returned with a glass and a pitcher of water. "Will there be anything else, sir?" she asked, placing the tray on the table that separated the sofas.

Nigel looked to Lady Beckett for direction on any additional needs, but both agreed this would suffice.

"Thank you, Mrs. Chapman," Nigel replied, "I believe we're much better now."

"Yes, thank you," Lady Beckett repeated. "I'm afraid I'm not myself and it is so very kind of you to see me like this. Is Lord Coats at home?"

"I'm afraid His Lordship has been called away on an urgent matter," responded Nigel soothingly, "but I'm Nigel Coats, his nephew. Is there any way I can be of some assistance to you in his absence?"

"I don't know," she replied, obviously a little disappointed. "It never occurred to me he wouldn't be here."

"I don't want to appear indelicate to your situation," interjected Lily politely, yet underlining the importance of the question, "but what led you to believe he *would* be here?"

"Where are my manners!" said Nigel sharply, jumping to his feet and startling the others. "Please allow me to introduce my associates," He walked round the sofa to where Lily was standing. Placing one hand on Lily's shoulder and the other on Ernie's, he continued. "This is Miss. Lily Corbitt and Mr. Ernie Bisquets."

"How do you do," Lady Beckett replied kindly, nodding at each in turn and managing a slight smile.

Nigel continued on around the sofa, stopping in front of the fireplace. "With respect, Lady Beckett, Lily does raise an interesting question." He nudged the logs with the poker, causing the fire to flare up, then placed a fresh log on top of the embers.

The fire tended to, Nigel completed his stroll by sitting back down next to Lady Beckett. "We're a private club, or business, if you wish, of very little relevance or interest, save to the curators of a few London museums. Patterson Coats is the president of the club and only recently relocated us here to Conduit Street. I've traveled a great deal with my uncle and to the best of my knowledge we've never met, nor can I remember him ever mentioning your name. You say you've come to ask his help over this matter of a missing uncle, so I hope you can understand our surprise." He looked over at Lily, raised an eyebrow and finished, "And I can assure you it's surprise, not suspicion."

"Of course," said Lady Beckett, appearing much more composed. "I quite understand your confusion. I'm here because of this." She searched about in her purse for a few moments, eventually pulling out a small card and a folded piece of paper.

She handed the card to Nigel. He recognized it immediately as his uncle's calling card. On the back, written in his uncle's hand, was their address.

"It was in Paris," she began, loosening her coat and settling back into the cushions of the sofa, "and quite by chance, that I met your uncle. I was attending a benefit Tuesday evening, where I was to meet my Uncle Jacques. He's not really my uncle, but a very close friend of the family since I was a little girl. My parents will be gone five years this December, so Uncle Jacques is the only family I have left. He has a small business, restoring antique frames and mirrors, and it occupies much of his time. Without exception, we make arrangements to meet once a month. It's something I look forward to and can always count on.

"Just last week he mentioned he was expecting to be in Paris Monday and Tuesday of this week for business. When I told him I was attending a hospital benefit at the Musee d'Orsay on Tuesday, Uncle Jacques insisted we make arrangements to meet. We share a passion for fine art, so I thought it a lovely idea to meet at the museum last night and then return to London today by train. He agreed, and I was so looking forward to seeing him. I waited all evening at the benefit, but he never arrived."

Emotion once again overtook Lady Beckett and she struggled to regain her composure. "I'm sorry. I called his studio a number of times, but with no answer. It's not at all like him to go missing or break a promise. Uncle Jacques is older, and I worry so about his health."

"That's quite understandable," replied Nigel. "The museum is very large. Is it possible he was just unable to locate you in the crowd?"

Lady Beckett shook her head. "He has done a great deal of work for the Musee d'Orsay, so he is very familiar with the layout. I walked through each gallery with the hope of finding him, but to no avail. It was on my third time through—and near the end of the evening—that your uncle approached me and introduced himself. He apologized for intruding but said he couldn't help but notice I was extremely upset. I explained what was causing my anxiety and he very kindly offered his comfort and assistance.

"After completing our search of the galleries, and at Patterson's suggestion, I called my hotel to enquire about messages. The desk clerk informed me a message had been left for me earlier that evening. Your uncle was kind enough to escort me back to my hotel where I was given this note."

Lady Beckett unfolded the piece of paper and handed it to Nigel. He read it quietly to himself and then handed the note to Ernie. "What do you make of this?"

> *Dear C,*
> *Sorry, my plans changed.*
> *Please forgive my feeble old mind.*
> *I'll call,*
> *J*

"Seems a fair explanation," Ernie replied after reading the note out loud and handing it up to Lily. "So, he hasn't called?"

"No, not at all, and I have been to his studio a number of times, but without result. Patterson offered his assistance if I was unable to locate Uncle Jacques today. He suggested I contact him and then wrote his address on the back of his card."

"Well, that certainly explains it," said Nigel contently, "and let me assure you we join Patterson in his concern for you and the wellbeing of your uncle. I'll be talking to him this evening, and I will explain the current state of your situation."

Lily handed the note back to Nigel. "I'm sorry, Lady Beckett, but have the police been able to shed any light on his disappearance?"

"No," said Lady Beckett, without hesitation. "And I would rather not bring them into this if possible."

There was a very awkward pause.

"If that is your desire," Nigel said breaking the silence. "And unless evidence of foul play is turned up, we will respect your wishes."

"If you must know," Lady Beckett directed her remarks to Lily, "my uncle has not always been on the right side of the law. He's never been proud of his past and he gave up that life many years ago. I just want to find him without embarrassment, or casting undo suspicion on him."

"You mean in light of the attempted robbery at the Musee d'Orsay?" Lily pressed.

"I'm sure your uncle had nothing to do with that business," Nigel interrupted in an aggravated tone, also responding to Lily's skepticism. "And with that aside, may I inquire, during the time you spent with my uncle did he mention anything about how our time is usually engaged?"

Lady Beckett gazed at Nigel with repose. "He explained briefly that you deal in antiques."

"Yes, quite right," said Nigel, taking a small pad and pen from his pocket. "We deal primarily with locating antiquities, but we are not without resources in other areas. Where does your uncle have his studio?"

"There is a small alley across from St. Paul's off Ludgate Hill," Lady Beckett said, watching Nigel take notes. "I'm not sure of the number, but it is on the right hand corner, at the end. He has the third floor loft. Here, I've put his telephone number on the back of this card."

"I know that place, but..." Ernie paused, sensing it might be to his benefit to finish this thought later as he caught the attention of both Nigel and Lady Beckett.

"Go ahead, old man," coaxed Nigel, "You know that place, but...?"

Ernie recovered enough to fabricate an unassuming ending for the sentence and change the subject. "I know that place, but I never 'ad much reason to spend time there. Did you mention your uncle's last name?"

"Millet, Jacques Millet," Lady Beckett said, returning her attention to Nigel.

"Thank you." Nigel replaced the pad in his pocket. "I will make a few inquiries regarding your uncle's whereabouts and ring you tomorrow. Let us agree to contact each other before then should any pertinent information present itself. As I mentioned earlier, I will speak with my uncle this evening about this matter. In the meantime, and as difficult as I'm sure this must be, you should return home and wait patiently for word from your Uncle Jacques or from us."

"Yes, perhaps you're right." Lady Beckett stood and buttoned up her coat.

Nigel noticed Mrs. Chapman loitering in the foyer and he waved her in. "Mrs. Chapman will see you out," he said after Ernie and Lily had bid Lady Beckett good day. Without another word she followed Mrs. Chapman to the foyer.

Ernie opened his mouth to speak but was cut off by a wave of Lily's hand. It took a moment but he finally understood why when he noticed Nigel peering through the curtains down at the street to verify Lady Beckett's departure. Nigel turned back with a pensive look, walked over to the sideboard and began sifting through the newspaper.

"Here it is," Nigel said quietly to himself. He picked up a section of the paper and began to read the highlights of an article out loud as he walked back over to the fireplace. "Let me see...*attempted robbery at Musee d'Orsay...older man of average appearance...apprehended at the scene...Police baffled...disappeared before being questioned...'The Fifer' by Manet not harmed...museum officials relieved.* Lily, there is a slight chance you could be right about this museum business, after all."

"Slight chance? There's a *slight chance* you're an idiot."

Ernie did his best to hide his laughter, but he found the situation far too comical to contain his amusement. "Sorry, squire. I'm not..."

"That's quite all right, Bisquets," replied Nigel.

"And if you're not quite sure about Nigel being a pompous ass, I'll be more than happy to detail his qualifications."

"The two of them sound like an old married couple, don't they Mr. Bisquets?" remarked Mrs. Chapman who had returned and was busy clearing the table from lunch. "You're going to give Mr. Bisquets the wrong impression."

"Quite right, Mrs. Chapman," answered Nigel. "Lily. Ernie. My apologies to you both."

"I'm sorry, too," added Lily, as she and Nigel sat down across from each other on the sofas. "So, you agree there is more to this business at the museum than what the newspapers' report? I'm not sure how she fits into this whole thing, but I think Constance Beckett knows more than she's reporting, also."

"You could be right, Lily. Either she truly believes his disappearance and the robbery attempt are just a coincidence, or she realizes he has slipped back into his old ways and she wishes to find him before he becomes a suspect. I'll be very interested to hear what my uncle has to say about Lady Beckett and this museum business."

"Ernie," Lily mused, "you were about to say something before, but changed your mind rather abruptly. You mentioned your familiarity with the alley by St. Paul's, but never quite finished your *original* thought."

"That's right, Miss," Ernie replied cautiously. He knew her question was relevant to the discussion about the visit by Lady Beckett, but he was reluctant to reply for fear of revealing details of his own past. However, with respect to the trust Patterson Coats placed in him, he dismissed his reluctance and continued. "Not only the alley, Miss, but I'm familiar with the very building she mentioned. Seems there's an old forger what lives there. The lady's right, he makes a modest living restoring frames, but for the right price he'll include a fine piece of art. I knows of a few occasions when he's been questioned about a forgery, but no charges were ever brought against 'im. She said he's on the right side of the law, but I guess that depends on which side of the fence you're standing. In polite society he may be known as Jacques Millet, but I knows 'im as Jackie Miller."

"Patterson was right about you." Lily smiled.

"Apparently he was," Nigel agreed, visibly puzzled over the source of such knowledge. "How did you…"

The ringing of the telephone in the foyer interrupted Nigel's thought.

Mrs. Chapman entered the room. "Pardon me, sir, his Lordship is on the telephone for you."

"Excellent!" Nigel jumped to his feet and followed Mrs. Chapman out of the room.

"Don't worry about Nigel," Lily said with a reassuring smile once she and Ernie were alone. "It doesn't matter how you come about information. What matters is what you do with the information once you have it. Ernie Bisquets, I think you're going to like this side of the fence."

A smile slowly came to Ernie's face. He was a bit alarmed that his past didn't appear to be a complete secret but relieved that, at least to Lily, it was of no concern.

From the foyer they could faintly hear Nigel on the phone with his uncle. Their conversation drifted off to lighter channels as they waited patiently for his return to hear what Patterson Coats would shed on this business.

Five

NEWS FROM PARIS

A T A TIME when a mobile phone and voice mail are the preferred forms of communication, Nigel was quite satisfied with the reliability of the telephone on the hall table and Mrs. Chapman to answer the calls. It wasn't that Nigel was a philistine, but just that he regarded his daily needs the tortoise to technology's hare. He had a mobile phone, but those who knew him knew there was no sense calling it because Nigel would never think to answer it, or for that matter, even have it with him. He valued his time and committed it completely where needed, and that only after careful consideration. If for no better reason than to prove Pavlov wrong, he was not about to surrender his privacy to any one at the ring of a bell. This he considered his silent protest to a world growing ever smaller and continuing to spin out of control.

Nigel picked up the receiver from the hall table. "Hello, Uncle? I didn't expect to hear from you so early in the day." He sat down on the chair next to the table.

"I'm sorry if I'm interrupting, but I'm not sure how my afternoon is going to go, so I thought now a good time to check in."

"Oh, it's quite all right, we were just entertaining an acquaintance of yours...Lady Constance Beckett."

"Very good!" came the spirited reply. Patterson was not known for any outward show of emotion, so Nigel was convinced her arrival at their door must have a greater significance than just a women in search of a missing uncle. "She lost no time in securing our assistance, did she?"

"Apparently not. She arrived just as we were finishing our lunch. Not to appear naive, but I must admit I was taken in by her apparent grief. Ernie didn't say much during the visit, but Lily was determined to—"

"Oh yes, Ernie Bisquets," Patterson interrupted. "Sorry, but that was another reason for calling early. I'm very happy he arrived. Has Mrs. Chapman got him settled in?"

"Yes, but he seems a bit overwhelmed by everything. I assume this to be quite a different household than he was accustomed to in Suffolk, but nothing he can't get used to. He's quiet and polite, I like that, and when he does speak it has relevance. I know how you think, Uncle, so I am quite sure there is a specific purpose to his employ?"

"You know me very well indeed, Nigel. Ernie is very reserved about himself, but he has entrusted me with an intimate knowledge of his past. I have assured him that information will remain private until he feels comfortable enough to share it with you. He is pretty sharp though, so I am sure he has figured out by now it's the diversity of his background I intend to leverage."

"He did seem a bit confused about his role here, but between Lily and I, we have laid out the basic structure of our activities without going into too much detail. Bisquets appeared receptive and his only comment was asking for an assurance from us that we were not going to involve him in any unlawful acts."

"I'm very happy to hear that," said Patterson with a quiet, satisfying laugh. "I believe Ernie Bisquets will prove himself invaluable to our organization, much the same way you and Lily have. Now about my new acquaintance, you were saying…?"

"Oh yes. Lady Constance Beckett. She does seem very troubled by the disappearance of her uncle, but Lily is less than convinced of her motives."

"I agree. When we met at the Musee d'Orsay, she seemed quite angry—not concerned, as she would have us believe—that her uncle wasn't there. I believe they had arranged to meet at the museum, but not for a pleasant evening of wine and art."

"So, you believe these two and the attempted robbery are related in some way?"

"For now, let me say I have my suspicions. There have been a few new developments concerning the attempted robbery, but I am not at liberty to divulge them at this time. I'll know more when I speak with the curator later this afternoon. Meanwhile, has Lady Beckett given you any indication where you might look for her uncle?"

Nigel pulled the card from his pocket. "As a matter of fact, she gave me the address of his flat here in London. It's in the alley across from St. Paul's. I'm not familiar with it, but Bisquets tells me he knew of an old forger named Jackie Miller who lived down that very alley."

"Well, there you have it," responded Patterson with a laugh. "It appears Ernie has jumped right in and uncovered what could turn out to be an important piece in this puzzle."

"Lily and I are going up there to have a look later today. I wasn't going to include Bisquets because I felt plunging him that deeply into our work didn't seem prudent at this time."

"To the contrary, I believe it will help establish the intent to which he plans on contributing to our activities. He has the background and certain skills that can be utilized in our endeavors, but it's his decision alone to travel down this road. If he's to be one of us, he needs to make the commitment, and he needs to make it of his own volition. I have presented him with the opportunity, so let's see what he does with it. I think he is capable of more than just being a valet. If you would, please ask him to join you this afternoon."

"Very good. I'll take care of it when we're done here."

"Thank you Nigel, I can always count on you. Now, when will you be speaking to Lady Beckett again?"

"Tomorrow," Nigel replied, after thinking about it for a moment. "Yes, I told her I would ring her tomorrow. Can I relay any message from you?"

"No, and it would be best if she thought me removed from any inquiries into the whereabouts of her uncle."

"That's easily accomplished. We told her you had been called away suddenly on an urgent matter so we will continue the charade."

"Brilliant!" Patterson said briskly. "I believe you can relay a message for me, then. Please give Lady Beckett my apologies for being called away and my assurance that she can rely completely on you, as I do."

"Thank you, Uncle. Should I ring you later after we return?"

"I think it might be interesting if I ring Ernie later for the update. I haven't had an opportunity to speak with him since our last meeting in Suffolk and I'm sure he must have a few questions for me. And if you wouldn't mind, mention to him I would be very interested to know what he thought of the note Uncle Jacques left for Lady Beckett. If I'm correct about Ernie Bisquets, I think you'll be very surprised by his answer."

"I'll do just that."

"Then it's settled." Patterson hesitated for a moment before continuing in a more solemn tone. "There is one more thing, Nigel. I fear the people involved in this affair are not as docile as they would have us believe. Trust no one and take every precaution for your safety and that of Lily and Ernie. You and I will talk again tomorrow."

Nigel said goodbye and returned to the lounge. Lily and Ernie were very eager to hear what Patterson had to say, especially his thoughts regarding Lady Beckett. Nigel wasted no time conveying the essential points of the conversation and concluded much the same way his uncle had, with a warning for their safety.

Lily took the warning in stride. Why should this business be any different than anything else they've done?

Ernie, on the other hand, looked about the room with some trepidation, convinced the impending danger was peering out from the shadows and sizing him up for a fitting end. His nervousness didn't go unnoticed by the others.

"It's quite all right, old man," said Nigel soothingly. "You'll find my uncle has a flare for the dramatic, and things are never quite as dire as he portrays them. Besides, Lily is tough as nails and just as sharp."

"He's right, Ernie," Lily replied, returning Nigel's haughty smile with a contemptuous one of her own. "Not about me, but about the level of danger with our current situation. We have Lady Beckett's tale of woe and Patterson's insight on what happened at the Musee d'Orsay. Neither of these appear to be posing much of a threat at this time, so why don't we dig a bit deeper and see if we can separate the fact from fiction."

"Excellent idea," Nigel agreed briskly, stretching his neck out in the direction of the foyer to see if Mrs. Chapman was within earshot. "Mrs. Chapman? Are you there? We'll be leaving for a while and should return close to supper."

"No need to shout." Mrs. Chapman peeked her head around the pillar in the doorway. "Mind your time. I'll be making Cornish pasties and serving them promptly at seven, so it'll be bubble n' squeak for the lot of you if you're late. Mr. Bisquets, I'm counting on you to keep them to the task."

"Sorry, mum, but I don't believe I'll be—"

"Nonsense, Bisquets," Nigel interrupted, slapping Ernie on the knee. "We wouldn't think of going without you. As fortune would have it, Mrs. Chapman, Bisquets knows the place, so we'll be there and back in no time at all."

"It's been a while, squire," Ernie replied hesitantly. "It's not a bit hard to find, at all, and I'm sure I'd just be in the way."

"Not at all, Ernie," Lily chimed in with enthusiasm. "I think having a third opinion will be refreshing. Besides, this will give you a nice insight into our little club."

"Miss Lily makes a very good point," Mrs. Chapman interjected, and then disappeared back into the kitchen.

"I believe she does," agreed Nigel. "When I mentioned to my uncle we would be venturing over to St. Paul's to take a look about, he presented a similar *raison d'être*. He mentioned he would ring you this evening for an update. He feels quite guilty about his absence and thought this would give him the opportunity to express his apologies personally, and see how you were getting on."

"That's very kind of 'im, it is," replied Ernie sincerely. "I'm still a bit overwhelmed at everything that's happened to me in the last few weeks, but I know I owes my good fortune to His Lordship. I'd be a right proper fool if I didn't show my gratitude for what he's done for me. It's a bit queer this bird and her missing uncle. If Jackie Miller has his hand in the soup, as well, we're in for a bit of a treat. If you don't think I'd be a bother, I think I would like to go along with you."

"Good show old man." Nigel gave Ernie a nod of approval.

"Yes, I quite agree," responded Lily, seeming just as pleased with the decision. "I'll just get my camera and we can go."

"There's an extra Mack in the closet over there," Nigel said, pointing across the room. "I'll just get mine and when Lily returns we'll hail a cab and be on our way."

As Ernie was getting the Mack from the closet, Lily returned with her coat and camera in hand. Nigel came walking back in from the foyer waving the note Lady Beckett had given him.

"I almost forgot" — Nigel, handed the paper to Ernie — "I know I showed you this earlier but my uncle seemed very interested in what you really think it means."

Ernie unfolded it and read it aloud once more.

> *Dear C,*
> *Sorry, my plans changed.*
> *Please forgive my feeble old mind.*
> *I'll call,*
> *J*

Ernie handed it back to Nigel and helped Lily on with her coat. "Well," he started, looking from one to the other, "if he is just a dotty old uncle, I'd say the note is perfectly innocent and she should be hearing from him any day now. But if there are sinister forces at work here, the note tells a different story. If you read every third word it says 'Sorry…changed…my…mind…J', and that, squire, smells like a double-cross."

"Remarkable." Nigel scratched his head and reread the note. "Just remarkable. What do you think of that, Lily?"

"I think Patterson knew just what he was doing when he invited Mr. Bisquets to join our little club."

With a big smile, Lily took Ernie by the arm and the three of them were ready to head off to St. Paul's.

Six

REKINDLING AN OLD FRAME

THE WEATHER WAS overcast and cold in Paris that afternoon Patterson Coats was meeting with Marie Bussière, the acting curator of the Musee d'Orsay. He was a close friend of Bussière and someone she had called on in the past to handle delicate matters for the museum. He traveled in the right circles and over the years had secured the confidence of those around him through his discretion and extraordinary abilities in bringing the most puzzling of transgressions to a successful conclusion. His social standing afforded him access through many doors and commanded the attention and cooperation of those he spoke with. So, to the people and institutions that sought his services, having Patterson Coats in control of the situation also assured tight management of the information related to the problem. His calculated release of details assured them the public would be informed of the result without the public embarrassment of the problem being drawn out for weeks in the papers.

To some, the embarrassment of the affair was a far greater crime than the crime itself. To those people, the final punishment affords little or no satisfaction, and for what satisfaction there is, it is quickly consumed by the ongoing regurgitation of the incident itself by the media. They are affluent and heavily insured and can afford to lose anything they own, anything except their public face. So, for the protection of their most prized possession, they turn to one of their own.

It was understood there was never to be a discussion of monetary compensation for this service, but the successful conclusion of the affair brought with it the polite understanding of a donation to the East London Adventurers Club. The amount of the pledge was at the discretion of those in receipt of the services rendered, or in most cases, an amount determined by their insurance provider. Either way, most gave gratefully and without hesitation. There were, on occasion, some who saw Patterson Coats as someone who looked to profit from their misfortune. He would simply remind them that they had sought his help and cheerfully add, "I profit only in the knowledge that a wrongdoing has been corrected. You are in no way obligated to compensate my organization for any part we may have played in protecting your good name and reputation." After additional thought of how they led their lives, these curmudgeons would eventually come to the conclusion it was in their best interest to just write the cheque.

Yet they had no reason for concern. Patterson Coats was a man of honour, and he would lock away their secrets with or without a contribution...because that is what honourable men do. The thought of betraying a confidence would never enter his mind, even if the aforementioned arrangement were completely reneged on. His character was above reproach and the highest officials often sought his advice and insight on situations. It was this, and his past relationship with Marie Bussière, that brought him to the left bank of the Seine on that chilly October afternoon. As he stood by the sculptures at the entry plaza he heard a familiar voice call his name.

"*Bonjour*, Patterson," Marie Bussière called out, waving as she crossed the Rue Bellechasse. She came running up to where he stood and kissed him on the cheek. "You look as handsome as ever."

"I would suggest you get those beautiful eyes checked." Patterson offered Marie his arm and they walked toward the entrance. "It's wonderful seeing you again Marie."

" I saw you last night at the gala," she said, taking the kerchief from her head and stuffing it into the pocket of her overcoat. "You were with a rather striking woman, so I didn't want to intrude."

"I'm afraid you give me more credit than I'm due. That was Lady Constance Beckett. I think you'll find her of interest, as it appears she is even more anxious to find your missing burglar than the Préfecture de Police."

"What! She knows about the robbery?"

"Indeed she does," replied Patterson with a smile. "Though she has no idea that we know. Lady Beckett is under the opinion that the museum and the police believe they apprehended the intruder before he could make off with Manet's painting, and that is just what we want her to believe right now."

"This is why you suggested we take a closer look at the painting and not say a word until we spoke?"

"Precisely," replied Patterson as they entered the museum.

The grandeur of the central alley of the Musee d'Orsay was breathtaking, and a fitting location for the art displayed within its walls. Originally a rail station designed to greet passengers arriving for the world fair of 1900, Laloux would be proud of the care taken to restore his cast iron pillars and decorative stucco. Though the daily train schedule has been replaced with a gallery guide, the destinations remained. One need only gaze into the paintings framed on the walls and to find themself transported to another place, another time. The porters and conductors were now magnificently carved sculptures that were illuminated with natural light from above, and they still command the attention of those passing by. At one time the overtaxed Parisians were irritated at the idea of another museum in a city bursting with these institutions, but once they stepped inside they could see this was not just another museum.

As they proceeded toward the impressionists' galleries, workmen could be seen high above in a crane replacing the panes of glass that had been broken out the night of the robbery. Despite the size and awkward appearance of the crane, the repair was drawing very little attention, save from the children who didn't share their parents love for the art around them. Most people hadn't read of the attempted robbery, others didn't care.

"You know my brother will be furious when he finds out about these latest developments...and even more so that you're involved."

Patterson paused at the doorway to the gallery where the painting was displayed. "I've told your brother that he takes his position as the Prefect de Police far too seriously. Besides, according to the papers, the police have dismissed this as an *attempted* robbery. He's made it clear he'll not be looking any further into it."

"And you wonder why he doesn't like you," Marie said with a smile, shaking her head. She entered the gallery.

"Oh, I don't wonder about that at all," Patterson replied quietly, following her in.

Through the doorway was the gallery that housed the Impressionists before 1870. There, hanging with Pissarro and

Boudin, was Manet's Le Fifre. It was a large painting, ninty-seven centimeters by one hundred sixty-one centimeters, in an ornate gilded frame.

"It's one of my favorites," said Marie gazing at the painting, her arms folded and head tilted to one side.

Patterson leaned close and whispered in her ear, "And when we get the real one back I'll assist you in hanging this one in your flat. It will make very interesting dinner conversation."

"What would make better dinner conversation," said Marie suspiciously, "was how you knew this was not the original."

"I never said it wasn't, I just suggested you take a closer look at it."

"Yes, I know," she said briskly, a little irritated with the evasive answer. "When I received your message after the gala, I had Emory—you've met Emory, our art expert—do just that." She glanced around. After seeing they were alone in the gallery, she stepped forward, ran her hand slowly over the frame and continued. "It's the most remarkable thing. It's perfect. The painting. The frame. Even the marks on the canvas that rest against the inside of the frame matched exactly. After hours of examination, and just when Emory was about to conclude this was the original, he noticed a discrepancy in a small label on the back of the frame. The original label had a misspelled word while this one does not.

"It was against my better judgment, but I called you and had the painting put back in place so as not to raise any suspicions. That was this morning, now it is afternoon." Marie took Patterson by the arm once more and with a coy smile continued. "Why don't we go over to my office? We'll have coffee and you can tell me what is going on...and where my painting is."

"How can I refuse such a charming invitation?"

"You won't think it so charming when the museum directors find out that painting is a fake."

"No, that won't do at all," Patterson said, leading Marie out of the gallery. "I would certainly never compromise your integrity or position with the museum. I suggest you tell them what has happened, and that I am looking into the matter. They know me and the methods I employ. That should mollify them for the time being. You can also tell them I am following up on a lead, and that I do not believe the painting to be in any danger."

"So, you think this Beckett woman had a hand in this?"

"Let's have that coffee," Patterson said with a reassuring wink, "and I'll tell you what I know about Lady Constance Beckett."

The two of them continued through the central gallery and turned down the hall toward the administration offices. Along the way they chatted about the state of their current lives. Working too much. Traveling too long. They both agreed it would be nice to see more of each other, but they also knew their lives were separated by more than just the channel.

Patterson sat down on the sofa in Marie's office while she poured their coffees. They'd met at Oxford, she as a student and he a lecturer. Marie was twenty years his junior, with premature gray hair and big brown eyes. She was attractive, intelligent and seemed to adore Patterson. He was flattered by her fondness of him, and in return he shared those same feelings for her. Years ago they had been more than friends so he buried those feelings deep inside for fear of acting upon them. Marie and her husband of twelve years lived in Paris. Her married name was Lafarge, but she continued using Bussière for personal reasons. She kept that life separate from her time with Patterson. Her marriage was a fact neither saw reason to discuss, but both secretly would welcome its absence.

She handed him his cup and sat down beside him.

"So, tell me about your new friend," she began, settling comfortably into the corner of the sofa. "Does she have the painting?"

"I would say not, but I believe the gentleman she refers to as her uncle—the same person she was waiting for at the gala—knows exactly where it is. I'm also convinced she was the money and brains behind the theft but not the intended recipient of the painting."

"I'm confused. Did you know her? There were hundreds of people at that affair, what made you suspicious of this woman?"

"These charity functions are expensive and always attended by the same select group of people, only the venue changes. When you go to enough of them you become familiar with all the faces. You also know when one doesn't belong. There she was amongst her peers, yet this woman knew no one. In that group you are either adored or despised, but never ignored. That itself hinted that something was amiss with her.

"Even the painting was alluding to her incongruity that evening. Due to it being the central focus of the robbery, the painting was attracting quite a bit of attention, except from Lady Beckett. As your Fifer proudly peered out from the canvas at his admirers, she looked away with contempt and only feigned interest at any mention made of the matter.

"She appeared to be waiting for someone and concerned at first by this person's absence. Her concern quickly turned to anger, and she did a poor job of hiding it. I was intrigued, so I introduced myself and offered assistance. She was reluctant at first, but finally introduced herself as Lady Constance Beckett. She explained she was waiting for her uncle and very concerned about his whereabouts. To be brief about the remainder of the conversation, she said they were staying at the same hotel and had arranged to meet at the museum. When her uncle failed to appear by the end of the evening, I escorted Lady Beckett back to her hotel. There was a note at the desk from her uncle explaining his plans had changed, but I suggested she contact me the next day if she still had not heard from him. I knew if my suspicions were correct, it wouldn't be long before she came knocking at my door. That is when I left word at the museum suggesting they contact you and give that painting a closer examination."

"So, who is Lady Beckett and who is her uncle?" asked Marie.

"I'm not sure about her. I made a few inquiries, though, and it appears there is no Lady Constance Beckett. I believe it is a convenient, self-anointed title. As for the man, she referred to him as her uncle, but explained that he was an old family friend she's known for years. I believe you know him, too. His name is Jacques Millet. Through information recently brought to Nigel's attention, I believe he is also Jackie Miller, an old forger with a flat in London."

"Jacques Millet?" Marie gasped. "Why, I don't believe it. Jacques has been doing restoration work on our frames for years. He's such a charming little man. Surely Nigel is mistaken."

"Charm is a powerful weapon in the hands of a criminal. The smart ones realize that and it is their crimes that are the most difficult to expose. I'm fairly certain of the accuracy of the information and Nigel is out right now confirming it. If indeed I'm right, this would also explain that exceptional forgery now hanging in the Impressionists' Gallery."

"I suppose it would," Marie said pensively. "I'm grateful you're here—and for your interest in what is unfolding—but I am not completely clear how you knew this attempted robbery was not what it appeared. The police were satisfied with the results, except for the culprit disappearing from the back of the van. I'm sure they found that quite embarrassing."

"I gave it little or no thought at first, but the police account of this business raised some very interesting questions. The fault I find in their investigating is they seem very accepting of the most bizarre of circumstances when a criminal is caught in the act and the actual crime is averted."

"You've seen the police report?" Marie interrupted.

"Yes, but don't worry. I slipped in under your brother's radar and discussed the report with Inspector Duquenne. It was all rather abrupt. Her Majesty suggested I look into the matter, especially since the painting in question was on loan from the Royal family."

"Oh, so that's it," Marie said sharply. "I was wondering why such a trivial matter as an attempted robbery in Paris would command the attention of Lord Patterson Coats. Please assure Her Majesty the French are quite capable of—"

"Before you make too much of this," interrupted Patterson in a calming tone, "her concern was prompted by questions I raised. It had nothing to do with the ability of the French police. More to the point, if it wasn't for the questions and concern your visitors to the museum would be enjoying nothing more than an incredible copy of a priceless work of art. And what of the greater crime? If not for the suggestion of my involvement, I would have missed yet another opportunity of seeing you."

Marie settled back into the sofa, her irritation less than appeased by his rationale but her stern scowl slowly softening to a smile. "Well, I suppose you're right. I'll contact the board and our insurance carrier. Your involvement should satisfy the request for these latest developments being withheld from the public for the time being, but if they insist on involving the police I will have no choice but to contact them immediately. I don't even want to think what my brother will say."

"Agreed," said Patterson, lightly slapping Marie on the knee. "I will compare notes with Nigel and ring you tomorrow. Now, I think we've given this robbery business enough of our time."

"Yes, we can leave it at this for now, but"—she tapped his chest with her finger—"it's your head if any harm comes to that magnificent work of art."

"I assure you, it has my complete attention."

"Very well. Now, speaking of Nigel..." Marie began in a hushed tone, sitting attentively at the edge of her seat. "How are Nigel and Lily? Has he noticed her yet?"

"I'm sad to say that train has yet to leave the station." Patterson laughed. "They continue to bicker like an old married couple, but Lily has yet to get him to the altar."

"I so like them together," Marie sighed. She paused for a moment. "And tell me, Chief Inspector, did I read you have retired from service?"

"Yes. I'm getting too old for that nonsense." Patterson placed his cup on the table behind him. "Besides, there seems to be no end to the trouble showing up at my door on Conduit Street. To keep one step ahead of it, I've hired a most unusual chap. His name is Ernie Bisquets and he is possessed with rather extraordinary talents."

"And where did you meet this unusual chap?" Marie asked with a smirk.

"He picked my pocket one morning walking through Grosvenor Square." It was completely out of character but Patterson became very animated as he continued his story. "As he approached me we exchanged greetings. He was carrying an armful of books, which he fumbled a bit and eventually dropped on the pavement at my feet. It took only a moment. I helped him up with the books and with a wink and a nod, and oh yes, my billfold, he was on his way and 'round the corner. Two hundred pounds gone in an instant—and it was worth every shilling!"

"Let me understand this—" Marie said, her voice filled with laughter. "You hired a man because he picked your pocket? I think Her Majesty has more to be concerned with than she thinks!"

"No, not for picking my pocket," Patterson replied lightheartedly, "I hired him because he was so adept at his craft. I also believe, if given the chance, he will find life much more rewarding on this side of the law."

"I have always admired that in you," Marie said softly, her hand on Patterson's arm. "Your unwavering battle over evil."

"I wish it were that simple," he said, waving off her compliment. "The habitual criminal proves evil will not be beaten back easily. Each time we catch them, judge them and incarcerate them, they are left with even less than what originally drove them to wrongdoing when we release them. We smile and commend each other over the time and money we devote to the rehabilitation of these offenders, but society has no intention of forgiving anyone. Just ask them, that's God's job."

"It saddens me to hear you speak like this."

"I haven't given up, I just need to step back from the realities of our society before our failures overpower my desire to continue trying to make a difference."

"And you've chosen this Ernie Bisquets to be your standard bearer?" asked Marie, smiling.

"Yes. Since that day in the square I have made it my business to learn more about him and observed his day-to-day activities from afar. I'm a pretty fair judge of character and I've concluded he is more a victim of society than a threat to it. Here's a man standing in the water worried about the storm and not realizing the undertow is about to drag him under. I've decided to intervene on his behalf, with a selfish hope by doing so I can also save myself. I'm not fool enough to think I can control or change his life, but I can control the choices presented to him, which in turn can change his life. And that, my dear Marie, is just what I've done."

"Would you care to elaborate on these choices?" she whispered back.

"I'll not bore you with the details," replied Patterson through the pleased look on his face, "but when given the choice to turn in another or atone for his past, he chose the latter ending up with a stay at Edmunds Hill. I choose to believe it was character that led him to this choice and not just an attempt to save his hide. This was the first of many choices afforded him and to date he has stayed the course, confirming my belief in that character."

"Is he aware of what is going to be expected of him?"

"I'm not expecting anything from him," Patterson said with an innocent grin. He rose to his feet. "But I will extend my heartfelt thanks, and those of The Queen, if he so chooses to contribute to help in what you refer to as our fight against evil."

"I wonder if he knows how good a friend he has in you?" Marie took Patterson's offered hand and rose herself.

"Again you give me more credit than I'm due," he said earnestly. "More than once we have been stifled in our attempts to gain information from those who are less than willing to cooperate with anyone remotely associated with the law. To have someone who can walk amongst them opens a whole new dimension for us. My motives may sound very selfish, but the decision is still with him. And if he so chooses to refrain from assisting in our business dealings, a situation as my valet will remain without contempt. Ernie Bisquets is a decent chap who was never afforded proper choices. I have given him the opportunity of starting a new life with new choices. At what level he chooses to live that life is his. Either way, he will earn an honest living."

"You can be very persuasive when you want something. Just be sure about what you are introducing him to before you push him into something you both may regret."

"Have a little faith, my dear," said Patterson with a reassuring wink. "I have removed myself from the equation for the time being. He is getting settled in at Conduit Street, and I have yet to speak with him. Nigel and Lily will be paying a visit to the studio this afternoon where your charming little man repairs frames, so we will see just how curious Mr. Bisquets is about our work and the opportunities laid before him."

"I am still amazed over Jacques' involvement in this business," Marie mused as she and Patterson walked toward the door. "Please let me know what Nigel learns from his visit."

"We'll talk later this evening." Patterson kissed Marie on the cheek. "I'll be in Paris for the next day or so if you need me. Until then, *adieu.*"

Seven

A MOVING EXPERIENCE

NIGEL OPENED THE door of the cab waiting at the curb and Lily and Ernie climbed in. A figure in the shadows across the street caught his attention and he hesitated getting in himself.

"You there!" he called out across the top of the cab. "I say, you there!" he called out again even louder, since his first attempt to make contact was ignored.

A bit frustrated, Nigel started across Conduit Street but two buses going by hindered his efforts. As they passed he watched the elusive stranger disappear around the corner. Seeing no reason to turn his curiosity into a chase, Nigel climbed inside the cab and instructed the cabbie on their destination of St. Paul's.

"Who was that?" Lily asked, still straining to get a look at who or what had captured Nigel's attention.

"I have no idea," he replied, fixing his overcoat as he settled back into the seat. "But I find it very odd indeed. Earlier, when Lady Beckett had left, I glanced out the window and noticed a rather large man standing across the street. He stood a few buildings down, just in view from the alley, looking about in a nervous way and obviously attempting to conceal his interest in our flat. I dismissed it at first, thinking he may have come along with Lady Beckett, but seeing he was still there after she climbed into a waiting car I believe he might have had a different agenda."

"Do you know him, Ernie?" asked Lily, catching him by surprise with the question. "Ernie? You look like you've seen a ghost. Are you all right?"

"Sorry, Miss," Ernie stuttered, noting the puzzled looks on their faces. "No...I didn't see anybody...I think I'm just a bit overwhelmed at all the goings on."

"Well," Nigel said, "a bit of fresh London air will do you good, then. We'll be there in just a few minutes. You say you know this place where we're going?"

"Yes, yes I do, squire," Ernie replied quietly, struggling to put a less concerned look on his face. "There's an old man—Maunder, I believe his name is—what takes care of the building for the owner. He'll know what Jackie Miller's been up to, but it won't be easy getting 'im to talk. He's a prickly sort, suspicious of everybody. He even hates the people he knows, so I can't image how he'd treat a stranger."

"You let me take care of that," Nigel said confidently, dismissing the warning with a wave of his hand. "You'll find I have quite a way with people."

"Yes, I'm sure he'll rue the day he tries to cross you," said Lily with a laugh, poking Ernie in the ribs with her elbow.

Ernie responded with a slight chuckle and Nigel shot them both a stern glare. Lily smiled and stuck her tongue out at him. There was an awkward pause, and then Nigel shook his head and laughed right along with them.

"You laugh now, Bisquets," said Nigel through his smile, "but she'll be having a bit o'sport with you soon enough."

They turned from Shaftesbury Avenue onto New Oxford Street. The sky had cleared partially and the late afternoon brought with it a crisp bite to the air. The traffic was its usual mess as they entered Holburn Circus. Eventually, the cab turned down Limeburner Lane, finally pulling over on Ludgate Hill near Creed Lane. Nigel paid the fare and the three of them got out and proceeded the short distance on foot to the address mentioned by Lady Beckett.

The typical flocks of tourists were milling about the steps of St. Paul's Cathedral near Queen Ann's statue. Nigel, Lily and Ernie crossed over St. Paul's Churchyard and started down a narrow street. Two trees loomed up over a tall brick wall that lined the right side of the street, giving an ominous appearance to the building at the end that they were approaching. Suddenly, they were quite alone.

In front of them was a two-story, brick and limestone building, with a third story dormered out of the slate roof on all four sides. It appeared to be part of the cathedral outbuildings, with its Baroque ornamentation and Latin inscription around the mid-level frieze.

They continued down to the corner and turned on to Carter

Lane. Lily and Ernie waited on the pavement as Nigel walked up the marble steps to the main door. There were doorbells above two postboxes. One had a tarnished brass plaque over it, long obscuring the name of the occupant. The second had a scrap of white board tucked beneath the brass cover of the button and bore the name *Miller*.

Nigel pushed the button a number of times, but no one answered. He looked back at Lily and Ernie and shrugged his shoulders. It was an unusually loud, piercing bell, that resonated down through the soles of their shoes. Nigel indicated he would try once more, but as he turned he was startled by a little, wrinkled face peering through the partially opened door.

"You push that bloody button again," the scowling little man snapped in a voice as piercing as the bell itself, "and I'll break that finger off, I will!"

"Are you Miller?" Nigel demanded, wasting no time in jamming all of his fingers into his coat pockets, out of reach of the gentleman at the door.

"And who might be askin'?"

"I'm Nigel Coats, and these are my associates—"

"No! Piss off," the little man shouted back, red-faced and barely missing his nose as he slammed the door shut.

"Apparently he doesn't understand that *way* you have with people," said Lily casually, glancing up at Nigel and thoroughly enjoying the situation.

"What an impertinent little man!" Nigel shouted. Then waving the very finger alluded to earlier at Lily, he said, "And I'll have none of those cheeky remarks from you!"

"Beggin' your pardon, squire," Ernie interrupted, cautiously sharing in the amusement, "but I believe that was Maunder."

"Oh, it was, was it?" Nigel turned back toward the door, his finger at the ready. "Well, we'll just see about that." He paused before ringing the bell and, after what was surely a brief reflection on the virtues of having all ten fingers, opted to knock instead. And knock he did.

The door creaked open slowly, as if to underline the depth of the little man's irritation. At this point the scowl on his face had deepened into a glower. "I can see I'm going to have trouble with you," growled Maunder, hiking up his trousers and puffing out his chest. He was just short of five feet, but every inch looked meaner than the one below it. His right eye drooped and the scar on his cheek, and notch of skin torn from his left ear, gave further testimony to a life lived hard, and without compromise.

"See here, now," Nigel shot back, appearing both angry and nervous. "Maunder, is it? We've come to see a Mister Miller and if you don't—"

"Bisquets?" exclaimed Maunder, pushing Nigel aside and bounding down the steps. "Ernie Bisquets? Bloody hell, why it is you! Last I heard you was up—"

"Yes, up in Suffolk," Ernie quickly interjected. "It's good to be back in London."

"Yes, I'm sure it is," replied Maunder, giving Lily a long look with what possibly could have been a smile.

"So, it's Jackie you're looking for, is it? Owes you money, does he? And who's this?" continued Maunder with a malicious grin, pointing his thumb over his shoulder toward Nigel. "Your muscle?"

"Something like that," replied Ernie.

"He's not here," Maunder said, "but for a fiver you can go up. The door's open. Popular guy, old Jackie is. Some woman's been here twice looking for him." He sneered at Nigel who was holding out a five pound note and still standing by the door. "You probably knows her. Snooty bitch she was. Just follow the stairs." He snatched the note from Nigel's hand and checked it twice, just to be sure. "And don't nick a thing, I'll be checkin' yer pockets on the way out."

Lily smiled and followed up the stairs behind Nigel.

Maunder took Ernie by the arm and held him back. He waited until the other two were out of sight to begin. "I don't know what game you got going with these two," he said quietly after pulling Ernie down close to him, "but I'll be expectin' my share for helpin' you like I am."

Maunder held out his hand, indicating a small down payment was in order.

"I don't have much," Ernie replied, reluctantly pulling a twenty-pound note from his pocket, "but I'll see you're taken care of later. Just tell me what you know about what Jackie's been up to."

Maunder glanced around, grabbed the note from his hand and pulled Ernie close once more. "Jackie said he had a big job in Paris and if all went well he wouldn't be back. He paid me two hundred quid to borrow the lorry on Sunday and brought it back two days later. I heard him walkin' round the flat that afternoon and that was the last I seen 'im."

"So, you did actually see him yesterday?"

"Well..." Maunder grumbled, scratching his head and thinking for a moment. "Not exactly. Friday was the last I seen 'im. Like I says, he mentioned some Paris job and gave me two hundred quid to borrow the lorry in the courtyard for a day or so. He had two crates in his flat. One we left there and one we carried down and put in the back of the lorry. Bloody heavy it was, too. Sunday morning I found an envelope with the money in it stuffed under my door. I looked out after I found it and the lorry was gone. When I went out for my paper early yesterday morning it was back in the courtyard. One of the crates was in it, but I thinks it was empty. He must have gotten back some time overnight. I heard Jackie-boy moving things around in the flat a bit later, but when I went up to ask how it went in Paris, the door was open and he was already gone. His clothes, his tools and the other crate. Gone." Maunder looked around yet again and then tapped his pointy finger into Ernie's chest. "You be careful, Bisquets. That big gorilla has been lurkin' about, too. Every time that bird showed up lookin' for Jackie, I seen him down the street watchin' us. That Dragonetti is trouble. If he's got something going on with Jackie, you better keep out of his bloody way."

Ernie jumped back with a start, looking up and down the street. "It *was* him," he said quietly to himself, visibly shaken by this news.

"If you crossed him already, Bisquets," said Maunder through his tobacco-stained smirk, "maybe you oughta pay me now."

"I haven't crossed anyone," Ernie replied flatly, shoving Maunder's outstretched hand out of his way. "I just don't want to see him, that's all." He started up the stairs to rejoin Nigel and Lily but paused at the door and looked back. "Did Jackie know that woman who's been knocking up for him?"

"I've known Jackie a lot of years now. If he did, it's news to me."

"Thanks Maunder." Ernie gave another quick look down the street before heading up to the third floor.

When Ernie got to the landing at the top of the stairs, there was an open door to the right, revealing a small toilet and two steps up to another open door. That was the door to the flat and he heard Lily and Nigel moving about inside. He knocked and poked his head through the door for a look.

"No need for that, Bisquets," Nigel said, waving him in. "It's just us. It appears our boy Miller is long gone. We'll take a quick look 'round and see if he left any clue to his whereabouts."

Ernie cautiously stepped through the narrow doorway. It was a fairly large room with a wide chimney coming up through the center of it and disappearing again through the peak. Three knee walls were wainscoted and darkened with age; plaster continued up the roofline to the peak. There was a fifteen-foot square space one could walk around upright; otherwise it was necessary to crouch so as not to hit one's head. There were windowed dormers on three of the four walls and two ceiling lights illuminated the space, but did very little to diminish the dreary atmosphere.

It was sparsely furnished with a small table and two chairs, a single bed and a rather large cabinet on chest against a full height wall. On the table was an old hotplate and a well-used copper kettle. There were magazines and papers bundled along the wall in front of them, along with paper boxes filled with odd pieces of frames and the assorted refuse generated by a tradesman of this sort. At the opposite end of that wall was a generous closet, which Lily was busy investigating, while the cabinet, also along that wall and almost obscured from view by the boxes piled on and around it, captured Nigel's attention.

"Remarkable," Nigel mumbled to himself, as he pulled away the bundles and rubbish from around the cabinet. "Just remarkable." He stepped back to admire the treasure he had just revealed. "This is an early 17th century, Queen Ann cabinet on chest. This should be in a museum."

"What are you talking about?" Lily asked, poking her head out from the wardrobe.

"This!" Nigel crowed, holding his hands out in presentation of the piece. "This! I'll wager there aren't ten of these in this condition in the world. If Miller knew his way around museums, he also knew the value of this piece. Why would he leave it behind?"

"Maybe it's a fake." Lily joined Nigel in front of the cabinet.

Nigel took off his coat to take a closer look. The key was still in the lock on the beveled mirrored door so he slowly opened it. Inside were ten chevron-banded drawers and a bookshelf. Pulling out the drawers one at a time, he turned them over and over, examining every inch. He ran his hand over the secondary wood panel holding the mirror in place and lightly scratched at it with his fingernail. The patina came off quite easily, as it should if it were genuine. He continued on to the lower cabinet, opening the top desk and then the remaining three drawers. The brass handles appeared original to the piece and the secondary woods were correct to the period. The large bulbous feet were solid and in a condition expected for its age. Satisfied with his inspection he stepped back and smiled.

"I believe this is the genuine article. But again, it begs the question, why was it left behind?"

"It is rather large," Lily remarked, looking back towards the narrow door.

"The top separates from the drawers below," Nigel said. He got down on all fours and pushed the debris away from around the bottom. "It seems he was intending to move it, there's a dolly under here. What do you make of this, Bisquets? Bisquets?"

Nigel and Lily looked around, but Ernie was no longer in the room. They listened for a moment and heard the sound of someone tapping on the wall just inside the closet. The tapping stopped and Ernie emerged from the closet with a puzzled look on his face.

"Sorry. Did you say something?"

"We were remarking how odd it was for Mr. Miller to leave this valuable antique behind," Lily responded curiously as she watched Ernie resume his tapping, but this time on the wall where the papers were stacked.

"Valuable, is it?" Ernie replied thoughtfully, tapping his way down the wall, around the cabinet and ending on the landing through the narrow door.

"Bisquets, what are you doing?" Nigel asked with a raised eyebrow, waiting patiently for some explanation to this strange behavior.

"Dormers, squire," Ernie answered, one hand on his hip and the other scratching his head. "Where are the other dormers?"

Nigel had to mull over the question for a moment. As he did so he looked carefully at the other three walls and then responded. "You're right, Bisquets, where are the dormers?"

Lily looked on in wonderment as both Nigel and Ernie began tapping on the wall. "I think you've both lost it," she said quietly to herself, plopping down on one of the small chairs next to the table.

"Give a hand!" Nigel shouted, instructing Ernie to put his back into moving the cabinet. The wheels began to creak and slowly they pushed the massive cabinet along the wall. As they did so a shaft of light burst forth across the floor from the windows in a concealed room. Lily was on her feet in a moment and pushing right along with them. They rolled the cabinet far enough to allow them to pass through the opening.

"Dormers!" Nigel smiled, slapping Ernie on the back. "Absolutely brilliant, Bisquets! Now, let's see what else Mr. Miller left behind."

Lily's nature was to go charging forward, but a cautioning glance from Nigel was enough to keep her in check for the moment. Nigel went in first, with Ernie and Lily a step behind. Through the opening, paintings were visible leaning against the wall below the missing dormers. As they crept forward, elaborately carved frames came into view. Nigel and Ernie started toward an easel to the right, but Lily looked back to the opposite wall.

Without warning she grabbed Ernie's arm and let out a piercing scream. There, strewn amidst a pile of frames, was the body of an old man.

He had white hair and looked to be in his early sixties, and was dressed in a dark, wool suit. His face was contorted from the trauma that had befallen him, the pain still visible in the cloudy gray eyes that stared at them. He had a chalky blue complexion, that intensified in the orange glow of the late afternoon sky. He was slumped to one side, with an outstretched arm lying across the wooden box that was holding him upright.

Lily turned her head away and buried her face in Ernie's shoulder. She was tough, but she had no intention of ever getting used to the sight of a dead body.

Ernie's gaze was fixated on the body. His mouth was open but he was unable to utter a sound. In all he had seen through his life, this was his first glimpse of the cruel side of death. He barely realized when Nigel led he and Lily back through the opening.

"Bisquets," Nigel started slowly and with intent, "it's important that you get hold of yourself and do as I say. Please ring Scotland Yard and ask for Inspector Flannel. Tell him where we are and that we need him and the medical examiner at once. Do you understand?"

It took a moment for Ernie to compose himself, but he turned to Nigel and nodded his head rapidly. "Yes. Very good, sir."

"I'm okay now, Nigel," Lily interrupted, forcing a smile. "I'll call down to the Yard."

"Very good. Ernie, why don't you ask that prickly little man Maunder to join us. I'm sure the inspector will be curious to know if he had a hand in poor Miller's demise."

Ernie started toward the door, but stopped and looked back at Nigel with some confusion. Instead of going after Maunder, he peered into the hidden room for another look at the body.

"What is it, old man?" Nigel asked to his questioning expression. "Did you say Miller?"

"Yes. I assume that's the remains of Jackie Miller lying in there?"

"I can see how you might, sir," replied Ernie, in an apologetic tone, "but I used to frequent the same pub as Jackie Miller, and I can assure you that ain't him."

Eight

A BRUSH WITH DEATH

LILY FINISHED HER conversation with Scotland Yard and snapped her phone shut. "Did you say that isn't Miller?" she asked, perplexed.

"Yes, Miss. He's about the same age, but Jackie Miller...he's a bit on the heavy side, he is, and wears thick glasses."

It took Nigel a moment to comprehend what Ernie had said. He peered into the room where the body was and then back at Ernie, repeating this several times. It was clear in his expression he was churning the information over in his head. Finally, he looked over at Lily with a satisfied expression, prepared to proceed.

"Lily," Nigel said, "I'd like Bisquets to stay here with me and take a look around that room before the constables arrive and muck it all up. Would you mind asking Mr. Maunder to join us? I believe he'll respond much more favorably to a request from you, anyway."

Lily was composed, now, and though she didn't relish the idea of another encounter with the cheeky Mr. Maunder, she understood the significance of Nigel's request in relation to the discovery of the body. After placing her coat on the bed she went off to locate him. Ernie tossed his Mack onto the bed as well and, with a certain amount of apprehension, followed Nigel back into the concealed room.

The sun was finishing its descent, so Nigel found himself feeling about on the wall for a light switch. It took only a moment to locate the fuse box. After pulling the handle down, two bright lamps overhead threw light in every corner of the room. They both shielded their eyes, squinting until they adjusted to the sudden brightness.

As the room came into view, there was a four-foot high knee

wall in front of them with the three *missing* dormers above. Leaning against the wall were a number of half-finished canvases, most of which were of the same subject—Manet's *Le Fifre*. There were two large, wooden easels at the end to the right, layered with what looked like a lifetime of paint dabs. In the corner, between the easels, was a Regency chiffonier. It was rosewood with pleated silk doors flanked by spiral twist columns. The white marble top was stained from the pigments mixed on it and littered with detailed photographs of what must have been the original Manet painting and frame. One of the doors was slightly ajar, revealing boxes of additional photographs and bottles of organic material and mediums used by artists to make their paints. A collection of mortars and pestles were arranged on shelves above the chiffonier.

At the other end of the room was a workbench with an assortment of woodworking and pottery tools scattered on top. There was a glisten in the corner caused by a small packet of gold leaf and a few bottles of rabbit glue. Neatly stored underneath were boxes of rubber mold sections, lengths of aged wood and, for lack of a better description, the skeletal remains of old frames. The body of the unfortunate man was propped up in the corner opposite the workbench. The bright lights in the room did little to diminish the eerie effect of his presence. The horror of the events that led to his sudden end lingered in his eyes, and his chalky white hand reaching out still sent shivers up their spines, despite the brave faces they put on for each other.

"Buck up, old man," Nigel said soothingly, laying his hand on Ernie's shoulder. "Those who knew this man will mourn him. We'll serve him best by establishing how and why this happened. Now, the inspector will be here soon, so it's important we identify and decipher any clues this room may hold, but be careful not to disturb the crime scene. He has a great respect for our work in antiquity, but he considers us nothing more than bothersome amateurs in ugly business like this. He tolerates us out of respect to my uncle and their mutual service to Queen and country. Oh, he'll be cordial enough all right, maybe even look interested when we offer our assessment of the situation. Then with an indiscreet nod to one of his constables we'll be escorted out, along with our chance to make some sense of this poor chap's death and what role he may have played in the attempted theft of the painting in Paris. What say we have at it?"

With a furrowed brow, and chewing a bit on the inside of his cheek, Ernie forced a smile and agreed timidly. "What should I do?" he asked, looking about the room with every intention of ignoring the body.

"Touch nothing," Nigel said seriously. "Inspector Flannel and his men will want to see this room exactly the way we found it. He'll probably—"

"Inspector Flannel?" Ernie interrupted, tugging nervously at his coat.

"Yes. Inspector Derby Flannel," Nigel replied, as he leaned down for a closer look at the stack of unfinished paintings between the dormers. "Detective Inspector, actually. He's a bit somber for my taste, but quite adept in the field of criminal investigation. Have you heard of him?"

Ernie nodded but could not speak. He knew very well whom Nigel was talking about, and he shook at the thought of how the good inspector was going to react when he found him there. This could ruin everything.

"There's no time to dawdle," Nigel continued sharply. "Lily will be back with Maunder any moment, and we'll need some time with him, too, before the inspector arrives."

"Sorry," Ernie replied, shaking off the vision of his reunion with the detective inspector. "What is it we're looking for?"

"Clues, my good man." Nigel glanced back over his shoulder at Ernie. "We need to know just who this poor chap is, what his relationship was with Miller and Lady Beckett and what, if anything, he had to do with this business in Paris."

Ernie took a few more steps into the room and with great effort forced himself to look at the body. "His name is Thomas…" he said quietly. and with some hesitation. "And…I believe he was a guard at the Musee d'Orsay, squire."

Nigel stopped what he was doing and looked back at Ernie in amazement. "Good God, man, how do you know that?"

"The wool coat," Ernie said in an even lower voice, pointing down to the poor chap on the floor. He cleared his throat and continued. "It's stitched into his coat pocket. His name, too."

"Excellent, Bisquets!" exclaimed Nigel, startling Ernie with his enthusiasm. "Let's have a look."

Nigel bent over the body, moving around a bit so as not to block the light. Indeed, the museum name was stitched on the pocket, but something seemed amiss. Nigel took a pencil from his pocket, slipped it into the end of the sleeve and raised the arm up. The dead man's hand was barely visible. It wasn't as evident on the outstretched arm, but the sleeves were at least two inches too long. He then pinched the shoulders and tugged a bit in an outward direction. There was more cloth than there was shoulder. Stretching the coat out also revealed a bloodstain on the shirt in the upper right chest area.

"That's a bit queer, isn't it?" Nigel said, patting the shoulders back to the way he'd found them, then rising to his feet. "There's an entry wound and blood on his shirt but no bullet hole on the front of the coat. Not only did someone shoot this man, but they also went through the trouble of changing his clothes afterwards. Curious indeed. Let's see what else Thomas can tell us."

Ernie stepped back to examine the body and the general area where it lay. "They've never been worn," he said, eyeing the dead man's shoes intently. "Look at the soles. Not a scratch or a scuff." He bent over to get a closer look. "The trousers are fairly worn, and in need of a good press, they are, but these shoes are just from the box. Look."

Nigel bent down close to Ernie to see for himself. After a careful investigation he looked at Ernie and nodded in agreement.

"What's all this?" snarled Maunder miserably.

"Jesus, man!" Nigel cried, alarmed at the abrupt intrusion. "You'll put us both in a grave sneaking up like that!"

Maunder started to reply. Ernie and Nigel stood up revealing the body and his predictable retort was interrupted by the sight. Maunder paused for a moment, then threw a sneer in Nigel's direction.

"I knew you was trouble," he said, barely acknowledging the unfortunate man and showing no concern at all for his tragic end.

"So, Maunder," Nigel said, watching his response closely, "just what can you tell us about this fellow here on the floor?"

"He's dead," came the short, biting reply. "And it looks like there is just enough room next to him for a friend."

"We'll see how cheeky you are when Inspector Flannel arrives," Nigel said smugly, content that he retained the upper hand.

Maunder dismissed the remark with a grunt and retired to the main room to gawk a bit more at Lily. Nigel indicated to Ernie that he should stay close to him and he complied, passing Lily on his way through the doorway.

"So, what have you deduced?" she asked curiously, craning her neck to look about the room. The shock of finding the body had passed, and she approached the situation now more abstractly, as was her style.

Nigel turned to her and pointed toward the body. "It seems

our poor friend here was shot and then dressed in the uniform of a museum guard. The stitched name on the coat is Thomas, but we have some reservations of it relating to this fellow. Curiously, the trousers are a bit shabby, probably his own, but the coat and shoes appear to be new. As for a connection with the attempted theft...?" Nigel looked about the room and continued. "We have a body dressed in a museum coat in a concealed room with discarded canvases, paints and framing. I'm sure our friend here could have told us much about this museum business but somebody had other ideas."

Nigel turned back around in time to see Lily going through the pocket of the dead man's trousers.

"What are you doing?" he cried gruffly, trying his best not to be heard in the other room. "Have you lost your mind?"

"You said these were probably his own pants," replied Lily pleasantly, "so let's see if they can tell us anything."

Lily pulled her hand out of a pocket and with it came what looked like a rail ticket. She was wrong to disturb the body but careful enough to only handle it by the edges. She held it out for Nigel to see. He jotted down the information from the front of the ticket in his notepad.

"What does it say?" she asked briskly, rising to her feet.

"It's his rail ticket from Paris to London," replied Nigel slowly, genuinely more interested now that Lily had produced something of significance. "It looks like he intended to be in London only one day."

Content he had all the information transferred he suggested she replace it before they were interrupted.

Together they walked out into the main room where they found Maunder talking to Ernie, making every effort not to be overheard. He stopped hastily as they approached, giving Nigel a loathsome sneer from the left side of his mouth while curling up the other side into a smile for Lily.

They all four looked up at the sound of heavy footsteps on the landing.

After a moment, in walked a constable, followed by a rather serious looking individual. He glanced from one to the other of them and just shook his head.

"Nothing good can come of this," he said gravely. He tipped his hat to Lily and shook Nigel's hand.

"Good afternoon, Inspector Flannel," Nigel said.

The inspector then walked right up to Ernie. "And who might

you be?" he asked, as well as answering his own question with the look he threw at Ernie.

"Uh...Bisquets, sir," Ernie stammered nervously, extending his hand to the inspector. "Uh...Ernie Bisquets."

"Yes you are," came the inspector's cold but quiet reply. He made no attempt to shake his hand and Ernie slowly withdrew it.

"Terribly sorry, Inspector," Nigel said openly, unaware of the inspector's response. "This is Ernie Bisquets. He's with us. My uncle has asked him to join the East Londoners. I fancy you'll be seeing a bit more of him around London in the future. He's just back from—"

"Suffolk?" Inspector Flannel asked in an almost accusing tone, tapping his pipe on the top of his umbrella.

"How did he—" Nigel began, addressing Ernie with the inquiry.

"I believe your uncle mentioned it over lunch the other day," replied the inspector, cutting short the question and the suspicion. "You're the new valet, I believe." He gave Nigel a quick glance and continued past Maunder in silence. The impertinent Maunder had no cheeky remark for the inspector; he just cowered in his shadow as he walked by.

"Miss Corbett," said Inspector Flannel dourly, "you said something about murder?"

Lily nodded and pointed the inspector toward the entrance to the concealed room.

Ernie didn't understand why it happened, but he was relieved the inspector took such little interest in him.

Maunder saw the disinterest in him as an opportunity to depart, so he slowly crept toward the stairs.

"I suggest you stay," Inspector Flannel warned him, stopping at the entrance to the room and looking back over the shoulder of his green tweed coat. "It won't go well for you, Maunder, if I have to come looking for you."

Maunder stood motionless at the doorway. "I guess I ain't goin' nowhere," he whispered miserably, and then rejoined the others.

With a jerk of his head, the inspector indicated to the constable he was to keep an eye on Maunder. He then disappeared behind the Queen Ann cabinet on chest.

Nine

QUESTIONS FOR YOUR ANSWERS

Detective Inspector Derby Flannel had an unwavering allegiance to the law. It was often the topic around the station, but by no means to his face, that he had never been a child. He'd been born a Scotland Yard inspector and, when coming of age, became a Detective Inspector. August, his given name, had been long forgotten, except by a handful of people he had allowed to share his personal life. Derby was an epithet he'd acquired from the conspicuous adornment he chose to wear. It was rather fitting to his station in life and certainly singled him out from amongst the others of his profession. He quite literally had made a name for himself.

He had no interest in the common man, save a portentous nod in response to a greeting on the street. If you had ever stepped on the wrong side of the law, he could read the misdeed in the expression on your face. With one raised eyebrow and a sideways glance, he could size up anyone who crossed his path.

He was about six foot, with a long drawn face. Bushy eyebrows hung over two slits where his eyes were assumed to be. His hair was short, receding and as coarse as his demeanor. A thick gray mustache concealed his thin lips and curled down at the ends giving the appearance of a perpetual frown. No one could ever remember a time when they saw him smile, or even show any expression of amusement. Any attempt at idle conversation with him was met with a grunt. He spoke very little, but when he did, it demanded your full and complete attention. No matter where he went Detective Inspector Derby Flannel needed no introduction. He was, by all appearances, the law. In a green tweed coat and a black derby, he was a man to be respected and certainly never crossed.

Nigel pulled Lily and Ernie aside and left Maunder to contemplate his own situation. "Lily, would you ring up my uncle and inform him of these latest developments? A dead man in a museum uniform is certain to raise many questions and even more speculation by the press. We certainly don't won't to embarrass the Musee d'Orsay, so it's important that they are ready for any inquiry regarding this discovery."

Lily pulled her phone from her pocket and very quietly slipped off to the privacy of the stairwell. Ernie was still fidgeting a bit, preoccupied with what the inspector was up to.

"How are you holding up, old man?" Nigel asked encouragingly, but Ernie was too consumed and never heard the question. "It's getting interesting," Nigel continued a bit louder and leaning in close to his ear, "isn't it?"

"You calls it interesting," Maunder, eavesdropping on the conversation, snarled under his breath, "I calls it a bloody nuisance!"

"Sorry," Ernie replied in a low voice, ignoring Maunder and leaning his head toward Nigel. The truth of his background still loomed ominously over the situation, but his concern about that was now buried in the shadow of his curiosity. "What do you think he makes of it?"

"Here's Lily," Nigel replied. "What say we poke our heads in and find out?"

Lily returned, giving a reassuring nod that the information had been passed along as requested, and that she, too, was anxious to hear the inspector's thoughts. Together they walked over and squeezed into the narrow opening like a gaggle of nosey-parkers. Maunder stayed behind, still mumbling under his breath.

The inspector was crouched next to the body. He had the rail ticket Lily had found earlier in his hand, and with his pencil in the other he had pulled back the victim's coat to examine the wound. An abrupt pause acknowledged the group's presence behind him, but ignoring them he then proceeded to pull the body forward and then from side to side, examining it and the floor around it. Satisfied with his evaluation, Inspector Flannel carefully settled the body back into the pile of frames as it had been found. He slowly stood up and took a small pad from his vest pocket. The inspector looked at the easels at the opposite end of the room and the canvases leaning against the wall in front of him. He made a few notations on his pad and casually looked through the stack of canvases.

"It seems someone was an admirer of Manet," postulated Inspector Flannel, addressing the curious group. "When you were poking about in here, did you manage to find his glasses?"

"Glasses?" Nigel repeated sheepishly, obviously puzzled by the question. He stepped into the room.

The inspector pointed at the victim's head with his pencil and continued, "The marks below his temples and on the bridge of his nose suggest glasses...rather heavy ones, at that."

"Brilliant," Nigel said quietly, bending down for a closer look and then standing back up. "No, I can't say we did." There was an awkward silence, which led to Nigel noticing the inspector's questioning glance in his direction. "You're probably wondering what we were doing here in the first place."

"Rest assured, I was getting around to that," Inspector Flannel said with conviction, pulling a pouch of tobacco from his coat pocket and filling his pipe.

"We came by the body quite by accident," Nigel said simply, pointing back toward Ernie. "It was Bisquets here who found this concealed room. We came inquiring about the whereabouts of a Jacques Millet and, quite by accident, stumbled upon this poor devil."

"Crime just seems to follow your little group, doesn't it?" replied Inspector Flannel reproachfully, puffing at his newly lit pipe.

"If you're referring to that nasty business with Queen Nefertitis's necklace," Nigel continued, put off a bit by the remark, "*that* trouble found us! Our involvement here is purely accidental, and on request of a Lady Constance Beckett. She met my uncle at a reception at the Musee d'Orsay, and has asked for our help locating her uncle. She was oddly cautious in what she told us, but she suggested this flat could possibly shed some light on his whereabouts. Through additional information we've gathered today, we believe Lady Beckett, and an uncle she refers to as Jacques Millet, may have some involvement with the attempted theft at the Musee d'Orsay. Stumbling across this room has only strengthened our resolve to that end."

"Well, you've certainly been busy," said the inspector, jotting down a few notes from Nigel's narrative. "So it hasn't escaped your attention that this is the address of a small time forger named Jackie Miller?"

"No. Bisquets made mention of that and we believe Jacques

Millet and Jackie Miller are one and the same."

"I'm sure he did," replied the inspector under his breath, looking out into the room where Ernie and Lily stood waiting. "And is Mr. Bisquets under the opinion that this is Jackie Miller?" The inspector looked back at Nigel and pointed to the body.

"No, just the opposite," countered Nigel, answering his insolent glare. "There's a resemblance, but he is relatively certain this is not Miller." Nigel stepped closer to the inspector to avoid being heard in the other room. "You seem agitated more than usual, and in particular, with the addition to our group. Is there something the matter? Is there something I should know about Bisquets?"

"Not at all," replied Inspector Flannel impatiently, dismissing the question with a wave of his hand. "It's just one more of you mucking about my crime scenes."

"I can assure you, Inspector," Nigel shot back curtly, "our intention was not to contaminate your crime scene. As I mentioned before, we came looking for Jacques Millet on request of Constance Beckett. She is unaware of our suspicions of her, so our objective was to act as quickly as possible to locate her uncle and uncover a connection between them and the attempted theft in Paris. In light of these current developments, I would imagine you are anxious to speak with them to establish their role, if any, in this unfortunate man's demise."

"Do you have a way to contact this Lady Beckett?" asked Inspector Flannel, barely acknowledging Nigel's discourse.

"Yes…Yes I do." Nigel rifled about for the card she'd given him, finally pulling it from a pocket of his coat. "Here."

"Thank you," grunted Inspector Flannel. He copied the information onto his pad, handed the card back to Nigel and continued firmly. "I'll appreciate your stepping aside to allow me to investigate this properly. It's murder now, not just a missing person, but for your efforts in uncovering this mess I'll at least tell you this. The wound and the absence of blood say this man was shot at close range, but not here. His original clothes were replaced with what he now has on, save his trousers. The shoes are intriguing, not because they've never been worn, but because they are two sizes too large. Mr. Bisquets is entitled to his opinion, but I'm not convinced this isn't Jackie Miller. Death has a way of changing a person's appearance, and I'm sure it's been some time since he's seen Jackie Miller. To be sure, I'll have his fingerprints checked through Interpol and let you know what I find out. Fair enough?"

"As you wish," replied Nigel reluctantly. "If you would allow me, my uncle is in Paris at this moment so we can get him this man's description and have him check with the museum. I'll contact you directly with any information they can furnish."

Inspector Flannel nodded in agreement. "There are two crimes here," he began solemnly, tucking his pad back into a pocket. "A murder, which falls in my jurisdiction, and the attempted theft of a painting, that is primarily the responsibility of the French authorities. With the information you have provided, and the circumstances this room has revealed, it's reasonable to believe they are related. I will contact the French authorities after I have filed my report and share these developments with them. I had my constable ring up the medical examiner, so while we wait for him why don't we see what light Maunder can cast over this dark business."

Nigel agreed and together they rejoined the group in the outer room. Two additional constables had arrived and were talking quietly by the landing. Maunder was pacing back and forth, muttering under his breath, while Lily talked to Ernie. They all turned their attention to Nigel and the inspector as they emerged from the room.

Nigel quietly asked Lily if she would take a photo of the victim's face, while the inspector approached Maunder.

"You know, Maunder," said Inspector Flannel in a calculating tone, putting another match to his pipe, "the law frowns upon those who willingly harbor criminals or criminal activities."

"Rubbish!" Maunder shot back, getting a bit shirty. "I ain't done nothin' and I can't be arsed. Maunder stepped toward the inspector. He raised a fist to make his point, but a sharp glance from the inspector hastened a retreat. "I'm just the custodian of this dustbin, paid by the church, I am, to look after things. I don't know what's goin' on here, or who killed that old punter, but that's your problem, ain't it?" Maunder curled up the left side of his lip enough to reveal a decaying smile.

"Bloody hell!" Nigel cried out, pointing at the man coming through the doorway from the stairs. "That's the chap I saw this afternoon watching our flat."

Standing back upright, after ducking down to enter the room, a very large and stout man looked at the group now staring at him. The constable who had ushered him in was barely visible behind him, but peeked out enough to be heard.

"I found this one lurking about in a doorway down the lane," the constable stated, inching his way into the incredibly crowded room.

With a nod, the inspector acknowledged their entrance, but turned his attention to the two constables by the landing. "Why don't you take Maunder, here, downstairs. I'm sure there's more he would like to tell me, but he just needs a little time to get his thoughts together. I'll be down when I'm done here."

While this was going on, Ernie eased back behind Nigel, trying his best to blend into the shadows. He knew very well who the big fellow was and the last thing he wanted was to engage in any conversation with him. Lily got a sense for what was happening and she closed the gap between her and Nigel to further conceal Ernie's presence.

"Well, isn't this interesting," said Inspector Flannel contently, looking back at the concealed room. "In that room I have a dead man, and who should be found lurking about the scene but my old friend Dragonetti."

"That's why you dragged me up here?" inquired Dragonetti dryly, brushing at his coat sleeve without ever looking up at the inspector. "I'm surprised to see you grasping at such an unfounded accusation."

We are cursed as humans to quickly formulate an opinion about the people we meet from nothing more than their appearance and lot in life. Such was the case with Nigel and Lily who, after doing so, were visibly surprised at how soft spoken and articulate Dragonetti was for so large and frumpish a man... especially a man who obviously was no stranger to the law. Nor did he appear to them as a threat, but they would readily concede they didn't know him the way Ernie did.

"Why would I waste my time accusing?" responded the inspector warningly. "If you took part in this little drama, I'll know soon enough, and then I'll just arrest you."

That was enough to raise Dragonetti's head, but he responded with only a smirk.

"This is Nigel Coats," Inspector Flannel continued, now that he had his attention. "He believes he saw you earlier this afternoon outside his flat on Conduit Street. That would make this quite the coincidence, so, since you have graciously consented to join us, I was wondering what you find so interesting about his flat and this flat?"

"That good-looking bird," Dragonetti said casually. "I noticed her going into the flat on Conduit Street. I thought about chatting her up when she came out again, but she drove off before I had the chance. I followed her and she went up the block and backed into a small alley just up the street. After a while your friends here came out and she followed after them. I was curious, now, so I followed her here. It was nice entertainment for the price of a cab ride."

"Lady Beckett is here?" exclaimed Nigel.

"Relax Guv'nor," Dragonetti said dismissively, irritated with the interruption. "She took off when Constable Crabbe yanked me out of the shadows and walked me up here." He paused, looked over at Lily and smiled. "So, what's your story, luv?"

The inspector gave a nod in the direction of the constable standing next to Dragonetti. He jerked his head towards the door and stretched out his arm to usher them down the stairs, as if indicating the show was over and he needed to make room for the next tour group.

Lily ignored the question and grabbed their coats from the bed. Nigel informed the inspector he would ring him later and bade him goodbye. Nigel and Lily started down the stairs, with Ernie close at their heels, his head ducked in an attempt to hide his face. He was almost at the stairs when Dragonetti stepped in front, blocking his way. The inspector was busy filling his pipe and didn't notice what was happening at the doorway.

After a cautious glance to confirm the inspector's disinterest, Dragonetti leaned down close to Ernie. "Now we're even, so stay out of my way," he whispered, and slowly stepped away.

Ernie began to tremble, but nodded his head rapidly in agreement as he stumbled back against the wall. He felt his way to the landing and bounded down the stairs, catching up with Lily and Nigel at the bottom.

"There you are, Bisquets," said Nigel, as he helped Lily on with her coat.

"Are you okay?" she asked. "You look rather flushed."

"Yes, Miss," Ernie replied, winded from his abrupt descent. "Lost my footing, that's all."

"Thinking about those Cornish pasties, eh Bisquets?" said Nigel briskly. "We better put a good foot to it, it's nearly seven."

Together they left, walking back towards St. Paul's churchyard in search of a cabbie. Nigel and Lily were quietly comparing theories about what had transpired up in the flat and contemplating their next move. Ernie just followed along, outwardly expressing interest in their thoughts but inwardly relieved that fortune had yet again spared him the embarrassment of having to explain his past.

For the first time in his life he felt he mattered to someone other than himself, so it had gone beyond just hiding his past. Ernie now felt he was deceiving those who had afforded him their trust and respect, asking only for the same in return. Nigel and Lily had certain expectations of him, based on what they believed to be a truthful accounting of his character. If they were accidentally confronted with his past would they see him in the light Patterson Coats had cast upon him, or recognize him as a deceptive, common thief, newly released from Edmunds Hill?

This was more than he was willing to continue to wrestle with. He got it in his mind that when he spoke to His Lordship that evening he would inform him of his intention to disclose his past to the household, and accept whatever consequences that action resulted in.

Ernie was so lost in that thought he hadn't noticed the open door of the cab.

"Are you coming, old man?" said Nigel from inside.

With a nod, Ernie smiled and climbed in. The weight of his past was enough. He certainly didn't want to add to it by being responsible for them missing Mrs. Chapman's Cornish pasties.

Ten

TODAY IS TOMORROW'S PAST

I T WAS TEN minutes past seven when they arrived back at Conduit Street, and Mrs. Chapman was waiting for them patiently at the top of the stairs. As he tossed his Mack over a chair Nigel remarked on the wonderful aroma that filled the air. Lily agreed and the two started off to the dining area.

"Are you coming?" asked Nigel, glancing back at Ernie.

"He's offered to help me with the tray, he has," answered Mrs. Chapman abruptly through her quintessential smile. "You'll find a lovely bottle of wine in need of *your* attention on the table, so off with you, now."

With a click of his heels and a playful salute, Nigel turned and ushered Lily through the lounge to the dining table in search of the aforementioned bottle.

Mrs. Chapman took the Mac from Ernie's outstretched arm, not a bit fooled by the smile he had struggled with for the benefit of the others. Twice he motioned as if to speak to her. Each time she paused and leaned close to listen, but each time he refrained with a shake of his head. With the coats put away Mrs. Chapman scurried off to the kitchen with Ernie once again hurrying to keep pace with her.

As they walked through the swinging door, they were met with a blast of heat emanating from the cast iron Imperial. The kitchen was a monument to the Victorian era, right down to its black and white octagon tile floor. The room was lit with beautiful ornate gas fixtures that had been electrified, but remained in their original positions. The refrigerator was the only modern convenience, with wood panel inserts making a fair attempt at masking the awkwardness of its necessity. Ernie stood by the large butcher block-topped table in the center of the room, waiting as Mrs. Chapman took the plates down from the cupboard.

"I don't belong here," Ernie said softly, finally breaking the awkward silence.

Mrs. Chapman looked back and smiled, but continued preparing the meal.

"I'm lying to these fine people, I am, and they deserve better than the likes of me. It's only a matter of time before they see me for the scoundrel I am." Ernie took the tray that Mrs. Chapman was now holding out and, with his head lowered, he continued. "It was only by the grace of God that Flannel didn't out my past. Next time I won't be so lucky. And then what do I say? *Yes, he's right. I'm a common pickpocket. Sorry Guv'nor.* I knows how it'll be. Every time something's misplaced, he'll look at me and wonder if I nicked it."

"Is that what you think?" replied Mrs. Chapman, the sparkle in her eyes softening with disappointment. She took hold of Ernie's chin and raised his head as she lowered her voice so as not to be overheard. "It's a nutter, you are. No one here will give a damn about the man you were, because they've already decided about the man you're capable of being. And if someone does say you were a common pickpocket, all you need to do is correct them."

"Correct them?" Ernie muttered, confused by the statement.

The sparkle was slowly returning to Mrs. Chapman's eyes. "Why yes, correct them. You're anything but bog standard. His Lordship—no finer man walks this earth—told me you were the best he'd seen in a long time." A broad smile now stretched across Mrs. Chapman's face as she held out a small leather object. "Or at least since I been on the pension."

Realizing what the object was Ernie all but dropped the tray as he checked from pocket to pocket trying to locate his billfold, but to no end. With a quiet laugh Mrs. Chapman tossed the billfold on the tray and turned her attention back to the pasties, which she had warming on top of the old Imperial. Balancing the tray with one hand, Ernie took up the billfold and placed it back in his pocket, very much confused but smiling and impressed with the demonstration.

One by one Mrs. Chapman placed the pasties on plates and arranged them on the tray. "Everyone has a past, Mr. Bisquets," she said, looking over the plates one last time. "You'll find mine not too different than your own. Remind me one day over tea and scones to tell you the particulars. For now, you should listen to

His Lordship and let yours go."

"But what about Inspector Flannel?" Ernie replied, doing his best to keep the heavy tray level. "He's not one to bury the past of someone the likes of me. It's just a matter of time."

"There's one thing I'll tell you about my Derby," said Mrs. Chapman modestly, turning Ernie towards the doorway, "he knows he'll never taste my ham an' cabbage again if he does dredge up your past. It's his favorite, you know, and he looks forward to it every Sunday when I'm off. Now off you go, they'll be getting impatient if we dawdle any longer."

"You've been very kind to me since I arrived," Ernie said, the cheerfulness returning to his voice. "And if you say it's okay, then I guess I'll leave that baggage back at Edmunds Hill."

With a smile Mrs. Chapman gave him a shove and the weight of the tray pulled him right through the swinging door and into the dining area.

"There you are, old man," said Nigel, seated at the head of the table, his serviette tucked hastily into his collar. "I'd given you two—and those pasties—up for lost."

"Sorry, squire." Ernie held out the tray for Mrs. Chapman to serve the much anticipated fare. "I had a few questions and Mrs. Chapman was kind enough to let me distract her from her duties for a moment."

"No need to explain, Bisquets, I'm just having a bit of sport with you."

With the meal in place and the tray under her arm Mrs. Chapman excused herself, and Ernie took his seat at the table. Nigel handed Ernie a glass of Merlot and for the first time since his arrival he genuinely felt relaxed. It hadn't gone unnoticed by Lily who looked over at him with an approving smile. All three had worked up their appetites, so they wasted no time putting their utensils to work. Nigel soon settled back in his chair ready to discuss the day's activities and sketch out their next move.

"I think it's safe to say," he started, sipping at his wine, "that we've had quite the day and much of what we have uncovered is thanks to you, Bisquets." Nigel raised his glass and was promptly joined by Lily. "If you hadn't noticed the absence of the windows in that flat we may never have found that hidden room or that unfortunate man's body."

"You're very kind, squire," Ernie replied, embarrassed by the attention.

"Not at all, you've earned this modest hurrah. And to go a bit further I'll say my uncle's intuitive senses about people have once again been spot on."

"I don't know about that, sir," replied Ernie, intently looking from one to the other, "but I must admit I've found this whole business rather exciting."

"Nothing like a murder to get the blood going," Nigel said, then pausing for a moment he realized what he'd said, and he broke into a hearty laugh.

"Forgive him" — Lily shook her head. — "You'll find Nigel has an adept ability to amuse himself."

"Quite all right, Miss," Ernie replied, trying hard to refrain from joining in Nigel's amusement.

"You'll find Lily doesn't share in or, for that matter, appreciate, my sense of humor, but I can see I've found an ally in you."

"If Ernie is to update Patterson," Lily said patiently, "maybe we should review where we stand with this inquiry?"

"Quite right you are, Lily," replied Nigel briskly. "Bisquets, feel free to correct me if I've captured something incorrectly." Nigel took the small note pad from his pocket and flipped through the pages. "Here we are. I believe it is still safe to assume that Jacques Millet and Jackie Miller are in fact one and the same, and that he may or may not be lying dead in a pile of frames. Lady Constance Beckett is indeed trying to locate this man, not out of concern for his safety, but for reasons we believe related to the attempted theft of the painting at the Musée de Orsay. Our old friend Detective Inspector Flannel is checking the fingerprints of the dead man, whom he believes to be Jackie Miller, but we're less than convinced. Maybe something will turn up with the description we gave my uncle. And then there was that rather large chap...what was his name?"

"Dragonetti, squire," Ernie responded in a low voice.

"Yes, that's it, Dragonetti. Is that his first name or last name? No matter," Nigel continued, waving off the need for a response. "I'm sure Inspector Flannel will have more to tell us about his involvement in all this. Now, have I missed anything?"

"What about that prickly little Maunder?" Lily wrinkled her nose.

"Oh yes, Maunder." Nigel gave Lily an encouraging wink. "He's quite a looker, that one. I think you might have a chance with him," He quickly sat back, beyond her reach, in anticipation of her response.

Lily's face flushed at his teasing, but with exceptional self-control she looked past Nigel's remark and slowly repeated her question directly to Ernie.

"Maunder's a bit dodgy, Miss, and always on the pull, but he hasn't the nerve for the rough stuff. He'll pick at the crumbs, all right, and talk it up at the pub over a pint, but he runs the other way from trouble. I believe he hasn't a clue what happened to that poor bloke or where Jackie Miller might be."

"On that subject," Nigel said, refilling and nodding at the glass of wine in front of Ernie before relaxing back in his chair, "Inspector Flannel mentioned to me he felt the body we found was, in fact, Jackie Miller."

"It's possible, squire," Ernie agreed. "It's been some time since I've seen him."

"Yes, Inspector Flannel thought as much."

"I'm very anxious to hear what Patterson makes of the photo I sent him," Lily said brightly. "Maybe he'll look familiar to someone at the museum?"

"If you're ready, old man," suggested Nigel, "I believe my uncle should be calling any moment now. There's a telephone on the desk in his study across the hall. Feel free to take the call there, you'll find it much more private than the hall."

Ernie nodded, and as he rose from the table, the front bell rang. From the hall a familiar voice could be heard. No sooner had Ernie reached the doorway than Inspector Flannel stepped through.

"Don't leave on my account," said Inspector Flannel gruffly.

"I'm…er…not," Ernie stammered, inching his way around the man. "I'm…expecting a… call. His Lordship, you know."

"Inspector Flannel," Nigel called out, rising from his chair and extending his hand. "We weren't expecting you this evening. Please, join us. Can I get you anything?"

"Good evening, Miss," the inspector replied, addressing Lily as he tipped his hat. "Nothing, thanks. I'm just on my way back to the Yard, and I thought you might like to know your body is one Thomas Fournier. He came up right away because he was a night watchman at the Musée d' Orsay. The medical examiner believes he met his end some time yesterday."

"Brilliant!" Nigel exclaimed. "It seems we're spot on about the connection between the attempted theft at the museum, Jackie Miller and the demise of that poor chap."

"Well, I'll just leave you to your afters," said the inspector. "If you don't mind, I'd like to have a word with Mrs. Chapman."

"By all means," said Nigel, starting to grin. "I should have known we weren't the only reason for this impromptu visit. Just the same, thank you for the information. If we scare up anything additional, we'll be sure to give you a ring."

With a grunt and a tip of his hat he bade them both good evening and quietly made his way toward the kitchen. "One other thing," added the inspector, pausing at the door. "The number you gave me for Lady Beckett is no longer in service. We checked and it doesn't seem she ever existed. Maybe your new mate has something to say about that." That said, he was gone.

"You know, Lily," Nigel said, frowning slightly as they watched the door swing closed behind the inspector, "I believe the good inspector is a bit unchuffed with Bisquets. We may need to look a bit deeper into this."

"I think you're making too much of it," Lily said coolly. "You know how the inspector is. He barely tolerates us."

"I can understand him barely tolerating you," replied Nigel with a smirk, "but he and I are thick as thieves, we are. In fact, I'm thinking about getting a derby of my own. Or maybe a trilby, like those chaps in the cinema."

Lily just rolled her eyes. "The only things thick about you two are your heads."

Eleven

WILL THE REAL MR. FOURNIER PLEASE LIE DOWN

A S ELEGANT AND impressive as their public rooms were, Patterson Coats' study exhibited a dramatic, yet somber, atmosphere. Resting quietly on the walls between the coffered ceiling and the richly decorated oriental carpets were the memories and accomplishments of this unpretentious group. In very modest frames were the photos of past and present members, receiving what were most likely handshakes of gratitude for services rendered. There was nothing to indicate what those services might have been, but the people and private settings in which the photos were taken spoke volumes of how significant and appreciated their efforts had been.

These images looked out over a leather topped, three drawer, Regency writing desk with an equally superb matching chair. In this otherwise tidy room, the desk was awkwardly cluttered with papers and leather bound books, but the telephone was easily visible by the light cast upon it by the black tôle lamp. Flanking the tall windows that overlooked Conduit Street at the other end of the room, was a stylish pair of mahogany library chairs with scrolled arms and dark leather upholstery. The only truly personal item displayed was a pierced silver frame, holding an intimate photo of Patterson and Marie Bussière. It sat on a Regency whatnot of small proportions between the two chairs.

Such was the sum total of the room. Where the whole of the flat was a testament to their achievements in antiquities, this was indeed a room imbued with the discretion the club had built its reputation on.

The photos captured his attention as Ernie entered the study and walked over to the desk. He wasn't sure who anyone really was, except for the few where he recognized Nigel and Lily, but he was quite sure if they were on the wall they were significant. As he looked from photo to photo he felt around behind him for the chair and slowly sat down.

The phone rang suddenly, startling him. He paused for a moment, and then picked up the receiver. "Hello?"

"Ernie, so good to hear your voice," replied Patterson. "Please forgive my absence, as I mentioned before, I had every intention of being there. But how have you been getting on? I hope the arrangements I've made for you are to your liking."

"You've been more than generous, sir," Ernie replied humbly. "More than the likes of me deserves, I can tell you that."

"Nonsense. I'll have no more talk like that. You've earned this and, if your first day is any indication, much more. I've spoken with Nigel about Lady Constance Beckett's visit and the note from her uncle. I spoke only briefly with Lily but she made it a point to tell me how impressed she is with you. But I'm not surprised in the least. I've been impressed with you since that day in Mayfair when you pinched my billfold."

"B-but...h-how did you know..." Ernie stammered.

"I wouldn't be very good at what I do if I didn't know things," Patterson interrupted with a slight laugh. "I have a great deal to tell you about that day, but we'll leave that for another time and a glass of Malmsey."

"Anything you say, Guv'nor. I do want to properly thank you for all you've done, 'specially getting me out of the Hill."

"Edmunds Hill is for criminals," Patterson reminded him quietly, "and I don't think you see yourself spending any more time with that lot. You're too talented to waste your life looking over your shoulder, wondering when our mutual friend, Inspector Flannel, will knock up for you. You're also much smarter than that, and I would imagine by now you've even deduced I have no need for a valet."

"Since you mention it, sir," said Ernie respectfully, "I thought it a bit queer, what with my rooms and Mrs. Chapman and all."

"Once again I'll ask your forgiveness," continued Patterson with conviction, fully indicating the gravity of what he was about to explain. "This is not the conversation I intended to have this evening, but because of the nature of our business it is imperative that I be certain of an individual's character before I reveal anything related to the ELAC. You've had a glimpse today of what lies ahead if you intend to continue on this path laid before you, but I'm sure you'll understand that before I can allow you to continue I'll need to know what your intentions are?"

"You can trust me, sir. I ain't done nothing wrong." Ernie was surprised by the sudden change in the tone of the conversation.

"No, of course you haven't," Patterson said soothingly. "I have every confidence you have—and will—continue to act with honor and integrity. It's more complicated than that. I'm afraid there's a greater danger in this museum business than I originally anticipated, and with information recently brought to my attention I may have put your life in jeopardy. Nigel and Lily are no strangers to the perils involved with this aspect of our work, and they willingly accept these risks. You, on the other hand, have been duped, so to speak, by me—but with the best of intentions."

"Duped?" Ernie hesitated for a moment, and then continued. "In what way, sir?"

"Your diverse background has afforded you certain talents and abilities which can prove invaluable in our profession. For this reason I've selfishly plucked you from the life you were leading and dropped you into ours, with the hope that you would embrace the opportunity to give back to the society you have for years made withdraws from."

"Blimey!" Ernie said slowly, doing his best to make sense out of what His Lordship just said, while not taking offense. "A bit blunt, innit?"

"I'm afraid so, Ernie, but the current situation has forced my hand. I'm acting in the best interest of my colleagues, and though you may disagree, I believe it's in your best interest also. Understand, there's a great deal more to it, and if you will indulge me for now, I assure you I will explain it all in due time."

There was a long pause in the conversation. Ernie was confused over what he was to do next. He wanted to answer, but he wasn't sure what the question was or if an answer was even in order.

"I wasn't always a bounder," Ernie said with some trepidation, finally breaking the silence. "I ain't never hurt no one, and I only took from those who could afford to lose it. That stay in the Hill was enough for me. I never want to see the inside of that place again."

"I understand that, but I need you to understand the possible dangers that lie ahead if you choose to join us."

"I ain't no coward, either," Ernie interjected sharply, then forced his voice back to a polite tone. "Sorry, I'm a bit knackered."

"Quite all right. Let's leave it there for now, but I'll ask a favor of you before we're done here. First, tell me about your visit to Miller's flat."

Ernie was still a bit confused but he went over the particulars in great detail, starting at his conversation with Maunder and following along to when Dragonetti was brought in. Patterson asked questions during the narration, interjecting his own thoughts at times. The dead man in Miler's flat was an important discovery and confirmed the connection with the incident in Paris.

Because of his uncertainties surrounding Ernie's future participation, Patterson was cautious not to allude to his evidence that the Manet had, in fact, been replaced with a clever forgery. They continued to talk over the details for the better part of an hour until they'd finally exhausted the subject.

"It seems you've had quite a day of it," said Patterson, sounding very much impressed at the degree of detail in Ernie's report. "I have additional information, but nothing we need to go over this evening. If you wouldn't mind, could you relay a few messages for me?"

"Of course," Ernie responded briskly, looking about the desk for paper and pen.

"Please tell Nigel that the acting curator of the museum spoke with Martine Evrard and Thomas Fournier, the two guards on duty that night." Patterson paused at times during his narration to give Ernie the opportunity to keep up with his notes. "They agreed to make themselves available to us tomorrow morning."

"Got it," said Ernie enthusiastically. "Anything else, Guv'nor?"

"There is the matter of that favor," replied Patterson, returning to a more serious tone. "I'm going to need you to make a very difficult decision with very little time. I was wrong, no matter how righteous my intentions were, to think I had the right to interfere with your life. So, be that as it may, I have taken steps to correct this. I would like you to take this evening to give careful thought to today's events and what might be expected of you if you so choose to become part of the East London Adventurers Club. I can promise you will see much more of the world than you thought possible, but the dark hand of evil will be forever at our door. At times we risk our lives for little reward, save the thanks of a grateful nation. Our triumphs are never spoken of in public, but we are held fully responsible for our failures in the media. The only respite from this aberrant side of our business is our work in antiquities. I find this particularly rewarding.

"I have made arrangements to have your criminal record

expunged. You'll find your passport in your room, along with £1000 and a travel voucher. If you decide you do not wish to continue along this path, you are free to leave in the morning without any negative reflection on your character.

"I would suggest, though, if you do intend to follow a different path, you holiday away from London for the next few weeks. This business may get a bit more unpleasant before we get to the bottom of it, and it would be best if we removed you from the equation. Either way, tomorrow you resume your life without my meddlesome interference. The path you take and what you make of that life is strictly your decision now. I hope I have impressed upon you the seriousness of what we do and the level of commitment required. I'll say nothing more; save I truly believe you have much to offer our cause, if you so choose to join us. Have you any questions?"

Ernie was dumbfounded. With his mouth open he just shook his head, giving no thought to His Lordship not being able to see him. "No," finally escaped from his mouth, though barely audible.

"Fine," said Patterson. "I think it would be best if you keep this arrangement between us. I know how persuasive Lily and Nigel can be, but it's important that you search inside yourself for the answer. Whatever you decide, rest assured you will have our full support. Tell Nigel I'll speak with him tomorrow. Good night, Ernie, and thank you very much for your help today."

Ernie sat at the desk for a few moments, still bewildered over what had just transpired. He finally hung up the receiver, picked up his notes and slowly made his way back to the salon.

"There you are, Bisquets," Nigel called out from the sofa. He and Lily both noticed the uneasiness in his expression. "Are you all right, old man?"

"Tired, squire," Ernie replied softly, handing the paper with his notes on it to Nigel, "just tired. His Lordship asked me to give you these messages. He got your photo, Miss," he continued addressing Lily, "and he'll be taking it over to the museum in the morning."

"Well, this is interesting," interrupted Nigel, holding up the note for Ernie to look at. "Are you sure about this name, Thomas Fournier?"

"Yes, sir," Ernie answered confidently. "He said he was one of the night guards and he agreed to meet with him tomorrow morning. Do you know him?"

"We met only once," replied Nigel, grinning. "I believe you

know him, too...he was that chap lying in the pile of frames this afternoon. While you were talking with my uncle, the good inspector informed us the fingerprints identified the dead man in Miller's secret room as Thomas Fournier, a night guard at the Musée d' Orsay. An exceptionally clever corpse this one, since he felt compelled to show up for work despite his debilitating affliction. Well, Bisquets, what do you make of that?"

"Miller, sir," answered Ernie sharply. "He looks enough like him, and it would explain the missing glasses."

"Brilliant!" exclaimed Nigel, jumping to his feet. "Exactly what I thought. I better ring my uncle back and suggest he have the other Fournier detained at once. If it is Miller, he has a lot to answer for. Lily, would you fill Bisquets in on the rest and our plans for tomorrow?"

"Have a seat Ernie," Lily smiled, tossing some pillows aside.

"Thank you, Miss,"

"We put you through your paces today, didn't we?" she continued, putting the note down on the table next to the sofa. Ernie smiled and settled back into the cushion as Lily continued. "When I first met Patterson, I thought he was the rudest man on this island. He was abrupt, with very little tolerance for the indecisive nature of people, and he had no problem letting you know how he felt. He is very calculating and once he makes his mind up about something it never occurs to him that it might not be possible. To his frustration, and sometimes ours, he expects the same behavior from those around him. He believes all people are capable of accomplishing anything they can imagine, yet many fail to achieve their dreams because they're not willing to take that first step. Instead, they sit back and allow fate to choose their path. *'If that's all they expect from life,'* he'll say, *'then there's more for the rest of us'*.

"After awhile I realized he wasn't the snobbish ogre I thought he was. He was just trying to impart to me the ability to achieve my dreams, and never be a victim of fate's fickle hand. He's a selfless noble who would willingly place himself between you and any evil that lurks in the shadows. No better friend could the Crown have...nor I."

"And no finer man walks this earth," Mrs. Chapman joined in, suddenly appearing with a tray. She placed it on the table in front of them. "Miss Lily likes coffee round this time, and I brought an extra cup in case you fancy one yourself."

"Thank you, mum," Ernie said. "You're very kind."

"You'll need a good rest tonight," Lily said as she fixed her coffee. "We're off to Paris in the morning to take a look around the Musée d' Orsay. We should meet with Marie Bussière. She may have additional information we might find of interest to this matter."

"Marie Bussière?" asked Ernie, sipping at his coffee.

"Yes, she's the acting curator at the museum. And did I mention our friend Lady Constance Beckett has dropped off the face of the earth? Inspector Flannel mentioned her phone number is no longer in service and he doubts that was ever her real name. She was the common thread between Miller, Fournier and the attempted theft in Paris, so losing her is going to make sorting this out a bit tougher." She glanced over at Ernie, hesitated, and then said, "Are you sure you're all right?"

"Sorry, Miss," Ernie said, yawning. "Just tired, I guess."

"Of course you are. We can talk more on the train tomorrow."

"If you wouldn't mind, Miss" — Ernie placed his cup on the tray and rose slowly to his feet — "I'd like to go up to my room, now."

"You go right ahead," Lily answered brightly. "I'll let Nigel know you've gone off to bed. Can I ask a favor of you before you go?"

"Yes, Miss, anything."

"Do you think you could call me Lily tomorrow?"

A very large smile came to his face, but it did little to mask the concern that still clung to him. "Yes, Miss, I'll certainly try." He gave a quick look around the room and with a wink and a nod he disappeared through the doorway.

Twelve

AN EARLY MORNING DELIVERY

THE FOLLOWING DAY brought with it the promise of everything wonderful about autumn in Paris. The early morning air was crisp, but not so that one had to cinch up their scarf. Small clusters of clouds hung in the distant sky, as if dabbed in by Renoir. The trees that lined the boulevards were brilliant with color, the leaves just starting to fall on the pavements left behind by the receding wave of tourists. The aroma of fresh breads and pastries hastened the step, playfully pulling customers through the doorways where vendors patiently awaited their arrival. It was no wonder Patterson Coats suggested to Marie that she meet him at his hotel and they walk over to the Préfecture de Police on the Île de la Cité.

Patterson was already out front talking on his mobile phone when Marie arrived. She wrapped her arm around the one he held out and together they started off down the street, quietly admiring all that is Paris.

"Forgive me," Patterson said, closing up his phone and tucking it away in his pocket. "That was Nigel with a bit of disappointing news."

"Everything's all right, I hope?" Marie asked, stopping short.

"I'm afraid it's my standard bearer, Ernie Bisquets." Patterson patted Marie lightly on the hand and continued. "It seems you were right, I did push him into something he wasn't ready for."

"I'm very sorry to hear that, I know you had such high hopes for his participation. What will happen to him?"

Patterson shook his head, not ready to answer the question. They walked along quietly, turning onto the Pont au Change. Ahead was the Boulevard du Palais, but they stopped for a few moments to watch the canal boats drift along the Seine.

"I am fully responsible for his current situation," said Patterson contritely, "so I've taken steps to undo what I've done. As far as the constabulary is concerned Mr. Ernie Bisquets is now, and has been, a law-abiding citizen of London. I returned his passport and gave him enough money to establish himself somewhere other than London. From this latest development you mentioned last night, it seems this business is deteriorating quickly, and I suggested it best that he get away from London for the time being."

"You shouldn't be so hard on yourself. Do you think he's in danger?" Marie asked softly, brushing back the hair from her face.

"Two men have been killed over this painting so far," Patterson stated firmly, "and I have no intention of allowing him to unwillingly be the third."

"The dead police officer that was found this morning could have just been a coincidence," Marie said as they continued on their walk,

"I doubt very much your brother would agree." Just ahead they could see activity in front of the Préfecture de Police. "I'm sure it's the one thing he and I will agree on. From what you told me on the phone this morning, the dead officer was the one who placed your thief in the back of the police wagon. The thief's escape would certainly cast suspicion in his direction, and then the officer went missing. The discovery of his body on the steps of the museum this morning is a message, not a coincidence."

"A message...but from whom?"

"From whom, indeed?" answered Patterson portentously. "The better question might be *for* whom?"

Marie looked down the street after hearing her name called by a familiar voice. "You think Jacques Millet is still mixed up in this, don't you?" she asked distractedly, waving to her brother in front of the station.

"Yes, I do, and I'm afraid he may not realize how truly dangerous the people he's dealing with are."

"*Bonjour,* Jean-Paul," Marie called out, greeting her brother with a hug.

"*Bonjour, Prefect* Bussière," said Patterson pleasantly.

"Well, *Monsieur* Coats," replied Jean-Paul contemptuously, ignoring the hand extended before him. "What brings Her Majesty's footman to Paris?"

"Please, Jean-Paul," Marie demanded, "is it so difficult for you to be civil?"

"It's quite all right, Marie," Patterson said quickly, addressing both questions. "My intervention in police business always brings out the worst in your brother. Why don't we just get to it and I'll make my stay here as brief as possible."

"Very well. Why don't I tell you about my morning? First I had a very interesting conversation with Inspector Flannel of Scotland Yard." *Prefect* Bussière motioned to an officer, who in turn pulled a car up to where they were standing. "It seems your little group stumbled upon the body of Thomas Fournier, a guard at the Musée d' Orsay." He held his hand up and shook his head, stopping Marie from interrupting him. "Then I received a call from Marie telling me the Manet *had* been stolen and replaced with a forgery." He opened both doors and indicated they were to get inside. "Now I have the body of one of my officers on the steps of that museum. But, then again, you already knew all of this. Didn't you?"

The three of them climbed into the car and her brother instructed the driver to proceed to the Musée d' Orsay.

"Thomas Fourier?" said Marie sadly, looking at Patterson sitting next to her and then her brother in the front seat. "I just spoke with him late yesterday…"

"That's not possible," *Prefect* Bussière interrupted, indicating to the driver to pull up next to the statues on the corner. "According to Inspector Flannel, Fourier was murdered some time Tuesday afternoon."

"But it is possible," Marie insisted, "because I called down to him in the main hall from the upper level. I told him I needed to see him this morning at nine o'clock sharp. He nodded his head and waved as he went on with his rounds."

"I'm sure you spoke to someone"—Patterson took her hand—"but you're brother's correct, Marie. I'm sorry. I meant to tell you this morning, but with the other news it just slipped my mind. After you and I spoke last night, Nigel rang and informed me about Fournier. They found him in a secret room in Miller's flat. At first they thought is was Miller, but the fingerprints proved otherwise. Lily sent me a photo last night for you to identify, but there's no need now."

"I can't believe Jacques Millet, or Miller as you know him, is capable of this." Marie sat back, amazed at what she was hearing.

"You and I need to have a conversation about this Miller," said *Prefect* Bussière sharply, addressing Patterson.

They arrived at the Musée d' Orsay in short order. A crowd was still lingering around the cordoned off area where the body lay. Recognizing Marie as the acting curator of the museum, the media hurled a barrage of questions at her when they exited the car, but she waved off comment and they made their way through the crowd and over to the body. After a brief conversation with the officers at the scene, *Prefect* Bussière instructed an officer to pull back the cloth covering the body. Marie gasped and buried her face in Patterson's coat.

It was a gruesome sight. The officer had been shot at close range. The pain engraved in his face hinted at the suffering he had endured before finally dying. His uniform was saturated with blood from the wound in his chest. Everything remained as it had been found. He had his wallet, his gun, and money in his pocket and a small piece of paper with a number written on it. Lying curiously next to the body was a small wooden fife.

"I'm sorry, Marie," Jean-Paul said to his sister as delicately as he could, "but this is police business. I need to know if this officer looks familiar to you, or if you remember him spending time in the museum?"

Marie just shook her head, making no attempt to look at the dead man's face again. The *prefect* motioned to one of the officers to cover the body, and then to one of the female officers to escort Marie into the museum.

"I'll stop in and see how you're doing after your brother and I have a chance to compare notes," Patterson told her.

Marie nodded and a slight smile came to her face. Jean-Paul grudgingly fumbled about at an apology, but she made no further attempt to acknowledge anything more her brother had to say. She turned and followed the officer into the museum.

Jean-Paul Bussière looked over; Patterson recognized the fellow saw the reprimand on the tip of his tongue, so he accepted there was no need to verbalize it. He escorted Marie's brother over to the low wall that acted as a base for a group of statues. They sat down.

"If it isn't already," Patterson started, "this business will be all over the media soon enough. It is to our advantage to put aside our differences and try to work to bring about a successful conclusion. You have a murder to solve, and I would like to see the safe return of the painting, so I suggest we sift through what we know and try to help each other."

This was murder, and Bussière was under no obligation to discuss any parts of the case with an outsider. Patterson Coats sat patiently waiting for the man's decision. He knew his commanding presence normally irritated Bussière, but this time it seemed to serve to convince the *Prefect de Police* that cooperation was in fact the best course of action.

With a reluctant nod of his head, *Prefect* Bussière began, "Suspicion about Officer Jules Delavau's involvement started to surface Monday night after the would-be thief disappeared from the police van. After a careful examination of the lock on the van we found it had been tampered with. Later, a check of the evening log indicated Delavau had asked to have a police van dispatched to Rue Bonaparte. This was ten minutes before the alarm went off, and only a few streets up from the museum. When the van arrived he gave some excuse about a false alarm. We believe this gave him time to tamper with the lock and it also insured he and the van would be first on the scene.

"Officer Delage, the van driver, told us he saw the thief only for a moment. He was dressed in black and had darkened his face with black grease paint. Delavau locked him in the back of the van and then hurried him off to the police station. It wasn't until the van returned to the station that the thief was discovered missing. Delage has been cooperating and we have no indications that he was involved. But that was the last anyone saw of officer Delavau...until he showed up on the pavement...dead. A *boulangerie* deliveryman, dropping pastries off to the museum, discovered him about 5:15 this morning. The number on the paper in his pocket..."

"A bank account?" Patterson proposed.

"Precisely," agreed *Prefect* Bussière. "We're checking on it now."

"Let me see if I can fill in a few blanks for you," Patterson said, very pleased with the openness afforded him. "We believe your thief was Jackie Miller, a suspected art forger, though no charges have ever been brought against him. An older man, known for his charm and skills, he's had access to the museum for some time as a trusted frame restorer calling himself Jacques Millet. He is, or was, in the employ of a woman introducing herself as Lady Constance Beckett, for the purpose of acquiring the painting by Manet. From information brought to our attention recently, we believe Miller used his resemblance to the museum guard, Thomas Fournier to gain additional access to the museum after hours. I would suggest he had knowledge of Miller's intentions, and a check of his bank account may confirm that. Fournier is most assuredly dead, so suffice it to say Miller is whom Marie engaged in a brief conversation yesterday in the main hall. In light of this latest development, I seriously doubt he'll be meeting us at nine o'clock."

Prefect Bussière, while jotting down the facts on his note pad asked, "This Lady Beckett, do you have an address?"

"No. She said she was staying at the Meurice, on Rue de Rivoli, but they have no record of a reservation, only that a note was left for her at the front desk on Tuesday."

"And this note?" asked Bussière slightly annoyed, looking up from his note pad. "Do you know what it said and who might have left it for her?"

"It seemed innocent enough and I believe Miller left it for her. Nigel has it. He'll be here this afternoon, so I'll see that the note gets to you." Patterson paused for a moment as Bussière put his note pad away in a pocket, then continued. "Thinking back to what I read in the initial account of the *attempted* theft, do we still believe our sixty-year old thief rappelled down through the ceiling thirty-four meters to the floor, with the idea of carrying off an incredibly heavy painting, after setting off every alarm, and before the French Police arrived?"

A smirk came to Jean-Paul's face, but disappeared quickly as he began to speak. "I agree. Things are not as obvious as they once appeared. What do you suggest?"

"I'm sure Inspector Flannel will share his ballistic report on Fournier," said Patterson, as the two men walked back over to the body. "I'd be very interested in how it compares to the report on Officer Delavau. That fife next to the body is a warning for Miller from whoever Lady Beckett is. It's safe to assume she doesn't have the painting yet, and for some reason Miller has no intention of giving it to her."

"So it's your contention Miller still has the painting?" asked *Prefect* Bussière, instructing his men to have the body removed.

"Yes, and I also believe he replaced it with the forgery long before Monday night. This man is a forger. Not a thief. Not a murderer. Whatever his game is, you can be sure the events of the last two days were not planned by him. We must get both murders in the news, especially with the reference to the Fifer with this latest. Let's hope he gets spooked enough to seek your protection. This woman is dangerous and most assuredly behind these murders, so with your permission I'd like to continue my search for the true identity of Constance Beckett. You have my word I will be forthcoming with any information I find regarding her identity or whereabouts."

Prefect Bussière was less than enthusiastic with his reply, but he agreed. They shook hands and Patterson started for the door to the museum. He only took a few steps before hesitating, and turned back toward the *prefect*. "By the way, I can only hope that one day my conduct and achievements in life might afford me the honor of being considered a *footman* to Her Majesty. Good morning, *Prefect* Bussière."

The tourists that were huddled in front of every vantage point inside the museum that overlooked the crime scene were starting to disperse. Patterson made his way through the crowd to Marie's office, finding her only slightly more composed than when she'd left him.

"You know, we could continue our walk," Patterson said, gazing down at her seated at her desk.

Marie just shook her head. "He gets me so angry sometimes."

"He has a very difficult job," replied Patterson in a comforting tone, taking a seat on the sofa. "So being a pompous ass will most assuredly guarantee a greater success rate."

Marie looked up, trying not to show her amusement at his left-handed defense of her brother. "You know," she said, leaning forward, unable to hold back the smile any longer, "he attributes your success rate to the same character trait."

"I have no doubt he does," replied Patterson playfully, brushing at his waistcoat. "But at least I pull it off in a tailored suit."

They both enjoyed the moment, however brief it was, but the concern soon returned to Marie's face.

"That poor officer," she said glancing out the window, her voice trembling slightly. "And Thomas. And what of Jacques Millet? Will he be next?"

"Fournier and this police officer were pawns," Patterson said bluntly, "sacrificed to make a point. Don't loose sight of the implication of their involvement with the theft of the painting. I'm in no way implying justification, but their deaths are a consequence of their actions. As for Miller, he's safe as long as he remains in possession of the painting. She wants it. He has it. It's that simple. There is a very good chance he'll come forward, for no better reason than self preservation."

"I hope you're right," she murmured. Marie looked at her watch and then, planting both hands firmly on the desk, slowly pushed to her feet. "It's almost nine o'clock and I've been told Martine Evrard is here as requested. Should I ask him to come in?"

"Yes, please. To put your mind at ease, your brother and I believe that was Miller you spoke to yesterday, dressed as Fournier."

"That was Jacques?" she gasped.

"We believe it was." Patterson rose to his feet. "I would be very interested to know what was so important that he would risk coming back into the museum."

"Truly remarkable," Marie whispered to herself as she walked over to the door and asked the guard to join them. "Martine," she continued, after showing him to a seat by the desk, "this is Lord Patterson Coats. He's here looking into the theft of the Manet."

"*Bonjour, monsieur.*" Martine removed his hat.

"*Bonjour,* Martine. I understand you speak English." Patterson paused, and Martine nodded. "Good. On Monday evening you were on your rounds at the far end of the museum when the robbery occurred?"

"*Oui.*"

"Did you have any conversation with Thomas Fournier that night?"

"*Non.*"

"Did you see him?"

"*Oui.*"

"You saw him, but you had no conversation with him?"

"*Oui.*"

"Is there any reason for this lack of conversation?"

"*Oui,*" answered Martine shortly, his tone becoming coarse as he continued. "Two weeks ago he insulted me. We work together twelve years, but now we just ignore each other."

"*Merci,* Martine," Patterson finished, holding out his hand. "You can go now."

Martine nodded, stood and walked toward the door.

"One other thing, Martine," Patterson called out, stopping him at the door. "I'm sorry to tell you this, but Thomas was killed the other day."

The bitterness that had lingered in Martine's eyes from the last question turned to deep sadness. He glanced over at Marie, who was struggling to hold back her tears as she nodded in confirmation. "*Merci, Monsieur,*" Martine said softly, gazing back at Patterson. "*Merci.*" Tears ran down his cheek as he turned and slowly walked out the door.

"He's lost a good friend," Patterson said, handing Marie his handkerchief. He waited for a moment as she composed herself. "I'm sure the insult was Miller's idea. As you can attest, the resemblance was probably convincing from a distance, but

Martine Evrard would know his friend of twelve years. He's sharp, that Miller."

"What will happen now?" Marie asked, handing back the handkerchief.

"There are a number of questions still unanswered," replied Patterson, buttoning his coat, "but I'm confident the painting is still safe for now. Have you spoken with the press yet?"

"I've arranged for a press conference at nine forty-five," she said, checking her watch once more. "We've kept them at bay long enough, and if I don't tell them what's going on soon they'll take it upon themselves to fill in the blanks." She paused for a moment. "Did you mention earlier that Nigel and Lily are coming to Paris today?"

"Yes." Patterson gave Marie a kiss on the cheek and walked her to the door. "If you wouldn't mind I'd like Nigel and Lily to take a look around. Miller had access to the museum disguised as Fournier, and he had a perfect forgery—so why go through the trouble of making it look like he broke in? All he had to do was switch the paintings. I'd like Nigel and Lily to have a go at that. For reasons of my own, I've yet to tell them this was an actual robbery, but I'll call them now on my way out of Paris and get them up to snuff."

"You're leaving?" Marie asked, quite surprised by the statement.

"Yes. Something has come up unexpectedly and I need to look into it."

"Please be careful," she whispered in his ear. With a comforting smile and a kiss on his cheek she added, "I'm very sorry you lost your standard bearer."

Patterson nodded his appreciation and walked off down the hall.

Thirteen

RIPPLES ON THE WATER

NIGEL HAD RUNG his Uncle Patterson before they boarded the train for Paris with the news of Ernie's departure. It had been only a brief conversation. Marie had just arrived and his uncle had said he would have to ring back later for the details.

The morning was dreary when the train pulled out of Waterloo Station. The journey to Paris started out very quietly, with only an occasional conversation between Nigel and Lily about the particulars of the murder and the elusive Lady Beckett. Invariably each discussion ended with how surprised they were that Ernie would just leave the way he had.

Leaving London's weather behind, a crisp, clear sky welcomed them as they emerged from the Channel. It was around ten-thirty, and still quite a distance from Paris, when Nigel's mobile phone rang.

"Hello, uncle.........Yes, we were quite disappointed also......... Mrs. Chapman heard him milling about early this morning, but when she went to check on him, his bed was made and he was gone. She said he took his valise, a change of clothes and his passport and travel voucher.........The money? No, he left the money behind with a note. I have it right here. It says *'Thanks, but I won't be needing this'*. Curious indeed. He's a nice enough chap, a bit odd, but very perceptive. I don't think we would have found the body without him.........Yes, you mentioned there was more to this story and you were very mysterious about our coming to Paris. Can you elaborate on it now?"

Nigel sat silently as Patterson explained what actually had happened at the museum Monday evening, the discovery of the policeman's body and why it was important they have a look around the museum. At one point he apologized for withholding certain facts, adding a brief explanation why. Nigel was quite surprised at how much more there was to the story, but it did much to strengthen the correlation between the theft and what they'd discovered in Miller's London flat.

Their conversation lasted the better part of twenty minutes, with Nigel hastily making notes of the details he thought pertinent and the questions still needing answers. Lily sat impatiently at the edge of her seat, leaning close to Nigel in an attempt to catch bits and pieces of what was being said.

"Yes, I understand, Uncle," Nigel said as the conversation came to a close. "I'll tell Lily and we'll go straight to the museum when we arrive in Paris. Sorry things didn't work out better with Bisquets. I rather liked him. I'll speak with you again after we return." Nigel snapped his phone shut, tucked it back in his pocket and shook his head.

"Well?" Lily asked, tugging at Nigel's sleeve in eager anticipation of the forthcoming details.

"Well is right!" replied Nigel sharply, settling back into his seat. He took a quick look around to make sure no one could overhear their conversation and began to explain the details as related to him. "It seems there is much more to this business than we thought. This was not an attempted theft at all, as the media first reported. It would appear that Jackie Miller, disguised as Thomas Fournier, managed to replace Manet's *Le Fifre* with a remarkable forgery, which at first went undetected for maybe weeks. Monday evening he attempted to steal his own forgery back, setting off multiple alarms, which brought the police. He was apprehended almost immediately."

"But the paper said he escaped before the police van reached the station," Lily interrupted, a little confused.

"That's correct," Nigel continued, looking around the rail car once more. "The French police believe one of their officers..." Nigel flipped back the pages of his notepad, paused for a moment and continued, "...here it is, Delavau, was working with the thieves. It certainly explains how Miller got out of the police van. They found Officer Delavau's body by the entrance to the Musée d'Orsay this morning, shot at close range. There isn't much he'll be telling us now, but my uncle is confident ballistics will tie this murder together with Fournier's."

"And what of Constance Beckett?"

"Our Lady Constance Beckett is as elusive as ever," said Nigel meditatively. "Her actions have certainly made her a prime suspect in this business, but there is nothing conclusive at this point to attach her to the murders or the theft. That, notwithstanding, my uncle still believes this woman to be incredibly dangerous and at the center of this villainy. He is turning his attentions to identifying and locating her, and has asked that we take a closer look inside the museum."

"What is it we're looking for?" inquired Lily eagerly.

"We're looking for the residue..." Nigel said quietly, carefully looking up and down the aisle before leaning in close to Lily "...of the *original* crime."

"Original crime?" she repeated, quickly craning her neck up over the seats for an additional look around. "What in the world are you talking about?"

"We've been presented with a rather odd collection of characters over the past few days, worthy of Daumier's pen." Nigel flipped casually through his notepad. "Emanating from this unsavory lot is an even more curious bouquet of circumstances." He tucked his notepad back into his pocket and continued, counting out the facts on his fingers. "A priceless Manet has been stolen from the Musée d'Orsay and replaced with a forgery by Jackie Miller. We believe Miller had two allies, Fournier and Delavau. One would give him unlimited access to the museum and the other would eventually aide in his escape. My uncle believes Miller switched the real Manet prior to the theft Monday evening for reasons not yet known. Then Miller orchestrates an elaborate sham to have everyone believe he broke into the museum on Monday evening to steal a painting he's already stolen. Fournier and Delavau are dead. A woman calling herself Lady Beckett is desperately searching for Miller, who, along with the original painting, is missing. So what we have is a slow, continuous ripple of crimes flowing away from the epicenter of the original crime."

"And what, pray tell, might that be?" Lily asked, raising an eyebrow as she settled back into her seat.

"Exactly!" exclaimed Nigel, folding his arms with a very contented look. "We've been following along basing our actions on the obvious, much the way everyone believed, that it was only an attempted theft. I think we need to step back and sift through the original facts and see if anything bobs to the surface. Remember, forgery is the art of deception and Miller excels at his craft. What happened to Miller and the painting is an important question, but it's not *the* question."

"That's brilliant, Nigel," replied Lily brightly. "We've held so tightly to that question, who knows how far we've drifted from the source."

"Spot on, Lily," Nigel agreed with a confident nod. "We need to get to the museum and see what else presents itself. There very well may be nothing more than the facts we have now, but I have a niggling doubt."

Quite pleased with themselves, and the course of action they'd decided on, their conversation drifted off into lighter channels as they enjoyed the remainder of the trip to Paris. By midday the train pulled into Nord Station and they found themselves in a taxi heading toward the Musée d'Orsay.

It wasn't long before they pulled up in front of the statues at the entry plaza to the museum. The area where the body had been found was still cordoned off, but the pallet of colors offered up by a beautiful autumn day in Paris had once again captured the attention of the crowds.

They proceeded inside and were very pleased to find Marie had left word that she be contacted on their arrival. The attendant at the visitor's desk rang her office and from down the adjacent corridor they heard her familiar voice.

"*Bonjour,* Lily." Marie Bussière waved as she approached them. "*Bonjour,* Nigel."

After a kiss on each cheek for each of them, they exchanged pleasantries for a few moments but the grave issues that had brought them together promptly seized the conversation.

"It's so wonderful to see you again," Lily remarked, as they started off down the corridor toward the central alley. "I only wish it were under better circumstances."

"Yes, this is certainly not the type of publicity the museum seeks," Nigel added, admiring the art as they walked along. "I hope you don't mind us having a poke 'round?"

"Not at all," replied Marie earnestly. "I was excited when Patterson told me you were coming. The museum directors and I have every confidence you will get to the bottom of this business and secure the safe return of the Manet."

As she spoke, they turned the corner and were immediately seized by the magnificence of the main hall. The natural light streaming in from above gave the marble sculptures an almost divine presence. Marie looked from one to the other of them and smiled, giving them a moment to take it all in.

"I've been here countless times," Nigel said in his most reverent tone, "but this gallery never ceases to take my breath away."

"This is your first time to our museum?" Marie asked Lily, taking her arm and leading her toward the Impressionists' Galleries.

"I'm embarrassed to say it is, Marie," replied Lily, looking back over her shoulder for Nigel. "Nigel has asked me a number of times to join him, but something has always interrupted our plans."

"Ah, there's hope for you two yet," Marie said through a mischievous grin.

"I hope so," Lily said optimistically, slightly blushing.

Nigel came bounding up behind them as they reached the entryway to the gallery that held the Manet.

"And what are you two smiling at?" he asked suspiciously.

"I was just remarking what a wonderful influence Paris has on a man and a woman."

"I think Paris could take a lesson or two from you in that department," said Nigel, biting his lip and ushering the two women along.

As they entered the gallery they were greeted by the portrait of Émile Zola, who seemed to look up from his book with an approving nod in appreciation of their purpose that day.

"When the media broke the story we had to remove the forgery," Marie said in answer to the questioning expressions on Lily's and Nigel's faces. "I've had it placed in my office for the time being."

"That's quite all right," said Nigel. "We're more interested in what the room has to tell us. Do you mind?" He indicated he intended to move in close enough to look behind one of the other paintings. "Thank you. In the week prior to the theft, did you have any alarm issues?"

"Alarm issues?" Marie asked.

"Yes. Any false or unexplained alarms?"

"Now that you mention it," Marie responded curiously, "during an electrical storm a week before the theft we had alarms going off randomly throughout the museum. It got so bad we turned the alarms off for twenty minutes until the storm passed."

Nigel looked over at Lily, who smiled and nodded her head in agreement. Marie glanced from one to the other of them, confused at first but quickly understanding the relevance of the incident.

"Are all the paintings secured in the same way?" Nigel asked, carefully pulling a thin wire into view from behind the Pissarro he was examining.

"Oui," replied Marie, cringing as Nigel continued to poke about behind the painting. "Careful. If you move that painting too much you'll set off the motion sensor attached to the top of the frame. That wire in your hand is for the secondary alarm. The painting is tethered to the wall with that, but the wire is long enough to allow the painting to be placed on a cart for light cleaning. If the painting is pulled too far from the wall it breaks the connection and sets off the alarm."

"Well we don't want that," Nigel said briskly, looking back at Marie and Lily as he tucked the wire back behind the painting. Pulling his hand back his sleeve caught on something sharp on the back of the frame, a sharp edge or nail head. Marie and Lily both gasped as the lower part of the frame was jerked from the wall and to the right. Nigel's sleeve tore from the weight, and the painting recoiled back against the wall with a thud.

The three of them stood motionless waiting for the alarm to sound, but nothing happened. They watched as the painting came to rest at a severe angle, but still no alarm. Nigel gave it a poke, and then another, and then took the painting in both hands and gave it a shake.

"What are you doing?" Lily finally blurted out sharply. "You'll set the alarm off!"

"No, I don't think I will," answered Nigel calmly.

"I don't understand," Marie said, amazed at what she'd just witnessed but composed enough to speak.

"It seems someone has disabled the motion sensor on this painting," explained Nigel as he straightened out the frame. "But why?"

"Maybe the Manet wasn't the only painting Miller intended to steal that night?" suggested Lily.

"Perhaps." Nigel stepped back from the painting. "Marie, I would suggest you have this painting examined and the motion sensors checked on all the paintings in this gallery. I'm not sure what we're dealing with, but Miller may deserve more credit than we've been willing to extend him."

"I'll notify security. I can close off this section and have them checked immediately." Marie hesitated for a moment and then asked, "You think Jacques Millet, or Miller, as you call him, intended to remove both paintings up through the glass on the roof?"

"Breaking the glass on the roof was a bit of theatrics," Nigel said, shaking his head. "It was a feeble attempt to have us believe that was the thief's point of entry. We believe he used his resemblance to Fournier to gain access to the museum, then changed into black clothes and darkened his face to appear as the thief. I would be very interested to see what sequence the alarms went off that night. It might confirm this, and help explain what happened next."

"I have the security report from Monday night on my desk," Marie said enthusiastically. "Maybe that will help?"

"Excellent!" beamed Nigel.

Together the three walked off to Marie's office, with Nigel lagging behind here and there as different pieces of artwork caught his attention.

Marie handed Lily the report while they waited for Nigel to join them in the office. As Lily looked over the report Marie took a moment to call security and arrange for all the alarms to be tested upon closing of the museum that day. Then she made a second call to Emory, asking that the Pissarro be checked at once.

"Sorry," said Nigel strolling contentedly into the office, his hands folded behind his back. "How does it look, Lily?"

"Umm... The motion sensor on the Manet went off first at 10:27, then at 10:34 the central gallery alarm went off. He was already in the museum when he broke the glass in the roof. I think he deliberately set off the alarms."

"Brilliant!" exclaimed Nigel. "Those theatrics must have been a last minute addition to his plan to throw off whoever he was stealing the painting for. For the time being let's assume Lady Constance Beckett masterminded this theft. Miller may have been hired to paint the forgery and arrange for the theft of the painting, but I don't believe he had any intention of allowing it to be stolen."

"I don't understand." Marie frowned. "You said Miller had already replaced the painting with the forgery prior to the attempted robbery. If all this is true, then where is the painting?"

"Miller underestimated Constance Beckett," Lily said coolly as she continued to study the security report. "I think he intended to have Beckett believe the robbery had been thwarted, and that would be the end of it. She either didn't believe it—"

"Or she didn't care," interrupted Nigel. "Either way, Miller was still on the hook to deliver the painting to her. His plan will be further disrupted when the discovery of the forgery breaks in the media. Killing Fournier was a message and an indication to him of how serious she is about acquiring that painting. Find Miller and you'll find the painting. The tricky part is finding him before she does."

"Killing the police officer is the sign of a determined woman," Lily added abruptly. "We may have to entertain the fact that Beckett in turn may be working for someone more powerful than herself."

"Yes," agreed Nigel, "that certainly would explain her tenacious effort to acquire this painting. We should leave you to your work, now. But if it's not a bother, we'll take another quick look in the gallery, and then poke our heads in before we start back for London."

"Take as much time as you need," replied Marie with a smile.

Lily handed Marie the report and together with Nigel walked back towards the central gallery. Halfway down the hall they heard a voice call out to them.

"*Excuse-moi, monsieur,*" said the voice, just loud enough to be heard by the two of them.

They both stopped and turned. "Are you addressing me, sir?" asked Nigel politely.

"*Oui,*" said the guard. "You are here about the theft, *oui?*"

"*Oui,*" Nigel replied, his curiosity raised. "Do you have any information regarding that?"

"You're Martine Evrard," Lily interrupted. "I saw your name in the security report. You were the other guard on duty Monday night."

"*Oui,*" said Martine quietly. "The older man this morning said Thomas Fournier was killed. Are you sure it was Thomas?"

"Who else do you think it could have been?" Nigel asked.

Martine leaned close to Nigel and whispered, "Jacques Millet."

The response surprised both of them. Nigel looked around for a secluded spot and, after finding an empty office, escorted Martine into it. Lily followed and closed the door behind them.

"What do you know about Jacques Millet?" asked Nigel.

"He was here Monday night."

"You're positive it was Millet?" Nigel continued excitedly.

"*Oui.* I saw him arguing with Thomas in the gallery."

"You saw him arguing with Thomas Fournier?" Nigel strained to keep his voice low.

"*Oui.* I was late starting my ten-fifteen rounds when I heard the alarm sound. I came back, and from the upper level in the central gallery I saw them arguing in the doorway to the Impressionists' Gallery. By the time I got down to the main level Thomas was gone and I heard the Police outside. I went back up to the second level and stayed out of sight, but I saw an officer come in and take Jacques Millet out to the police van."

"Brilliant!" exclaimed Nigel, pacing slowly in front of Martine as he listened. "What happened then?"

"Madame Bussière came in with the police," Martine continued. "I came down at that point and spoke with one of the officers. As we talked I noticed Thomas at the other end of the gallery speaking with another officer. He ignored me and just continued to talk with the officer."

"But the report said you didn't see anything," Lily scolded. "Why would you lie? People have died, including your friend Thomas Fournier."

"Thomas told me he was helping Jacques Millet with something, but he didn't want me to get involved. That's what started our argument weeks ago. He was protecting me, he said, and I see now I was wrong to doubt him. I'm just trying to protect him now." Martine dropped his head in remorse, unable to explain any further.

Nigel continued pacing back and forth, sifting through the new details given by the guard. He stopped finally and an expression of satisfaction came to his face.

"I'm in no way defending our friend, here," Nigel said, resting on the edge of the desk, "but on Monday evening this was nothing more than an attempted theft. The thief was apprehended and the paining was safe. A brief statement from each guard and there you have it." He paused, giving Martine a moment to compose himself, then continued. "Your loyalty to your friend is to be admired, no matter how misdirected the effort now appears. You are doing him a greater service by coming forward with the truth. We cannot undo what has been done, but we can use this information to help bring his murderer to justice. Of course, you know you must explain everything to Madame Bussière and the police."

Martine agreed with very little resistance and bid both of them *adieu*. They left the office together, Martine walking back towards Marie's office and Nigel and Lily towards the central gallery.

"You can be very sensitive at times," said Lily approvingly. She checked her watch. "We have time to take one more look in the gallery then we better head back to the station. As much as I would love to walk the museum, I think it best to get back to London by dinner. Mrs. Chapman told me this morning that Patterson was expected back at Conduit Street by nine this evening. It will be good to put all our heads together and sift through this mess."

"Yes, I agree completely," Nigel said as they walked toward the Impressionists' Gallery.

The gallery had been closed and the Pissarro had been removed while they were in Marie's office. A security team had begun to examine each painting, once again under the approving eye of Émile Zola.

Fourteen

NOTHING LIKE LOOKING UP OLD FRIENDS

MAUNDER WAS A vile little man, devoid of friend and conscience. His character was as crooked as his smile, but he was well known in the London underworld as a source of information. Anyone wishing to extract that information from him did so with contempt and then made every effort to leave behind any recollection of the transaction. To say he read the daily papers is an understatement. He dissected them, line-by-line and word-by-word. He could read an obscure article in the classifieds relating to a grieving woman's attempt to locate a lost article and by the time he was done he would know who had nicked it and how much they had gotten for it. Anyone else of questionable character would parlay this kind of knowledge into a handsome income, but to Maunder, the gathering of information was nothing more than a hobby that filled his otherwise empty afternoons.

Women found him most unnerving, cringing at the sight of his lascivious glare and fending off his endless advances. They certainly wouldn't have him over for high tea, but if someone nicked their silver tea service it's a good bet he'd know where to take the fairy cakes. He very rarely left his flat in the church building, so a person would have no other choice but to inquire for him there.

For someone who didn't drink, he was often the topic of conversation in the local pubs. Anytime there was a mention of him, it always ended the same way, "...*if Maunder shakes your hand, you'd better count your fingers*." It should be said once more, just to make sure there is no misunderstanding, Maunder was a vile little man.

"Oh, it's you, is it," snarled Maunder. The door creaked open just enough to allow his good eye to scan the immediate area while the words squeezed through. Satisfied with his observation he slammed it shut abruptly. A rustling indicated the security chain was being removed, then the door slowly creaked open once more.

Maunder looked more disheveled than usual as he stood in the doorway in a stained vest and tattered dressing gown. He stuffed his reading glasses into a pocket and stepped to one side to allow his guest to enter. "In with ya," he grumbled. "I don't need no more attention on my door stoop than I already got."

He closed the door and indicated for Ernie to follow him into his flat.

Ernie hesitated for a moment—surprised by the bundles of newspapers he could see through the doorway Maunder passed through to the right of the staircase. It was chock-a block full of bundles of newspapers neatly tied with green string and labeled with tags indicating a month. They lined the perimeter of the room, piled under windows and around the sparse furnishings. It gave the room the appearance of being much smaller than it actually was.

The shades were drawn, but a layer of dust over everything was visible. Given Maunder's appearance, and the room itself, Ernie was apprehensive about touching anything, but put his valise down at his feet. He was sure there was a reason for the collection of papers, but he had every intention of avoiding the subject for the time being.

Maunder had wandered off into the kitchen, but soon emerged with a plate in one hand and half a sandwich in the other. "You've interrupted my elevenses. I suppose I can give you half a sarnie," moaned Maunder miserably, holding out the dish with the other half of his roast beef sandwich on it.

"No thanks," replied Ernie, pushing the plate away and taking one step back.

"If you're here for that toff of yours," Maunder muttered, spraying the carpet with pieces of beef from his mouth, "you'll get nothing from me. I knew he was trouble the minute I laid eyes on 'im, I did." The little man pushed his papers aside and took a seat on the sofa. He waved at Ernie, suggesting he do the same, but if there was another seat to be found it was beyond him where it might be.

"I'm here for myself," Ernie snapped back. "I had nothing to do with this business and there are some pretty nasty people thinkin'

I knows something."

Maunder tucked the last bit of sandwich into his mouth with his finger and gave Ernie a suspicious look. "Goin' somewhere, are you?"

"I haven't been given much of a choice, have I?" Ernie explained as Maunder stood fast behind his wary glare. He sat quietly listening, pulling at his chin with his fingers, as Ernie continued. "I can pretty much figure out what Jackie Miller was up to, and I don't care. I just don't want to end up in a pile of frames like that bloke in his flat upstairs. Tell me what you know about that Beckett woman what came asking about Jackie and I'll be on my way."

The suspicion on Maunder's face slowly faded. He wiped his hand generously on his dressing gown and held it out like a bellman who had just carried your bags to your room. Ernie understood and slapped a ten-pound note in his palm. Maunder didn't retract his hand, he just nodded toward his open palm, indicating payment was not yet to his liking. Ernie took out a twenty-pound note and held it up. That got Maunder's complete attention.

"So, you wants to know 'bout that bit 'o crumpet what knocked up for Jackie-boy?" Maunder reached up for the note but Ernie pulled it back, implying service was to be rendered before payment. With a grunt Maunder settled back into the sofa and continued. "That bird's not one to tussle with. I don't knows 'er, but I knows of 'er, and you don't want any part of the likes of that. She's an evil one, she is, and there's always a couple of ugly plonkers with her ready to give out a good thrashing whenever she gives the nod.

"She operates out of Docklands, from what I can gather, but never the same place twice. Beckett you say? Maybe this time, but she uses whatever name strikes her fancy. She *acquires* things for people, she does, if you knows what I mean. And she doesn't take kindly to those who gets in her way."

Maunder's yellowed smile was that much more revolting with bits of beef stuck in it, so it was to Ernie's best interest to pay him and make it go away. Maunder snatched the note up and examined it like it was the first time he'd ever seen one. Satisfied, he stuffed it down into his pocket with the other bill.

"Those two crates Miller had," Ernie asked casually, "do you think he 'ad paintings in them?"

"Crates? Oh, yeah, could be," Maunder replied, after having to think back for a moment. He put his glasses back on and picked up his newspaper. "They was as big as me and thin…and bloody heavy, too. I helped him a few times before with crates just like them."

"Do you think he was capable of murder?"

Maunder put his paper aside and looked up at Ernie over his reading glasses. "If you wants me to think, I'll be turnin' the meter back on."

"Fine!" Ernie pulled another ten-pound note from his pocket.

"Ol' Jackie-boy wouldn't 'urt a flea," Maunder replied, quite pleased with the additional payment. "It was that bird and her thugs what did that bloke in. And if Jackie-boy knows it, I reckon you won't be seeing 'im 'round here no more. I thinks he has a flat in Paris."

"Why do you think that?" asked Ernie.

"He spent a lot of time there, he did," Maunder responded, a little suspicious of the question. "Like I said, he spent a lot of time there, days at a time. He wasn't much for hotels, so I don't think he'll be running into her there."

"I have no intention of running into her either," Ernie answered, making very little of the information and picking up his valise. He started toward the door, but turned back with one last question. "What about Dragonetti? Is he working for her?"

"He'll work for anyone who'll pay him, that one," Maunder said, picking up another section of the paper. "If I was you, I'd be lookin' for a semi-detached in Wales. If you're a jammy git, she'll forget all about you. You can show yourself out."

Ernie peered cautiously out the doorway up the street. Everything was quiet so he started off toward St. Paul's station. He was a bit nervous walking about that area, but soon enough found himself seated comfortably on a train heading to Oxford Circus. He had given careful thought to what Patterson Coats had said the night before, and had made up his mind about what he needed to do. It hadn't been an easy decision, but after talking to Maunder he knew he had made the right choice.

The train rattled along at a leisurely pace as Ernie thought intently about the events of the past twenty-four hours. Arriving at Oxford Circus, he was met with a light drizzle as he came up from the station. Once again he looked about for any sign of trouble. He was sure the danger His Lordship had alluded to was emanating from Lady Constance Beckett and her desire to locate Jackie Miller at any cost. He intended to spend the remainder of the day visiting his old haunts in the hopes of finding out as much as he could about her. His thought was the more he knew about her, the better he could guard against her surprising him.

He made his way down Oxford Street toward Bayswater, stopping into the lesser-known pubs along the way. Most of his mates were surprised to see him and, after exchanging pleasantries with them, the conversations came around to this woman calling herself Lady Constance Beckett. They all knew of her, but no one knew any more than what Maunder had told him. He did sense apprehension in all of them and a reluctance to speak openly about her.

By late afternoon he was exhausted and he ended up at the Mitre. It was a favorite pub of his, close to Paddington Station and adorned with baskets of petunias. He took a back booth and an order of bangers and mashed. An older chap put down two pints and took a seat across from Ernie in the booth.

"Bloody hell!" exclaimed Ernie, looking up and realizing who it was sitting in front of him. "Do you know how many people are looking for you?"

"Yes, I do," Jackie Miller replied, glancing around, "and if you'll keep your voice down there's a good chance they won't find me in here."

"Sorry," Ernie said, himself looking around at the faces in the pub.

"I don't have much time," Miller continued in a hushed tone, "but I was told by a mutual acquaintance you might be able to help me."

"I don't know what—"

"Just listen," Miller interrupted, leaning close so as not to be overheard. "Phynley Paine, that's who you're looking for, or whatever name she might be going by now. She brokers deals for some powerful people of dubious character and is utterly ruthless. I don't know what I was thinking to get involved with her, but I've made a right cock-up of it."

"They think you nicked that painting and killed a museum guard," said Ernie.

"Poor Thomas," Miller replied softly. "I never intended for him to get hurt, but I didn't kill him. He was dead in my flat when I arrived back that night. I really have to go, but I promise I'll tell you what happened the next time I see you."

"You must turn yourself in," urged Ernie.

"After you capture her," Miller replied sternly.

"Capture her?" Ernie blurted out.

"That's right." Miller rose to his feet. "You're a sharp lad from what I've heard. I'm sure you and that little group you're part of will think of something." He looked down below the table and spotted the valise. "Going somewhere?"

"Not really, I was…"

Miller leaned down close to Ernie and took one last look around the pub. "If I know you're asking around about Phynley, it's a good bet she knows, too. You're in this as deep as I am, now." He took a piece of paper from his pocket and put it in Ernie's hand. "That's her real name, mobile number and a location in Docklands where you can find her. Put it to good use."

"What about the painting?" Ernie asked, catching Miller by the sleeve.

"It's safe enough," Miller replied, yanking free. "You take care of this and I might even give it back."

Jackie Miller smiled and disappeared into the crowded pub.

Ernie sat staring, gobsmacked. He just picked at his dinner when it came, going over in his head what Jackie Miller had said. He wrestled with the information, and what he had to do next, and finally decided on a course of action.

After paying his check Ernie walked over to Paddington Station and purchased a box of envelopes and postage. He took one envelope out and addressed it to Lord Patterson Coats, 81B Conduit Street and placed the piece of paper Miller had given him inside. He tossed the remaining envelopes in a rubbish bin, put the postage on the envelope and dropped it in the nearest postbox.

Relieved he had done the right thing, he took a rail schedule from the information booth and walked over to the platform. He was still a bit nervous, looking everyone over twice as they passed by, but soon he turned his attention back to the newspaper he had nicked at Maunders, and finished the article about the theft.

In the distance he could see the headlamp of his train getting brighter as it neared the platform. Tucking the newspaper under his arm he stood up, blending in with the other travelers waiting patiently for their trains to arrive.

Fifteen

ALL TIED UP AND NOWHERE TO GO

THE TRAIN WAS running a few minutes late, so it was just past five o'clock when they arrived back at Waterloo Station. The sunshine that had brightened their brief stay in Paris had been gracious enough to follow them back to London, though the sun was dropping quickly in the autumn sky. Nigel hailed the first cabbie he saw and soon they were crossing Waterloo Bridge on their way back to Conduit Street.

They were tired from the trip so conversation was at a minimum. Nigel spent the time checking over his notes, occasionally mumbling a thought or two, while Lily sat contentedly gazing into the shop windows they passed. Traffic seemed to be moving slower than usual for the time of day, but that certainly could have been the result of being tired and anxious to get home. A few clever maneuvers on New Bond Street, a quick turn onto Conduit, and the cab pulled up in front of the stationary shop below their flat.

"It's been a long day," Nigel sighed, putting his notepad away.

Lily hopped out and waited on the pavement while Nigel paid the fare. Together they walked over to the door, but stopped short after noticing it was partially ajar.

"That's curious," Nigel said in a hushed tone, slowly pushing the door open. It was quiet inside and nothing appeared noticeably out of place. They cautiously entered; Nigel first with Lily close behind him. Nigel was two or three stairs up when the door closed behind them.

"Oh, Nigel," Lily called out.

"Not now, Lily," he replied quietly, waving her off behind his back as he continued slowly up the stairs. "I think I hear people talking up there," he added, straining to identify the voices.

Turning his head in the direction of Lily, Nigel was startled to see a rather nasty looking man standing at the base of the stairs. Lily's arm hidden in the grip of his large hand...but the pistol he waved in the other was very visible. He motioned for Nigel to continue up the stairs, giving Lily an unwarranted shove in the same direction. As they climbed the stairs one of the voices became very familiar.

At the top, they continued down the foyer in the direction of the voices, stopping at the pillared doorway of the lounge. Inside, they saw a woman talking to another nasty looking man as she scanned the books in the bookcase. With a less than polite shove they were pushed into the room.

"A very fine collection," the woman said casually, continuing to scan the books and making no other attempt to acknowledge their presence. "I would imagine these first editions would fetch a rather tidy sum."

"What have you done with Mrs. Chapman?" Nigel demanded.

"If I were you," she replied in a foul tone, slowly turning to address him directly, "I would be more concerned with what I intend to do with you if you don't tell me what happened to Jackie Miller."

The voice was familiar, but the look was completely different. Lady Constance Beckett had returned, but this time as a redhead. Her dark eyes, once softened with concern for her missing uncle, were now steel gray with a nefarious glare to them. The abrupt disappearance of Jackie Miller had a very negative effect on this woman, and it was evident by her demeanor she was prepared to do whatever necessary to locate him.

"I can assure you my good woman," Nigel said, not at all threatened by her remark, "we have very little information on the whereabouts of your little forger. I would suggest you keep better track of him in the future and maybe you wouldn't cock-up everything."

With her impatience growing and a furrowed brow, she motioned to the larger of her two henchmen standing behind Lily and Nigel. The brute responded with a sharp punch to Nigel's kidney. It sent him to one knee with a grunt. Lily helped him to the sofa, then turned and started toward their female antagonist. She stopped suddenly, realizing there was a pistol pointed at her.

"If you two are finished trying my patience," Beckett snarled, waving the pistol to indicate Lily would be better off seated next to Nigel, "I would like to discuss how you intend to locate Miller or my painting."

"*Your* painting?" Nigel grunted, still straining to regain his breath.

"That's right, *my* painting," growled Beckett. She hesitated for a moment to gain composure and then continued in a more civil tone. "I brokered a deal for that painting and it's taken six months to put all the pieces in place. The party I represent doesn't take failure lightly, so I'm not about to have Jackie Miller put my reputation—or life—in jeopardy. I paid him handsomely for that painting, and I am prepared to do whatever it takes to retrieve it."

"We've seen your handiwork," Lily muttered under her breath.

Beckett just smiled and ignored the implication.

Nigel had fully recovered from the blow and was sitting back on the sofa.

Lily looked around, taking inventory of their situation. There were two thugs. One of them paced back and forth behind the sofa, while the other watched out the window. Both had pistols and both seemed very eager to demonstrate their prowess with them. Constance Beckett had gone back to scanning the book titles in the bookcase, occasionally pulling one out for a closer examination.

Without the pistols, the threats and a missing servant, it was just another quiet night at 81B Conduit Street.

"What now?" asked Nigel, finally breaking the awkward silence.

"We wait," Beckett replied quietly, as if reading from a page of the book she had in her hands.

"We wait for what?" returned Nigel tersely.

"Not for what," Beckett corrected him, "but for whom."

"If you mean my uncle, it's a long wait you'll have indeed." Nigel said with a gruff laugh. "He's not expected back until tomorrow."

"I'm well aware of Patterson's travel plans." Beckett snapped shut the book. "I'm more concerned with the whereabouts of your other mate. I believe his name is Ernie Bisquets? The three of you left this morning. You've returned, so we'll just wait for him."

"Well, if that's what you're after," Nigel said, glancing at Lily with a smile, "you'll wait even longer. Bisquets left this morning with no intention of ever returning. One day chasing after you and your lot was more than he could handle. For all we know, he's already back in Suffolk. Now, I'll ask you again, what have you done with Mrs. Chapman?"

Constance Beckett circled around and took a seat on the sofa opposite them. "It was brought to my attention Mr. Bisquets had been asking around about me just this afternoon." She crossed her legs, brushed softly at her satin trousers and nestled back into the overstuffed cushions. "That doesn't sound at all like a man intending to leave town. I think we should wait just a bit longer, don't you?"

Lily smiled at the thought of Ernie's return, though she hoped he would avoid the grim circumstances they now found themselves in. Nigel completely ignored that prospect and was visibly perturbed over the evasion of his question about Mrs. Chapman. He started to get up, but Lily quickly grabbed his arm and pulled him back down.

"Relax," said Constance Beckett, "your Mrs. Chapman is just fine. She's tied up in the pantry. I left instructions with her for His Lordship...in the event the three of you fail to produce Miller or the painting. I'm sure she'll have no trouble convincing your uncle how serious I am about this. He should have no trouble putting the pieces together when he hears the name."

"So, what *is* your real name?" Lily asked, making it obvious she was not the least bit impressed with her captor.

"You mean you don't know who I am?"

"I mean we checked and we know there is no Lady Constance Beckett," Lily countered smugly.

"Well, you are a sharp one, aren't you?" Beckett said through a menacing smile. "If you must know, my name is Kathryn Fletcher and in light of the current situation I guess it wouldn't do any harm to include that I deal in antiques. Other people's antiques."

"And is that name supposed to mean something to us?" Lily replied, in a tone as unimpressed as she could muster for the occasion.

"You should quit while you're ahead, dearie," came the slow, drawn out response. She stared into Lily's eyes, underscoring the fact that she was in control and indicating it wasn't wise to provoke her. The point made, Fletcher resumed her smile and looked over at Nigel. "So, did you find anything interesting in Miller's flat?"

"You know, the usual things you find around a forger's flat," said Nigel casually. "Some paints...a few half-finished canvases...a dead body."

"Yes, that was unfortunate." Fletcher glanced over at her associate by the window, pursing her lips with disdain.

The displeasure on her face was obvious. Killing the man had been meaningless, but killing someone who could have led her to Miller or the painting was not acceptable. Nigel took advantage of the distraction and slipped the notepad out of his pocket and down between the cushions of the sofa. He wasn't about to give up any information to this woman intentionally.

"A terrible case of mistaken identity," Fletcher continued, turning her attention back to Nigel. "But you mentioned something about paints and half-finished canvases? I don't remember seeing any additional canvases. Maybe you could expound on that?"

Nigel hesitated for a moment. "No, not at all. Just making a point, that's all."

"You wouldn't be having a go at me, now, would you?" whispered Fletcher in a playful way, leaning forward so she could be heard. "The crate they found only had one canvas in it, and it was brought back to my warehouse."

"And where might that be?" Lily interrupted.

Kathryn Fletcher ignored the question, leaned back and continued, "I thought we had the Manet, so that man's death, as unintentional as it was, was of no consequence. All I lost was the money I paid Miller up front."

"No consequence?" Lily shouted, jumping to her feet. "You heartless bitch! You don't even know who you murdered."

It was apparent Fletcher was growing increasingly irritated with Lily. It only took a nod of her head to bring her associate around with the intention of removing her from the room. Recognizing her imminent danger, Nigel ordered, "Lily, sit down and keep quiet. Please."

Lily hesitantly obeyed and the woman seemed momentarily satisfied, waving away her man.

She returned her smile to Nigel. "Imagine my surprise when I found out I had a forgery. It seems Miller was a busy little man. I had a forgery, there was another forgery hanging in the museum and the original painting was nowhere to be found. Miller was also missing, but at least he was still alive. All of this certainly complicated matters but it presented certain opportunities, too. The gentleman I represent has already paid me and is expecting me to deliver the real painting within forty-eight hours. He is not someone you want to disappoint and he has made it perfectly clear he will either have the painting or my life. So you see, I have no trouble taking a life or two if it means preserving my own."

"What about the French policeman?" Nigel asked. "Is that your handiwork, also?"

"The only thing worse than a policeman," reflected Kathryn Fletcher softly, rising to her feet and walking back over to the bookcases, "is a corrupt policeman." She paused for a moment to take a closer look at one of the books, and then continued. "Miss Corbitt, why don't you take my colleague here and check on your Mrs. Chapman? Our introduction was a bit abrupt, so I'm sure she could use a pain killer. And if you wouldn't mind, I think we could all use a soothing cup of tea." She looked over at Lily and smiled. "Run along, luv."

Lily's face turned as red as her hair but she didn't say a word she just bit her lip and jumped to her feet. The henchman who was to accompany her went to grab her arm but she yanked it away and charged off to the kitchen.

"Bit of a temper, that one," Fletcher said to Nigel after the door had swung closed behind Lily.

"I don't know what you expect to gain by holding us hostage," Nigel said. "You already know more than we do. I had no idea there was another forgery. It seems you're right. Miller has been a very busy little man. To his credit, he has outsmarted both of us. You may have us, but he has your money and the painting."

"What I expect," she replied patiently, "is for Lord Patterson Coats to live up to his reputation and locate my painting. If not, I fully intend to live up to mine."

"If I may, how did you find out so much in so little time?" asked Nigel, once again ignoring the threat. "It was that big chap Dragonetti, wasn't it? He's been one step behind us since we got involved in this business. I told Lily, nothing good will come of this business with that bloke involved."

Kathryn Fletcher just smiled and turned her attention to one of the paintings. "Is that a Watteau? Exceptional."

"Yes, it is," Nigel said proudly. "Perhaps when you find Miller you might ask him to paint you one."

"Perhaps," Fletcher said quickly, running her fingertips lightly over the canvas. She stopped suddenly and turned toward Nigel. "Or perhaps I'll just take this one."

"How disappointing," replied Nigel, shaking his head. "Not only are you a murderer but it appears this cock-up is going to drag you down to the level of a common thief, as well. I'm sure that will do wonders for your reputation."

Kathryn Fletcher forced a smile and walked over to examine another painting. "I would suggest you not spoil our evening by trying to provoke me. I wouldn't waste my time inflicting any more pain on you, but Miss. Corbitt may not be as resilient to the same treatment. Do we understand each other?"

Nigel slowly nodded his head. "Perfectly."

The clock in the foyer chimed at six. Nigel checked his watch. He still had it set an hour ahead for Paris. As he adjusted it, he noticed the chap by the window signaling the approach of someone. He knew very well Patterson was expected back by nine that evening, but he'd told Fletcher they weren't expecting him back until morning in an attempt to throw her off. It would be just like his uncle to return early with news of a break in the case. The front door bell rang sharply in the foyer. Fletcher instructed her man to go downstairs before they buzzed their guest in.

Patterson would have used his key, so Nigel and Kathryn Fletcher were both curious about whom this might be. Nigel got up and walked over to the table.

"Find out who it is," Fletcher instructed him cautiously, "and don't forget our little chat."

Nigel pushed one of the ivory buttons on the small console on the table, "Who's there?" he called out.

There was a short pause, followed by static and a sharp reply: "Bisquets, squire, Ernie Bisquets. I've a bit 'o news about that Beckett woman."

Sixteen

TEA AND BISQUETS

"WELL IT SEEMS Mr. Bisquets decided to return, after all," said Kathryn Fletcher smugly, motioning to Nigel to buzz him in. "My sources are very accurate, so I was certain he hadn't left London. This should be very interesting. I can't wait to hear what he found out about *'that Beckett woman'*, can you?"

Nigel pushed another button on the console and the faint sound of the front door buzzer could be heard. Kathryn Fletcher stood with a smug look on her face as they waited for Ernie to join them. They could hear voices and the shuffling of feet getting closer.

"Bisquets, old man," Nigel said warmly, as the ruffian that met him at the door shoved Ernie into the lounge. "I'm delighted to see you again, but I'm afraid you've walked back into a greater threat than you left."

The confusion showed in Ernie's expression. He put his valise down by the desk and brushed off the sleeves of his coat. Even though Kathryn Fletcher had changed her appearance he was well aware of who she was.

"Yes, it is quite nice to see you again," Fletcher said to Ernie. She looked over at her henchman. "Did you search him?"

"A few pounds, passport and a change of clothes," was the coarse response.

Fletcher nodded and signaled her man to return to the window. "You must be exhausted, Mr. Bisquets. Why don't we have a seat and you can tell us all about me."

"Miss Lily and Mrs. Chapman?" Ernie whispered to Nigel as they walked over to the sofa. "Are they okay?"

"I believe Mrs. Chapman has a knot on her head," Nigel replied, shooting Fletcher a glare, "but Lily's checking on her now. She's a tough one, so I wouldn't be too concerned. But what about you?" Nigel took his seat on the sofa. "Mrs. Chapman told me you left, bag and baggage, and I can't say I blame you, what with a murder and all this museum nonsense going on. I even told my uncle you had decided to leave us."

"Not at all, squire," replied Ernie without hesitation. "I just needed a little time to think some things out. Miss Lily told me how important it was to find..." He paused, glancing over at Kathryn Fletcher, who was checking the time on her watch.

"Please continue," Fletcher replied, leaning back into the sofa opposite them. "We have a few minutes before the car gets here, and I can't tell you how excited we are to hear about your day. Isn't that right, Nigel?"

"Are we going somewhere?" he asked in an aggravated tone.

"Patience, Nigel," Fletcher said. "Everything in due time. Now, Mr. Bisquets, you were saying?"

Ernie looked over at Nigel, confused over what he should do. He tugged nervously at his coat, but after an approving nod from Nigel he finally continued. "Miss Lily said it was important that we find you, so I spent the day asking around. That's all."

"And what did you find out?" She asked softly, leaning forward.

Ernie looked over at the brute by the window. He was smiling at him, as if hoping for Ernie to say the wrong thing. Ernie looked back, cleared his throat and quietly stated, "It's a shame, mum, but nobody seems to like you."

Kathryn Fletcher appeared stunned by this revelation. With wide eyes and a gasp she threw herself back into the cushions and looked over at the man by the window. He was waiting for the nod, but his anticipation of delivering a good thrashing slowly disappeared as she suddenly broke into a hearty laugh. Nigel and Ernie were both amazed at how amused she was by the statement and couldn't help but join in the laughter. Fletcher was less than amused at their amusement and after a few moments the reality of the situation bobbed back to the surface and they resumed a quiet demeanor.

"You see, Mr. Bisquets," Fletcher said, abruptly changing to an icy stare, "one of the reason's I've been so successful is that people know I've earned every bit of my reputation, one life at a time. As I was telling your friend, here, before you arrived, I intend to deliver that painting, and I don't care who I have to bury along the way. It's in the best interest of you and your friends to tell me everything you know about Jackie Miller or where that painting is."

Suddenly the door from the kitchen burst open. Lily entered, tray in hand, her very nasty looking escort trailing close behind.

"I thought I heard you, Ernie," Lily said with a delightful smile. She walked over and set the tea tray down on the table between the sofas.

Ernie had stood up, being the gentleman he was, and was greeted fondly with a hug from Lily. "I'm very glad you're still with us," she added, then held him out at arm's length for a good look. "But I'm so sorry we've gotten you messed up in this."

"It's quite all right, Miss," Ernie replied with a smile, doing his best to put on a brave front. "It's rather exciting, really. Mrs. Chapman? Is she all right?"

"She'll be just fine," Lily said, glancing over at Kathryn Fletcher with contempt.

Ernie sat back down as Lily poured four cups of tea. She handed one each to Nigel and Ernie, pushed one over in front of Kathryn Fletcher and took the last one for herself. She walked around the sofa and sat down next to Nigel.

"Well, if you're all comfortable," Fletcher groaned, "maybe we can continue? Mr. Bisquets, you were going to tell us about your day."

"Not much to tell, really," Ernie remarked casually. "I walked all round tryin' to scare up a bit 'o scrap about who you were and where we could find you, but no one's talking. They're all scared."

"As well they should be," she remarked dryly under her breath. "And what about Miller?"

"I knows even less about him," Ernie replied, sipping at his tea. "They say he 'ad a big job in Paris, but nobody's seen him for days. If you're asking me, you'll be seein' Marley's ghost before you sees him again."

Ernie's account of his day was obviously far less than what she'd expected, as evidenced by the irritation on her face. Fletcher got up and walked across the room to the window where her henchman was watching the street. Their conversation was muffled as they both peered out the window. The other brute was lurking about in the foyer, paying no attention to what was going on in the lounge. Nigel took advantage of the distraction to quietly speak to Ernie.

"It's not that I'm not happy to see you old man," Nigel whispered, leaning in close to Ernie, "but what the hell are you doing back here?"

"I found him," Ernie whispered back out of the side of his mouth.

"You found him?" Nigel repeated, doing his best to keep his voice low.

Kathryn Fletched peered over at the three of them from across the room for a moment, but soon went back to her conversation with her thug.

"Actually, squire, he found me," Ernie whispered. He put his teacup up in front of his face to cover his mouth while he spoke. "I was at the pub and he sat down at the table. He gave me her real name. Said the painting is safe, but he wants us to capture her or he's not gonna show his face."

"What?" Nigel blurted out, almost dropping his cup.

"What are you three talking about over there?" Fletcher demanded, turning from the window.

"Nothing," Nigel responded quickly. "Burned my tongue, that's all."

Kathryn Fletcher motioned to her man in the foyer and pointed toward the sofa where they were seated. Soon they were under his watchful eye, and Nigel was unable to get further clarification about Miller's request.

"Exactly what are we waiting for?" Lily called out to her captor. "I'd like to know what you intend to do with us."

Fletcher glanced over at her, faintly annoyed, but ignored the question. After checking her watch once again she walked over to the bookcases to resume her inspection of the first editions. She ran her finger quickly over the titles as if searching for a particular book. When she found the one she'd appeared to be looking for, she pulled it out for a closer examination. She seemed very impressed with her selection, carefully turning pages and scrutinizing every aspect of it.

"Do you mind if I borrow this?" she asked in an irritatingly sweet voice, smiling at Nigel.

Nigel had no problem identifying the book in question; it was an early 1776 London edition of Common Sense by Thomas Paine. It was a favorite of his; a gift from a very appreciative client.

"I appreciate your asking and not just taking it," he responded cordially. "You'll find brown paper and a small leather satchel on the table. Please wrap it up in the paper and keep it out of direct sunlight. The satchel will protect it during transportation." He hesitated, then asked, "Not to question your intentions, but will I be seeing it again?"

"Well, let's just hope so," replied Fletcher in a dangerous voice.

With the book in hand she walked over to the table. It was obvious Kathryn Fletcher had experience handling rare books; she took great care as she wrapped it up in the brown paper. The corner of the satchel could be seen under a small pile of newspapers. She pulled it out, tucked the package neatly inside and secured the buckles on the front.

A grunt from the thug by the window signaled the approach of the car she'd alluded to earlier. With a nod, she acknowledged its presence and indicated it was time to relocate her three captives.

The group exchanged a nervous look, except for Lily who was too angry to give Fletcher the satisfaction.

"Let me make one thing perfectly clear"—Fletcher motioned for them to rise—"despite my reputation I don't take any pleasure in taking someone's life. It is, however, an unfortunate by-product of my business, and something that makes doing business that much more difficult. So, you see, leaving a trail of bodies only impedes my ability to locate the painting. That's where you come in.

"You've stumbled into a business deal I had with Miller. By reneging on our arrangement, Miller has placed my life in jeopardy, and the affect of that has unfortunately placed your lives in jeopardy. You'll want your coats."

Lily opened her mouth to speak but Fletcher waved her hand as if dismissing a petulant child. She waited patiently while they retrieved their coats.

"The man who contracted with me for the Manet is the Devil's twin," continued Fletcher as she buttoned her fur-trimmed jacket. "If I don't deliver that painting he will take matters into his own hands. No one seems to share the sense of urgency I have for finding that painting, so I've decided to turn the heat up. The police will plod along for weeks trying to figure out what happened, so that should keep them occupied. By dangling your lives in the balance I believe I can present Lord Patterson Coats with the incentive he needs to locate the painting quickly and allow me to complete my transaction."

"So, if my uncle does in fact retrieve the painting," suggested Nigel, looping his scarf loosely around his neck, "and is daft enough to give it to you, you're saying you'll just let us go?"

"That's the plan," Fletcher replied sharply. "I get the painting and we make all this go away."

"And what if he is unable to locate it?" Lily asked, smiling smugly.

"Let's just say I'll have no reason to return that book," replied Fletcher.

Lily lunged forward but was stopped immediately by Nigel and Ernie. She struggled for a moment to free herself from their grip but soon regained her composure. Unconcerned by her attempt, Kathryn Fletcher continued to don her gloves.

"You know, my dear," Fletcher finally said, giving Lily a sideways glance as she picked up the satchel from the table, "I may kill you just for the sheer pleasure of it."

"Let's all take a deep breath," Nigel said, turning Lily towards the foyer. "Where do you intend on taking us?"

"I have a car waiting outside," said Fletcher. "I would like the three of you to proceed to the car without making a scene. There is to be no trouble, do we understand each other? I'm leaving one of my men behind long enough for us to reach our destination. If you speak to anyone on the street, he has instructions to kill your housekeeper. If he doesn't get a phone call from me in twenty minutes…well, you get the idea."

"Yes," Nigel replied pensively. "You have our word."

The group proceeded downstairs and out to the pavement.

An autumn chill had returned to the air, but the early evening sky was clear and alive with deep orange clouds against a dark blue sky.

A black Mercedes embassy car had pulled up in front of the stationery store. The five of them climbed into the car and it pulled away into the London traffic.

Seventeen

SIGHTSEEING ON THE THAMES

Ernie, Nigel and Lily sat quietly in the back of the car as it eased out into traffic. It moved along at a casual pace down Regent Street and, after a few quick turns that tossed them about, continued on Northumberland heading towards the Thames. Kathryn Fletcher was seated in the front occupied with a conversation on her mobile. They listened intently and could occasionally pick up a word or two, but nothing that could be pieced together to give a hint of the topic or their destination.

"May I ask where we're going?" Lily called up to the front.

Fletcher ignored her and the driver gave only a quick glance at them in the mirror before making a left onto Victoria Embankment. They were heading east, now, at what would be considered a casual speed. The Thames was visible out the side windows. It glimmered from the lights on either side of the banks, and up ahead the Tower of London and Tower Bridge stood majestically against the evening sky.

"The Docklands, I wager," Ernie whispered, as they drove on a little bit farther.

"West India Quay, maybe?" Lily replied, leaning forward to look around Nigel, and making no effort to whisper at all.

"Plenty of activity there," Nigel joined in, "but not the place to stash a handful of captives. Limehouse. I'd put a fiver on Limehouse."

"You could be right, squire," agreed Ernie, looking out the window to get a glimpse of the road signs.

There was no reaction from the front seat to any of the destinations named. They turned off Commercial Road onto Branch and then continued slowly down Horseferry Road until they neared the entrance to Limehouse Basin. As the car came to a stop, a dark figure could be seen through the windscreen walking toward the car.

"It's a lovely night for a walk," Fletcher remarked in her usual haughty tone, looking back at her captives. "I'm sure I don't need to remind you about our earlier discussion. Right now, your Mrs. Chapman has only a slight bump on her head. I suggest you keep that in mind as we take a short stroll along the lock and meet up with another of my colleagues."

They climbed out of the car and started off along the walkway. The dark figure joining them was obviously there to enforce the rules and took his place behind their group.

Anytime the opportunity to poke an angry lioness with a stick presented itself, Kathryn Fletcher didn't hesitate for a moment. She threw a smug look at Lily and took Nigel by the arm, pulling him out ahead of the rest. Nigel was a bit surprised, and not at all happy about the advance, but he was unable to retract his arm due to the firm grip she had on it. He just shook his head, very much aware of Lily's displeasure, and together they walked along. On the other side of the lock, in the water below the Lock Keeper's office, another dark figure was signaling them from a small launch. They walked along the pier, down three short ramps and climbed aboard the craft.

The large marina was ahead of them at the far end of the basin, but they were motoring along in the direction of a small pier anchored separately in the center. It was around thirty feet long and made of aluminum with wood decking that had been weathered by the years. Black metal handrails came up on three sides, with two openings removed in the long side allowing access to board the longboat secured to it.

The basin was very well lit and it was easy to make out the lines of the craft. It was an exceptionally well-appointed canal boat, and typical in size at about forty-three feet. Along a side canal this might draw unwanted attention, but nestled amongst the expensive yachts in the marina it blended into the scenery. A black hull came up from the water and three black panels, trimmed with gold painted moldings, divided up the deep red upper section. A glow from the interior lights could be seen through the six brass portholes that ran along the side. As they approached the vessel they could make out a name painted in gold and wrapped around the transom — *Cerberus*.

Upon seeing the name, Nigel remarked, "Oh, that's not a good sign at all."

"No, it isn't," mumbled Lily to herself.

"Do you find something amusing about my longboat, Mr. Bisquets?" Fletcher asked, noticing the large grin on Ernie's face.

"Sorry, mum," Ernie replied cordially, shaking his head. "I ain't never been on a boat, that's all. Something I wanted to do once before I left this world."

"Well, let's hope it doesn't come to that," she said coldly.

"Yes, mum," Ernie replied softly, his smile drifting off into the night air.

The launch was tied up to the end of the pier where Kathryn Fletcher instructed everyone to quietly follow her man aboard the longboat. One by one they entered through a hatchway off the small aft deck and marched down five stairs. They were ordered to sit on the built-in that ran along the port side.

The interior was nicely detailed, as well; sporting mahogany built-ins with rich tapestry covers and polished brass trim. There was a narrow aisle that ran up the starboard side of the craft, with lighting running along the skirting boards. Looking forward a counter could be seen with stools jutting out from the galley and cabin doors ahead leading to a toilet and small stateroom. There was more than ample headroom and two skylights afforded a beautiful view of the moonlit sky. The cabin was well-lighted with a number of recessed lamps, including two small spotlights that illuminated a pair of Montague Dawson paintings. It was a remarkably comfortable vessel, as the look on Nigel's face would confirm.

"Now that we're here," Nigel asked, tossing his coat onto a stool in the galley and studying the paintings hanging above the built-in, "what do you expect to accomplish?"

"You're nothing more than leverage," Fletcher replied casually. "As I mentioned before, my only concern is locating the painting and delivering it to my client. To that end I can assure you I have no intention of killing you."

"So we're to believe," said Lily sharply, "that even though we know your name and where to find you, if Patterson gets you the painting you intend to let us go? Just like that?"

"That's correct," replied Fletcher, staring coldly into Lily's eyes. "But there are two sides to that coin, and I've left word behind of what I intend to do if he doesn't produce the painting. As for knowing where to find me—this boat wasn't here yesterday and it won't be here after you're gone. My time is running out, as is yours, so I'm giving His Lordship twenty four hours to produce the Manet."

"That's not much time at all," Nigel said softly.

"No, it isn't," replied Fletcher, adjusting her coat. "For your sake, let's hope he makes the best of it. You'll find provisions in the cupboards if you get hungry. My man will be on the pier… armed, should you feel compelled to take in more than the night air."

Kathryn Fletcher turned and walked back toward the hatchway.

"That's it?" Nigel called out, stopping her at the second step. "We're to just sit here until you come back for us tomorrow evening?"

"I'm afraid you misunderstood me." Fletcher smiled. "I won't be coming back at all. By this time tomorrow either my man on the pier will be gone and you are free to go, or I will be sending one of my colleagues back to deliver the bad news."

After addressing the last part of her explanation to Lily, Kathryn Fletcher smiled and disappeared through the hatchway. It was latched securely and they could hear the muffled sound of the launch motoring slowly away.

Nigel jumped up from his seat and peered out the porthole. "She's gone, but she left one of those thugs behind." He yanked the curtain closed and with one hand on his hip, and the other cupping the back of his neck, he began to pace up and down the narrow aisle.

Ernie quietly excused himself and went to the galley to put on a pot of tea. Lily sat fuming with her arms folded, muttering what she intended to do to Kathryn Fletcher if she ever got the chance. After a short while the whistle of the teapot got their attention and they joined Ernie in the galley.

"I found a tin of biscuits," Ernie said, making room between the cups on the table that folded out from the wall. Lily sat down across from Ernie, but Nigel chose to sip his tea as he paced.

"I must say, Ernie," Lily remarked, "I'm impressed with how well you're taking all this. Twenty four hours is not a lot of time so I'd be lying if I told you I thought we were going to get out of here with our lives."

"Don't you worry, Miss," Ernie said with a reassuring wink, "as long as the post is delivered on time we'll be back at Conduit Street for supper tomorrow."

"The post?" asked Nigel, stopping and looking back at Ernie.

"Yes, squire," he replied. "Remember when I said I saw Jackie Miller? Well he gave me a piece of paper, he did, with that bird's real name on it, the name of this boat and where it can be found."

"Brilliant!" Nigel exclaimed, throwing himself down on the stool next to Lily. Nigel's glee quickly turned to a look of confusion. "Sorry old man, but what does that have to do with the post and how will it help us now?"

"Simple, squire," said Ernie proudly, boasting a bit over his ingenuity. "I put the card in an envelope, addressed it to His Lordship, dropped it in a postbox and bob's your uncle! "

"Brilliant!" Nigel exclaimed again, even louder than the first time.

Lily smiled, but put her finger to her lips and pointed out toward the pier.

Nigel acknowledged with a nod and continued in a more controlled tone. "Good show old man. Mrs. Chapman is a creature of habit. She'll get the letters from the postman and promptly put them in my uncle's hands. It looks like Kathryn Fletcher hasn't seen the last of us."

"Who's Kathryn Fletcher?" Ernie asked.

"It would appear Constance Beckett's real name is actually Kathryn Fletcher," said Nigel, taking a biscuit from the tin. "It's all a bit confusing."

"That might be what she told you," said Ernie, shaking his head, "but Jackie Miller says its Phynley Paine."

"Phynley Paine?" questioned Nigel. "Why do I know that name?"

"She's a slippery one, she is," replied Ernie, stirring his tea. "There ain't a constable to be found that don't know the name Phynley Paine. The more outrageous the crime, the faster they are to blame her, but they never can put the two together in court. She's the devil's daughter, that one, and the blokes what works for her are even worse."

"Ernie's right," Lily agreed. "That's why we know the name, too. Half the police force doesn't even believe she exists. She's a myth. They see the name as a convenient way to explain an unsolved crime." Lily paused for a moment, then smiled big. "This has been quite a day. They won't be able to dispute her existence, now. We've had tea with her."

"Indeed we have," Nigel chimed in. He looked over at Ernie; surprised he wasn't enjoying the moment with them. "Why the long face, Bisquets?"

"Let's just pray the post gets there early tomorrow," Ernie said, doing a very poor job of holding back his uneasiness. "If it doesn't, even if His Lordship gets her the painting, she still has to kill us... you can't be a myth if somebody had tea with you."

Nigel looked over at Lily, having the same trouble concealing his acknowledgement of their fate. With a soft smile, she poured out a bit more tea for the three of them and they sat quietly for some time in thought.

Nigel startled the group by abruptly jumping to his feet. With his hands folded behind his back, he resumed his pacing. After a few laps he stopped and looked back at Ernie.

"You know, Bisquets, you never did say why you came back."

"I never left, squire," Ernie replied, looking from Nigel to Lily and back.

"But the valise?" Nigel asked, leaning back and banging his head on the curve of the wall. "Ow!...Mrs. Chapman said you left with your travel documents and a change of clothes, and without so much as a goodbye."

"I went back to see Maunder," said Ernie.

"Oh, that irritating little man," Lily mumbled to herself.

"Yes, Miss," Ernie continued, hoping Lily didn't notice his smile. "He might know me, but he doesn't trust anybody. I thought he might talk to me a bit more if he thought I was leaving town. He never misses a chance to look like he knows it all."

"And did it work?" Nigel asked eagerly, sitting back down across from Ernie.

"That and forty quid loosened his tongue right up," Ernie replied, nodding his head. "Maunder was certain Miller didn't kill that man. He thought old Jackie-boy had a flat in Paris. Said he spent a lot of time there. He also said he helped Miller move other crates like the one we saw. Oh yeah, that gorilla Dragonetti is mixed up in this business, too."

"I was afraid of that," Nigel noted.

"No sense brooding over this," said Lily briskly. "We have twenty-four hours to get out of here. Let's assume Fletcher, or whatever her name is, has no intention of letting us walk out alive, but she doesn't know we know that. We need to either neutralize our friend out there on the pier and make our way back to town, or be ready for whomever she sends back to kill us. Personally, I would rather not wait to see who she sends back."

"Lily's right," Nigel joined in. "It would be in our best interest to be far away from here should death come calling." He stood up and started looking through the cabinets. "Let's see what we can find on this boat and figure out how to employ it against our friend out there. Lily, why don't you see what that stateroom has to offer our cause?"

Lily grabbed another biscuit and headed off down the narrow aisle.

"Don't worry, Bisquets," Nigel said to Ernie, patting him on the shoulder before he leaned down behind him to get to the cabinets below the counter. "Lily and I have gotten out of worse situations… and now we are three. Why don't you take a look in the drawers under that built-in and keep an ear tuned to the hatchway."

Ernie got up from the table and walked over to the built-in. "Do you think it's possible to get out of here?" he asked, meeting Nigel's gaze under the table.

"Even if it seems impossible," Nigel said with a smile, "we must try. What counts is I believe it's probable, and I think Aristotle would agree."

Eighteen

TWENTY-FOUR HOURS TO GO

IT WAS SIXTEEN minutes before nine Thursday evening when Patterson returned to 81B Conduit Street. He found it remarkably quiet for the hour and even more suspicious was the absence of his usual greeting from Mrs. Chapman. He called out several times to announce his arrival, but his voice was met with little more than an echo. He placed his suitcase down by the door to his study and peered inside. Nothing looked out of place. The lounge was his next stop but there was no trace of his colleagues, except for the tea service out on the table and the half full cups.

Patterson continued through the flat cautiously, taking out his mobile and ringing Lily as he searched. There was no sense ringing Nigel because he was very absentminded about his mobile, but Lily always had hers close by. He held his mobile close to his ear and moved slowly through the rooms. As he approached the dining room table on his way to the kitchen, he heard Lily's mobile ring on the desk at the other end of the room. Something was certainly amiss and he was becoming increasingly concerned about their whereabouts...and more so, their safety.

He started toward the desk but stopped when he heard faint sounds coming from the kitchen. The kitchen door was hinged to swing both ways so standing to one side, and with guarded restraint, he pushed it open enough to survey the inside. The lamps in the dining area cast enough light into the kitchen to make out familiar objects, so with narrowed eyes he carefully examined the room. Satisfied with his observations he switched on the lights and continued into the room. It only took a few steps and he could see Mrs. Chapman bound and gagged in the corner next to the Imperial. Wasting not a moment, he rushed to her aid, cutting through the ropes with a knife he grabbed from the table.

"My word, Annie!" he exclaimed, pulling the gag from her mouth and helping her up from the floor. "Are you all right? Let's get you to a sofa."

A bruise was visible on her forehead, and red marks on her wrists gave testimony to a struggle to get free of the ropes that had bound her hands. With his arm around her waist to steady her, Patterson walked Mrs. Chapman out to the sofas by the fireplace. Leaving her for only a moment, he went back to the kitchen and returned with a large glass of water and a towel filled with ice.

"I'm so sorry, sir," she panted, taking the water from his hand. "I should have done something—"

"Nonsense," Patterson interrupted. "I'll not have you risking your life for any reason. Please take a deep breath and compose yourself, then tell me who's done this."

He had a genuine concern for her well-being so Patterson sat patiently next to her on the sofa, giving no indication of the urgency welling up inside him. She started to speak but winced as she put the towel with the ice in it against the bump on her head. The aspirin Lily had given her earlier helped, but the lump was still tender and a vivid reminder of the ordeal.

"It was that woman, it was. Called herself Fletcher this time, but it was her, I know it. Burst in here with a couple of burley blokes and did this to me."

"Fletcher?" asked Patterson.

"Kathryn Fletcher I believe I heard her say," replied Mrs. Chapman, in her short, crisp manner, "but it was that Beckett woman. Left one of those thugs behind and took off with the three of them. I heard his mobile ring about an hour ago and then the front door slammed shut. I've been tryin' to get free ever since. You must find them, sir!"

"The three of them?" inquired Patterson.

"Yes, sir." The color was returning to her cheeks and she looked up and smiled. "Mr. Bisquets, sir. He came in not long after Nigel and Miss Lily returned from Paris. Around six o'clock, I think."

"Bisquets!" cried Patterson, rising to his feet. "Under any other circumstances this would be excellent news, but it appears he has walked right back into the very danger I had hoped to safeguard him from. I'm afraid there's no hope of him escaping this ugly business, now."

Mrs. Chapman leaned forward and started to straighten up the teacups on the tray in front of her. "Don't you worry 'bout

Ernie Bisquets, sir. He's a sharp one, he is. He knows enough not to tell what he found out about that woman."

Patterson had walked over to the table by the windows hoping to find some clue to where they might have been taken. This last statement caught his attention and he turned back toward Mrs. Chapman and asked, "He had information about Beckett?"

"That's what he said," she replied, pulling the cleaning rag from the pocket of her apron. As she did, an envelope dropped to the floor. "That knock on the head must of left me daft. Here."

Mrs. Chapman picked up the envelope and held it out at arm's length.

"Now we're getting somewhere," Patterson said softly, taking the envelope from her hand.

There was nothing remarkable about it, save an outline of what looked to be a flat object, but he examined the envelope carefully before opening it. Inside was a note and a rather odd looking key. He took the note over to the lamp on the table and read it quietly to himself.

> I'll not waste your time explaining who I really am, except to say you'll have no trouble confirming my reputation for following through on my threats. As I'm sure you are well aware, Jackie Miller has failed to deliver on his promise of the Manet. This has made my client very angry and has put my life in jeopardy. To compensate for this I have your three friends neatly tucked away. The key in your hand disarms an explosive charge set to go off at that same location in twenty-four hours. You deliver the painting to me within that time and I will deliver to you the location of your three colleagues. I have every confidence in your abilities to rectify my situation. For now, you needn't worry about your friends, but you should be very concerned about when the twenty-four hours started. I'll be in touch. KF

"Do you remember what time it was that they left?" Patterson asked, tucking the key into his waistcoat pocket.

"I made a point to look at the clock. Not long past seven, it was," replied Mrs. Chapman, wincing slightly as she lifted the tray from the table. "Is it a clue? Are they going to be all right, sir? I don't trust that one, not after what she did to me."

Patterson didn't want to reveal the seriousness of the situation to Mrs. Chapman.

"It's important that you rest," he said brightly, tucking the note back into the envelope, "and take care of that nasty bump on your head. I don't want you to give this business another thought. Kathryn Fletcher is going to have her hands full dealing with those three, so I have no doubt they'll be back safe and sound by this time tomorrow."

"I'm sure you're right, sir. Would you like me to make you something?"

"No, thank you," he answered, giving her a reassuring smile. "Why don't you take the rest of the evening for yourself? I'll make myself something later. Right now I need to ring a few people and see what I can do to expedite their return."

"No finer man walks this earth," Mrs. Chapman whispered to herself, her round face glowing with appreciation.

Patterson went straight to his study and sat down at his desk. He looked through his address book for a moment and then dialed a particular number that was listed in his book without a name.

"There's been a rather dangerous development in this museum business," Patterson stated abruptly to the voice that answered.

"And what might that be?" asked the voice at the other end.

"Beckett is now going by the name Kathryn Fletcher and is holding my group ransom. She wants the painting stolen by Miller from the museum and has given me twenty four hours to locate it."

"Or what?" came the dry reply.

"I've been assured of a rather explosive response should I fail to produce the painting within the time allotted."

There was a short pause, and the voice at the other end of the line commented with little enthusiasm, "I've had no luck locating Miller—"

"Forget Miller for now," Patterson interrupted. "I believe our efforts would be better spent determining where this woman would hold my group."

"Fair enough. What do you know so far?"

"According to my housekeeper, less than an hour passed between when they left here and when the man who remained behind to guard her left. With travel time and getting them settled in, I would say they would have to be within thirty minutes of my flat. There were my three colleagues, Fletcher and one of her men. She would have to control them and how they traveled through the city, so you should be looking for a private car...probably a limousine. It would have been on the street around six thirty."

"That gives me a place to start. What should I do if I locate them?"

Patterson thought for a moment, then replied, "Call me on my mobile. Where they are being held will determine how we will approach them. I'll alert Inspector Flannel of the situation and your involvement in it."

"You mean my complicity, don't you?" the voice on the phone replied, followed by a throaty laugh.

"You leave Inspector Flannel to me," said Patterson dismissively. "He may not approve of your methods, but you have more than once played a critical role in his successful solution to cases others thought unsolvable."

"Just the same, I don't think he'll be having me over for tea any time soon. You mentioned three colleagues. Who's the third?"

"Ernie Bisquets," Patterson replied confidently. "He's just decided to join us and already he's made remarkable contributions."

"Well, let's just hope he lives long enough to enjoy your appreciation of his efforts."

"Call me with an update in the morning," Patterson responded, a little irritated with the attitude. "I'll make an additional arrangement in the event you come up blank, again. If any additional information should come to my attention overnight I'll ring you back, so keep your mobile close. Good evening."

Patterson leaned back in his chair to contemplate his next call. He knew very well Flannel wasn't going to be happy about the arrangement he'd just made, but he also knew his friend would support his decision because of the circumstances.

The call was brief, but the result was just as he had expected. Inspector Flannel also offered any additional police needed to apprehend this woman and her thugs.

As he was about to make his final call a soft knock was heard at the door of his study. Mrs. Chapman was standing there with a small tray.

"I thought we decided you were going to rest?" Patterson said with a warm smile.

"Beggin' your pardon, sir," she replied quietly. He could hear the sadness in her voice. "I can't get my mind off her taking them from us." She walked over and put the tray down on the corner of the desk. "I warmed up a bit of Shepherd's Pie and here's a glass of sherry to wash it down."

"I spoke with Inspector Flannel about this business," Patterson told her, prompting a smile. "We've worked out the details for an idea I have. He also mentioned he was very concerned for your safety and said he would knock up in the morning to see how you're getting on with that lump on your head."

"Rubbish!" she cried sternly, stamping her foot on the floor. "Never mind me, he should be looking for those kids, he should, and I'll be tellin' him that when I see him."

"I've also spoken with one of my contacts," said Patterson, sipping at his sherry, "and I have every confidence he'll have something to report in the morning. Until then I must insist you get some rest. You've been through quite an ordeal today and I'll need you at your sharpest tomorrow. Now, off with you. I'll clean up these dishes when I'm finished with this fine meal."

He could see in her eyes that the pain still lingered, but he also knew she was determined to do something to aid in the return of Nigel, Lily and Ernie. Mrs. Chapman was a woman of strong character and Patterson Coats had nothing short of admiration for her concern and devotion to those in her charge. She reluctantly agreed to his wishes and quietly retired for the evening, closing his door as she left.

Patterson had one more call to make, and that was to Marie Bussière. It was late, but this matter was too important to wait until morning. If his contact was unable to locate the three of them he had to produce the painting or all was lost. Marie had the second forgery and his intention was to have it transported back to London so he could draw Kathryn Fletcher out with it. He knew obtaining that painting was an absolute for her, so it might give him the leverage he needed to control the meeting place for the exchange. It was a gamble, but one he had to take.

Marie was reluctant at first, but finally agreed on condition that the French police were to be part of the capture. The missing painting was big news. It had thrust her and the museum into the media spotlight. They were being watched, and every move was being scrutinized in papers across France. Fortunately, Patterson Coats' involvement had yet to be discovered, but one wrong move transporting the forgery could expose him and his plans to rescue Nigel, Lily and Ernie. It was an uncomfortable position to put Marie in, and a great burden to place on her shoulders, but it was something she was willing to do if it meant saving their lives.

"I'm not sure how deep this woman's reach is," Patterson commented at the end of their conversation, relieved that Marie agreed to help, "so I think it prudent to alert as few people as possible."

"I'll contact my bother," Marie replied, "and have him arrange the transportation to London. Where should he take it?"

"I've spoken with Inspector Flannel about this and we worked out the basic details. Have your brother call him and make the final arrangements. I'm sure Jean-Paul will be much happier dealing with a fellow policeman, rather than me."

"You must get them back," said Marie firmly, her voice trembling slightly.

"With your help I will," replied Patterson softly. *"Merci,* Marie."

"Bonne chance, Patterson," Marie whispered tenderly.

With his plans in motion there was nothing left to do now but wait until morning. Patterson's mind was racing. At first he had no intention of entertaining the idea of sleep, but exhaustion was nipping at his heels. He took his small glass of sherry, loosened his tie and laid back on the leather sofa under the window.

Nineteen

A LETTER FROM HOME

THE MORNING BROUGHT with it a welcome crispness to the air. The bright sunlight streaming in through the window was enough to awaken Patterson by eight o'clock. He was a bit stiff from his overnight stay on the sofa but a hot shower, and the aroma of Mrs. Chapman's pork chops emanating from the kitchen, soon had him moving about again at his usual brisk pace. The events of the previous evening were still weighing heavy on his mind, so his first thought was to check on Mrs. Chapman. Additionally, he intended to reassure her everything possible was being done to affect the safe return of Nigel, Lily and Ernie. By eight thirty he was dressed and walking through the kitchen door in search of Mrs. Chapman and his first cup of coffee.

As he entered, he was surprised to see his friend Inspector Flannel seated at the table, apparently enjoying his second cup of tea.

"August! Do you have news?" asked Patterson, with hopeful anticipation.

"Nothing yet on their whereabouts, I'm afraid," Inspector Flannel sighed.

"Of course, it's still a bit early," Patterson replied, doing a very poor job masking his disappointment. Mrs. Chapman handed him his coffee and he suggested to Flannel they continue their conversation in the dining room.

"Forgive me, Annie," said Patterson, stopping suddenly at the door and turning back. "You gave me such a fright last night—how's your head feel this morning?"

"Don't you worry 'bout me," Mrs. Chapman said with a smile, "No sense having a hard head if you can't take a blow now and again. It's Miss Lily and those boys what needs you now, so off with you. I'll bring you both breakfast when it's ready."

Patterson smiled and joined Inspector Flannel in the dining room.

"Have you heard from our friend in Paris?" asked Patterson.

"That I have." Flannel drummed his fingers on the table. "The *prefect* was not at all happy about the arrangements, but agreed because of the severity of the situation. That forgery is evidence, you know, so I can understand their reluctance to release it to us."

"He needn't worry." Patterson finished his coffee and took his seat at the table, "I have no intention of losing possession of that painting. Without Miller, it's the only bargaining chip we have, at the moment. Has it arrived from Paris?"

The kitchen door swung open and Mrs. Chapman entered with their breakfast on her silver tray. "I'll only be a moment," she said apologetically, placing the plates out in front of them and refilling Patterson's coffee. "I've got work to do in the kitchen, so I'll be back for those dishes when you're done."

With a slight blush and a smile directed at Inspector Flannel, Mrs. Chapman tucked the tray under her arm and went back into the kitchen.

"Thank you, Annie," Patterson called after her. "Now, August, where were we? Oh yes, has the painting arrived?"

"Yes, It arrived a few hours ago in a small, unmarked lorry. I have one of my men with it now, waiting for instructions from me."

Patterson nodded his approval and the two men sat quietly picking at the breakfast Mrs. Chapman had prepared for them. Patterson was still wrestling with his decision to focus on locating his three colleagues instead of Jackie Miller and the painting. It had made for an unsettling night, which now intensified as the hours continued to tick by and there was no word yet from his contact. Inspector Flannel was equally concerned. He knew what this woman was capable of so this decision could have grave consequences for his friend.

When the inspector was finished he excused himself, asking to use the telephone in Patterson's office to check in at the Yard. The murder of Thomas Fournier was still a priority and he hoped a lead there might help in locating this Fletcher woman or even Patterson's three colleagues. Jackie Miller had proved himself elusive so far, but Inspector Flannel had men chasing down a lead he had turned up overnight on his whereabouts. Flannel didn't share Patterson's confidence in the agent he had employed to help locate Lily, Nigel and Ernie, but he was hopeful a positive result would be achieved through their collective efforts. The concern now was if that result would be realized in time.

Flannel wasn't gone long, but when he returned to the dining room the plates had been cleared and Patterson was engaged in a conversation on his mobile.

".........Yes, you made your point very clear and I assure you I am doing everything possible to locate the Manet.........I think you're being totally unreasonable asking for this in twenty-four hours.........Killing them will not solve your problem, it will only strengthen my resolve to bring you to justice and........."

Patterson's conversation was abruptly cut off. He slowly closed his mobile and tossed it on the table in front of him.

"Was that her?" asked Inspector Flannel, pulling his pipe out and packing down the tobacco.

"Yes," Patterson snapped, getting up from the table and walking over to the windows at the far end of the lounge. "It appears we have less than eight hours left to produce the painting, but it's of no matter. I don't believe this woman has any intention of releasing them."

"I think we've always known that," remarked Inspector Flannel softly, putting a match to his pipe. His years of dealing with the harsh realities of his job had all but erased the inspector's ability to lend comfort to his friend, but Patterson understood and appreciated all he was doing to support his efforts to bring about their safe return.

"It may not be her intention to release them," Patterson said briskly, "but I believe we may be able to change her mind."

"I'm not sure I follow," replied Flannel.

Patterson paced in front of the windows for a few moments, gathering his thoughts together. Mrs. Chapman had entered the room in the meantime, indicating she had the post and inquiring where she should put it. Without looking over, Patterson waved off her inquiry and pointed toward the dining table. Through her years of service to him she knew enough not to interrupt when he was deep in thought and followed his direction by putting the letters down on the table.

"August," Patterson began, "could you have the department issue a statement to the media indicating you have information regarding the whereabouts of a suspected forger and you intend to have him in custody later this morning? Add to that his suspected involvement with a murder near St. Paul's. If she believes we have Miller it may give us the upper hand in this deal. It's nine thirty now and Fletcher will be ringing me again at one o'clock with the instructions about our meeting and the exchange. At that point we'll have only four hours to locate them. We need to get this information out there quickly and hope she takes the bait."

"The media doesn't much like me as it is," Flannel muttered, "so I guess it won't matter much if *I* manipulate the facts for a change. I'm not quite sure how this will help in their release though."

"Fletcher is expecting us to produce the painting," Patterson continued, "but if we offer up Miller instead, in exchange for Lily, Nigel and Ernie, we just might catch her off-guard and draw them out into the open. Having Miller could possibly buy her time with her client."

"It certainly sounds feasible." Flannel patted at the pockets of his waistcoat in search of another match. "I'll take care of it, but what happens when she realizes we haven't got Miller?"

"We don't need Miller," Patterson smiled, "we just need her to believe we have him. We'll turn the game around on her. Remember, she doesn't know we have the other forgery, either. If we show up with what appears to be Miller and the painting we might surprise her enough to put a bit of distance between us and her before she realizes she's been had."

Flannel finally located his matches and relit his pipe. The two men walked back over to the dining table and Patterson handed Inspector Flannel his hat. "You're a good friend, August." Patterson warmly shook his hand.

"I'll just check on Mrs. Chapman one last time," Flannel said, waving off the compliment, "and then I'll be showin' myself out."

Patterson never appreciated the size of the lounge more than when he needed to think. When the need arose he was prone to walking slowly around the room with his head down churning over the facts in his mind. He placed one hand on his stomach and patted it slowly and rhythmically as he paced around the sofas, over to the windows, back to the fireplace, etc. It was a harmless old habit he was quick to deny with a smirk than acknowledge or devote any thought to its origin. He was engaged thus for almost two and a half hours, analyzing every scenario and response to ensure he would be able to react quickly when the time came. He hadn't even noticed Mrs. Chapman had entered twice to tidy up and refill the coffee urn he had all but emptied.

As the clock in the foyer chimed twelve Mrs. Chapman returned with a small tray of lightly toasted roast beef sarnies, a favorite of Patterson's. He looked up from across the room and smiled, checking his watch against the chime. As he walked towards the table his mobile rang.

"I was wondering when I was going to hear from you," Patterson answered. "What have you found out?"

"Everything seems to be pointing to the Docklands," the voice at the other end replied. "I'm going there now to check it out."

"That sounds promising." He hesitated for a moment and then added, "Whatever you do, do not tip our hand. I'll wait to hear back from you."

Patterson set his mobile down on the dining table and poured himself another cup of coffee from the urn on the sideboard. Checking his watch once more, he was beginning to worry over how quickly the time was passing, but it certainly explained why he was hungry. He could do nothing but wait and hope Fletcher was going to take the bait.

Picking up a sandwich from the tray, he started to look through the post Mrs. Chapman had left on the table earlier. He recognized the return address on one of the envelopes. It was Edmunds Hill Prison. He reached back for the letter opener resting on the sideboard when his mobile rang again.

It was Kathryn Fletcher, but this time she didn't give him a chance to speak.

"Listen to me very carefully," she began, "I'll not be made a fool. I heard the news reports about your apprehension of Miller and I know for a fact you have no idea where he is. I don't know what you intended to do next, but it's obvious you have no intention of producing the painting. Miller called me moments ago and I will deal with him directly now. You disappoint me Patterson, and you'll find crossing me is going to be a costly mistake. In doing so I'm afraid you have sacrificed your little friends. But all is not lost. I'll be preoccupied with Miller for the next few hours so you still have a chance to locate them, unless Miller doesn't produce the painting. If that's the case I'll be leaving London rather quickly and I'll have no choice but to send one of my men to clean up a few loose ends sooner than I expected. Do we understand each other?"

"Perfectly," Patterson replied.

The line went dead.

"Damn!"

Having Miller suddenly reappear and contact Fletcher was the one scenario he'd considered possible but had dismissed as improbable. It just didn't make any sense. Why would Miller surface now? He must realize how treacherous this woman was and that she had no intention of letting him walk away after she'd acquired the painting. His two accomplices were dead. What did he possibly think he was going to gain by giving her the painting?

The more he thought about it, the angrier he became, but not at Miller—at himself. This woman was cunning, but he was not about to have the lives of his colleagues slip through his hands without a fight. He was determined his plan to locate them would not fail, despite Fletcher's threats.

Patterson was a little more boisterous than he realized, enough to get Mrs. Chapman's attention. She poked her head in from the kitchen and quietly asked, "Is everything all right, sir?"

Patterson was so consumed with his thoughts that he didn't even realize she was there. She asked once more, again without a response, and slowly drew her head back in. As he was contemplating the conversation he had been tapping on the table with one of the envelopes, until the return address caught his attention once more. Using the letter opener resting next to his coffee cup, he opened the envelope and pulled out the small piece of paper. He read it, and then read it again.

At first he was confused. He looked once more at the return address and then read the note again. Suddenly, it all made sense. Patterson recognized the name on the note and laughed to himself when he realized who had sent it.

"Yes, Annie!" Patterson cried out, jumping to his feet. "I believe everything is going to be all right."

Mrs. Chapman rushed into the room, wondering what all the commotion was. She looked around but the room was empty.

"We must act quickly!" Patterson called out from the foyer. He pulled on his topcoat, hurried back into the room and continued, "There's a note on the table. I'll need you to ring Inspector Flannel and give him the information written on it. Tell him, and only him."

"Have you found them, sir?" asked Mrs. Chapman, trembling as she spoke.

"I believe so," he replied soothingly. He was elated with this new development, but he also understood exactly whom he was dealing with, now, and that was most unsettling. Even more unsettling was that he wasn't particularly certain the information in the note was, in fact, where they were being held, but at least it corroborated the information he'd been given by his contact. "Let's just hope this information is relevant and we get there before it's too late."

"Do you want me to call for a car?" asked Mrs. Chapman, picking up the note from the table.

"There's no time. I'll just hail a cab at the corner." Patterson started towards the foyer, then paused and looked back at Mrs. Chapman. He couldn't leave anything to chance now. Patterson knew who Phynley Paine was and it was very well known she had contacts inside the London Police. "Remember, speak only to August and have him contact me on my mobile."

"Very good, sir," Mrs. Chapman answered.

With a reassuring nod Patterson hurried off through the foyer and down the stairs to Conduit Street. Friday afternoons in London always rich with cabbies, he was seated in the back of one and talking on his mobile without ever breaking his stride.

Twenty

NEITHER FRIEND NOR STRANGER BE

THEIR SEARCH OF the boat had continued on well into the early hours of the morning—without result— until exhaustion finally overcame them. Ernie had fallen asleep sitting on the floor leaning against the sofa built-in, his head resting on his outstretched arm. At some point during the night Lily had placed a blanket around him and retired to the stateroom, too spent to continue. Nigel, on the other hand, had stayed at it until he'd been satisfied there was no logical reason to continue. Phynley Paine had left nothing to chance. The boat had been stripped of every tool and every article capable of being brandished as a weapon.

From that point on, Nigel had resumed his pacing up and down the narrow aisle, occasionally coming down far enough into the seating area to necessitate stepping over Ernie's outstretched legs.

When the fit was on him, he was very much like his uncle had been at that age, in that he was capable of going days with little or no sleep when pondering a problem. Paine's arrangements to dispose of them had him so consumed in thought that he had no recollection of when Lily and Ernie had abandoned their searches, nor did it matter. What mattered was that their time was dwindling and he needed a strategy if they were to survive whatever Paine had in store for them.

As silently as they had drifted off, Lily and Ernie were now starting to stir again. Lily was in the galley making coffee and cleaning out three egg coddlers she'd found in the cupboard above the small, two-burner stovetop. She was remarkably calm, but her concern for the situation still lingered on her pretty face.

"What time is it?" Ernie groaned, rotating his shoulders to

shake off the stiffness caused by his sleeping position.

"Eleven forty-eight," replied Nigel briskly, still pacing.

"Eleven forty-eight!" Ernie exclaimed, jumping to his feet and knocking his head against the roof of the cabin.

"Are you all right?" Lily asked, peeking out from behind the cabinets in the galley.

"He's fine," Nigel interrupted, waving off the question. He stopped for a moment, glancing from one to the other of them, and then continued addressing Lily. "What do you make of those ruffians employed by Paine?"

"All muscle, no brains," Lily replied lighting the burner. "And they're the only things keeping me from wringing her scrawny, little neck."

"Exactly!" Nigel answered. "Bisquets?"

"I would agree, squire," Ernie said, rubbing his head as he passed Nigel on his way to the galley and the coffee he smelled brewing.

He and Lily looked back at Nigel anticipating some type of explanation for his excitement, but he only placed one hand in the other behind his back and resumed pacing without uttering another word. Lily smiled. She had witnessed this before and knew Nigel would be sharing his thoughts with them as soon as he was satisfied they had relevance to their situation.

Lily had found eggs and fresh peppers in the small fridge. Using a plastic knife she'd found in a drawer, she diced up a pepper as best she could, mixed it together with the eggs, and filled the coddlers. One at a time she put them in the small pot of boiling water to cook. She served Ernie first then herself. There was no sense putting one in for Nigel when he was like this, but she prepared it and set it aside for the time being.

Ernie had never abandoned his hope that the letter he sent Patterson would arrive, but he quietly expressed his concern to Lily about whether it would arrive in time to help them. Lily, always confident no matter how dire the situation, assured Ernie there was more working in their favor than just his letter. Patterson Coats would never give up on them, and Nigel was at his best in situations like these.

"Are those coddled eggs?" Nigel suddenly asked, interrupting the quiet conversation Lily and Ernie were having.

Lily pointed at the coddler on the counter and nodded. He walked over, placed it in the boiling water and poured himself a cup of coffee.

"It's almost one o'clock." Nigel sipped at his coffee as he leaned against the counter. "If we are to do this we must act now."

Ernie was a bit confused, wondering if he had missed part of the conversation, but before he could speak Nigel continued his thought.

"We must assume her ruffians are as much aware of her reputation as we are, so it's to that fear we should address our actions." Nigel took the hand towel on the counter, grabbed the coddler by the ring on top and pulled it from the pot of water. Unscrewing the top and taking a seat next to Lily, he continued. "We should give our friend out there on the pier something to worry about. The last thing they want to do is draw attention to this boat…"

Lily looked up and smiled. "You're so right! Just imagine what would happen if people noticed flames coming out of the portholes in the stateroom. Alarms would sound, the Lock Master would call the fire brigade and all eyes would be on this boat, and, of course, our friend out there on the pier."

"Flames?" Ernie asked, startled by their enthusiasm to set the boat on fire.

"Exactly, Bisquets." Nigel responded, scooping out his egg with the plastic spoon Lily had handed him. "In here we have limited options, and if Phynley Paine gives our friend out there the nod to kill us, he's going to do just that. That hatch over there" — Nigel pointed with his spoon — "latches securely from the inside as well as the outside. I think some flames, a bit of smoke and his inability to get in here should be enough to send him fleeing back to his employer."

"Flames?" Ernie repeated, his eyes open as wide as was physically possible. "But—"

"Don't worry," Lily remarked with a slight laugh, patting Ernie's hand, "that thug will be long gone before we'll have to worry about the flames."

"Lily's right," Nigel agreed, finishing up his egg. "You and I will have no trouble breaking through that hatch once he's gone. The only reason we don't do it now is because he has a gun. Now, are we agreed?"

Lily was the first to say yes and jumped up to check on the man on the pier. Ernie thought about it for a moment and then, with a big smile, replied the same way, but as he got up from the table they could hear people talking outside. They couldn't make out what was being said but suddenly it was silent. The next thing they knew, the hatch was being opened. Lily walked back over to where Nigel and Ernie were standing. Her worst fears were realized when she saw the expression on Nigel's face. She turned around and there, standing before them with a pistol in his hand, was Dragonetti.

His huge frame blocked the hatchway, so getting by him was not in the realm of possibilities. Nigel took one step back, but Lily took hold of his arm when she realized what he was about to do. Nigel had no intention of going quietly, nor was he about to stand by and watch his friends die without at least trying to save them. He yanked his arm away from her and in an instant he plunged head first into the big man's stomach, knocking him back against the bulkhead with a crash. Nigel bounced off him and fell to the floor, but Dragonetti never lost his footing.

The gun was still pointed at Lily and Ernie so they stood motionless; amazed over what had happened and how Dragonetti had been unaffected. He just shook his head, appearing even more amazed than they were, then he grabbed Nigel by the collar.

"Are you mental?" Dragonetti cried, pulling Nigel up on his feet and tossing him back over with the group. "You could kill a bloke doing something like that!"

"And I suppose you've already decided how you're going to kill us?" Nigel demanded, brushing himself off and stepping between Dragonetti and the others.

"If I knew you were going to do something like that," Dragonetti replied smugly, putting the pistol into his coat pocket, "I would have, but then your uncle wouldn't give me the two hundred quid he promised for finding you, would he?"

"You're here to save us?" Nigel asked, scratching his head in wonderment.

"I'm here to save the bird," answered Dragonetti, giving Lily a quick wink. "But I guess I'll have to save you two blokes, also."

Nigel looked back at Lily and Ernie, and when he turned back around Dragonetti was pulling something through the hatchway.

"Let me help you," Nigel said, realizing he was dragging in the unconscious thug who had been outside on the pier. "My uncle sent you? How did he know where..." Nigel stopped in mid sentence, realizing it must have been the note Ernie had sent his uncle. He glanced back over his shoulder. Ernie smiled, and with a wink and a nod, he went to fetch their coats.

With Nigel's help, Dragonetti placed Paine's thug face down on the built-in. He then took a plastic wire tie from his pocket and bound the man's hands behind his back. "There." He turned back to the three of them and took his mobile out of his pocket, "That should hold him while I call your uncle. I have a power boat tied up to the pier and I suggest you get aboard quickly."

"What about him?" Nigel asked, pointing to the man on the sofa.

"If *his* uncle has two hundred quid," replied Dragonetti dryly, tapping the number into his mobile, "I'll save him next. Now get in the boat."

Nigel smiled and hurried out to join Lily and Ernie.

Within a minute or so Dragonetti was aboard and powering up the engine. As the group headed to the lock and out into the Thames, Nigel asked, "Where are we going?"

"Your uncle has a car waiting on St. Paul's side of the Millennium Bridge. I'll drop you there."

The Thames had very little traffic on it and the water was calm. Nigel sat down across from Dragonetti, basking in relief and enjoying the afternoon air. "I believe I owe you an apology," he stated after a brief pause. "It appears I was wrong about you and your intentions regarding this business we're mixed up in."

Dragonetti glanced back at Lily, who looked up and smiled, then slowly turned back around. "You're not wrong about me. I am what you think I am. That's why you get the girl and I get the two hundred quid."

"Don't sell yourself short, man," Nigel returned. "I understand completely the risk you've taken. You have put your own life in danger doing this and it is greatly appreciated. Phynley Paine is not a woman to cross at any price, so I must assume you know exactly what you are doing."

"Like I said"—Dragonetti smiled, but never took his eyes off the water ahead of him—"I did it to save the bird back there."

"If for nothing else, you will forever have my gratitude for that." Nigel held out his hand.

Dragonetti looked at the outstretched hand, then up at Nigel before rolling his eyes. "If I shake your hand, will you promise to drop the whole subject?"

With a smile, Nigel agreed. As the two men shook hands a huge explosion roared up from the Limehouse Basin, followed by a fireball shooting up into the sky. Dragonetti cut the engines and the four of them looked up over the transom at the black smoke now billowing up above the buildings.

"Bloody hell!" Ernie cried out. "What was that?"

They all exchanged nervous looks. Only Dragonetti appeared calm.

"That's the sound of Phynley Paine tying up loose ends."

Every small boat on the Thames was heading in the direction of the smoke...except for them. They sat quietly contemplating their good fortune as they got underway again, continuing off in the opposite direction up the Thames. Nigel took a blanket he'd noticed out from under the seat and wrapped it around Lily. They would look back now and again, and then look at each other. There was no need for words.

Boats were still racing by them as they passed under Tower Bridge, then London Bridge and finally Southwark. Up ahead they could see Patterson standing on the wall just before the Millennium Bridge. Dragonetti pulled up alongside and Ernie tossed a rope up to Patterson. The tide was in so the boat sat high enough for them to step up onto the stone wall. One at a time Patterson helped them up from the boat, giving Lily a warm embrace and Nigel a hardy handshake.

Ernie stopped to thank Dragonetti, but his attempt was brushed off. "I'm getting tired of saving your scrawny arse, Bisquets," he barked in a quiet voice, so as not to be overheard by the others. "You do right by His Lordship or the next time I'll be thinkin' twice before I pull you out of the fire." He looked at Ernie sternly for a moment, but then the right side of his mouth curled up into a smile. "Off with ya, before I change my mind and give you back to that wretched woman."

Ernie smiled back with gratitude.

With one hand on Dragonetti's shoulder Ernie extended his other and Patterson pulled him up onto the stone wall. "I got your letter," he said to Ernie, shaking his hand enthusiastically. "Brilliant, simply brilliant."

"I'm just glad it worked, Your Lordship," Ernie replied modestly.

"Ernie, if you are to be one of us I must insist you call me Patterson."

"Good luck with that," Lily chimed in. "I can't even get him to call me Lily."

"Well, we'll just have to see about that." Patterson laughed.

Dragonetti cleared his throat as loudly as possible. "If you wouldn't mind, I'll just be collecting my two hundred pounds and be on my way."

Patterson took an envelope from his breast pocket and handed it down to the outstretched hand waiting below. Dragonetti gave it a quick look and tucked it into his pocket. He started up the engine, gave His Lordship a mock salute and pulled slowly away.

"Patterson, how is Mrs. Chapman?" asked Lily, as they walked over to a waiting taxi. "She got quite a knock on the head."

"She's just fine," he replied, draping his arm around Lily. "I've called her and told her what's happened, leaving out the part about the bomb. She's looking forward to having you back at the flat."

"I'm looking forward to seeing her, also," Lily whispered.

"I don't mind telling you," Patterson said, addressing all of them, "I got a bit anxious when I saw that explosion. I'm glad Elgin got there in time."

Nigel stopped. "Elgin?"

"Dragonetti," Ernie replied. "That's his Christian name, but he never uses it. Thinks Elgin isn't the type of name a proper villain would have."

"Well, whatever he chooses to call himself"—Nigel glanced back toward the water as they neared the taxi—"I'm forever thankful he got there when he did. And he has rather a nice boat."

Patterson didn't reply; he just laughed.

"Have I said something funny?" Nigel asked.

Patterson opened the door to the cab and shook his head. "No, I just doubt very seriously if that is *his* boat."

Twenty-One

WHO WANTS SOUP?

Patterson excused himself from the conversation in the cab to make two calls on his mobile. The first was to check on Inspector Flannel. He had spoken to him after Dragonetti called and said he was on his way up the Thames with the group. At that time, Inspector Flannel was in route to the Basin, and Patterson was now concerned for his safety. He didn't reach the inspector directly but the desk sergeant told him that Inspector Flannel and a handful of CP's had arrived at Limehouse Basin minutes after the explosion, and escaped any injury. Patterson was relieved and explained he would check back with the inspector later that day.

His other call was to Marie in Paris. She had called earlier to inquire about any new developments and if there was anything more she or the museum could do to aide in the release of Lily, Nigel and Ernie. With things happening so quickly, Patterson hadn't had the chance to speak with her. When he did, she was delighted to hear all were safe and equally excited they once again were able to put their full efforts back into locating Miller and the Manet.

On a less positive note, Patterson explained to Marie the details of his last call from Phynley Paine. She expressed concern, but he assured her if Miller intended to negotiate for the painting he would have to expose himself at some point, and that was when he would be most vulnerable. Marie couldn't help but be uneasy at the idea of Miller selling the original painting to such an evil woman, but she had every confidence that Patterson and the East Londoners would not disappoint.

Marie also mentioned the museum directors and the Paris police thought it prudent that she make arrangements for a stay in

London. They would be more comfortable with her there until the forgery was returned to the museum. Their reasoning confused Marie but she intended to follow their wishes.

With the release of his colleagues it would appear that wouldn't be necessary, but Patterson suggested the forgery should remain in London until he could get a firm grip on their next move. He therefore insisted she stay at Conduit Street during her visit to London, and he would not be put off about it. With some reluctance she agreed, indicating it was only because of her desire to see Mrs. Chapman again, and spend a little time catching up with Nigel and Lily, that she would even consider it.

Marie bid Patterson goodbye, promising to ring back when she had firm travel plans. He snapped his mobile shut and tucked it back into his pocket. His thoughts of Marie completely captured his attention, and as the taxi sped through the city he stared out the window. He was unaware Lily was talking to him until he felt her tugging on his sleeve.

It took a moment to regain the present, but he finally turned to smile at her.

"Is everything all right?" she asked again, sitting back in her seat.

"How could it not be!" he exclaimed, slapping his knee. "The three of you are safe and none the worse for your ordeal, and I'm sure Mrs. Chapman will have something special prepared for your triumphant return. We'll eat, compare notes and plan our next moves."

Patterson paused for a moment. He was not a man easily overtaken by the grip of emotion, but he had to struggle slightly to maintain his composure. "We've been through a great deal together through these many years, but never have I felt so close to losing you than I did today. How dark a heart has to be to harbor such malevolence toward another human being is unfathomable. I give you all my heartfelt apology for failing to fully protect those who are so precious to me by underestimating the depths of this woman's wickedness."

"Rubbish," Nigel answered abruptly, but with reverence, surprising everyone with his outburst. It was very out of character for him. "This woman is wicked, I'll grant you that, but any danger we've encountered we've done willingly, and would do again when called on. You've done nothing that would necessitate an apology. If anything, we should be applauding you for your foresight in anticipating the treachery that was to rap upon our door."

Patterson was a bit confused at Nigel's line of reasoning, and his expression must have said as much.

"Ernie," Lily said confidently, answering the confused look on Patterson's face. "You had the foresight to introduce Ernie Bisquets into our small band of irregulars. Evil hasn't a chance now, does it?"

Nigel shook his head, and with a big smile, slapped Ernie on the knee.

Patterson let out a hearty laugh. "I suppose when you put it like that this woman has more to fear from us than we do from her. What do you say to that, Ernie?"

"I'm a bloody criminal," Ernie blurted out without warning, surprising even himself. He looked over at Nigel, determined to bare his soul and cast off his burden of deceit. "It's true, squire, You've been too kind, you have, and I don't deserve such praise. I'm a criminal, a bloody criminal."

All three of them sat motionless with their mouths open. Even the traffic seemed to stop over this impromptu declaration of repentance. Both Patterson and Lily raised a finger, prepared to explain, but the words weren't forthcoming.

"Well, of course, you are," Nigel said nonchalantly, finally breaking the silence. "The two things I know about Newmarket are: it's a great place to race a horse and a secure place to rehabilitate a non-violent offender. You're too tall to be a jockey, so I assume you've shimmied up a pipe or two?"

"Pickpocket, actually," Ernie replied slowly, not really knowing what else to say. "So...you knew, squire?"

"Not really," Nigel said, "but I know my uncle and his penchant for seeking out that which we lack, so there were times I suspected things were not as they seemed."

"You know, Ernie has been wrestling with this demon of his for a few days," Patterson interjected, feeling a need to defend Ernie. "It was his intention to tell you the other day, but I convinced him otherwise. I'll also have you know I gave him the opportunity to divorce himself of this group, but instead he chose to stay, setting out alone to identify who we now know to be Phynley Paine. Had it not been for that...well I don't want to even entertain how this day may have ended."

"I'll not argue with that," Nigel sighed, "and you certainly don't need to defend his character to me. A braver man there couldn't be, and indeed, no finer addition to the club."

"I'm so glad to hear you say that. We know you can be a bit prickly about things like this," Lily said with a smirk.

"A bit prickly?" Nigel shot back. "If you wish to talk about prickly, let's talk about your new friend…what was his name… Maunder? Now there's a prickly sort."

Patterson smiled at Ernie and just rolled his eyes as Nigel and Lily continued their bickering for the next few blocks. He thought about intervening but the bickering was a welcome sound, a sign that things were returning to normal.

"You know Ernie," Patterson said quietly, trying not to disturb the other two, "the decision to join my little group is still yours, and something that should be considered carefully. We're celebrating now, but the reality is, the death you escaped will linger over you until we locate the painting and bring this woman in front of a magistrate."

Ernie started to answer, but Patterson shook his head and threw a glance over in the direction of Nigel and Lily, indicating this was not the time.

"We'll speak more about this privately," he added, sitting back in his seat, "so we'll leave it at that for now."

Ernie smiled and nodded his head.

Nigel looked over, giving up all further attempts to gain the high ground in his discussion with Lily over the actual definition of *prickly*, and asked Patterson, "Did I hear you talking to Marie?"

"Yes," replied Patterson with a slight laugh, "She is coming to London for a brief stay and will be lodging with us."

"Wonderful!" Lily exclaimed. "When will she be arriving?"

"She'll ring back later with the details," said Patterson, "but I would expect to be seeing her no later than tomorrow afternoon."

The taxi pulled up to their flat on Conduit Street and everyone's attention quickly turned to a debate over what hearty fare Mrs. Chapman had in store for them. The ordeal had left them all tired, but not so that they would forego one of Mrs. Chapman's special meals. They were also very much aware that their vulnerability to harm was not necessarily over, only in check for the time being.

Having paid the fare, Patterson was the last to enter. As he climbed the stairs he could hear Mrs. Chapman, her voice filled with excitement and resonating through the flat. With a huge smile and tears running down her rosy cheeks she had her arms stretched around the three of them, giving no indication of an intention to ever let them go.

"Look at you!" she cried, finally holding them out at arm's

length for a good long look. "I'm ever so happy to have you all back." She pulled them all in again for another hug. Then with a big squeeze let them go, wiped the tears away and continued, "You must be famished. Off with you now...wash up...I've got a pot of Colcannon soup simmering on the Imperial and I'll not have it go to waste."

"Mmm!" said Lily, "You know that's my favorite, Mrs. Chapman."

Mrs. Chapman smiled and with a nod looked at Nigel and Ernie, "And you two have a large plate of steak and kidney pie, chips and salad waiting. Off with you now, before it gets cold."

Mrs. Chapman pushed the three of them on their way like children in from the cold, before they could say any more. With her hands on her hips, and standing next to Patterson, she watched them disappear up the stairs.

"I don't mind telling you," Patterson started as they walked toward the dining room, "that was a little too close. I know who we're dealing with, now, so I'll not make the same mistake twice."

He sat down at the table and resumed looking through the post from earlier as Mrs. Chapman poured out a cup of coffee at the sideboard.

"You mustn't blame yourself, sir," Mrs. Chapman replied, placing the cup and saucer down in front of him. "She fooled us all. I got a good look at that woman's eyes this time; black as Newcastle coal, they was. She won't be fooling us again."

"I'm sure you're right, Annie." Patterson smiled as he gazed at the envelope Ernie's note came in. "What do you think of our Mr. Bisquets?"

"Oh he's ever so sharp, that one," said Mrs. Chapman, arranging the table for dinner. "Will he be staying?"

"I hope so." Patterson tapped the envelope on the table. "He's resourceful and has exhibited a remarkable ethic and concern for others, most uncommon for his background. I believe he genuinely wishes to repay the society he, for years, has made withdrawals from. You could ask for no greater ambition in someone than the desire to do what's right for others, without expectation of reward for themselves."

"Whom are we talking about?" Nigel interrupted, entering the room and sitting down across from Patterson. "Bisquets? I must say, Uncle, I'm a bit put off you didn't inform me of his circumstances from the beginning. I might appear to be quick to judge, but I'm just as quick to admit my mistakes."

"Of course," Patterson said, putting the post aside. "I just didn't want to cloud the issue at hand. And to your credit, I had little doubt you wouldn't see right through the charade."

"I'll just be seeing to the meal," Mrs. Chapman said, having finished arranging the table and handing Nigel a bottle of merlot.

"Thank you," Nigel replied, taking the bottle from her. "You must join us Mrs. Chapman. You're as important to this group as any one of us, and it's—"

"You're very kind, sir," responded Mrs. Chapman cheerfully, putting a corkscrew down on the table and hurrying off in the direction of the kitchen, "but there's a meal to serve and pots to be cleaned. Besides you don't want some old bitty poking her nose about in the important business you have before you."

She got the last words out just as the door to the kitchen closed behind her.

"Nice try," Lily said, surprising Nigel with her presence at the table. "It's all I can do just to get her to have tea with me before bed."

"You remember Mrs. Chapman comes from a very proud family," Patterson interjected, handing his glass to Nigel, "who for generations have dedicated their lives to domestic service. Even if I were to insist, she would politely decline without thought to the consequence or loss of her situation here. We need to respect that. She's well aware of our feelings for her and I'm thankful she cares enough for us to ignore the shadow of evil that, on occasion, sees fit to darken our doorway."

"Sorry," Ernie stated quietly, after waiting for Patterson to finish. "Didn't mean to take so long."

"Not at all, Bisquets," said Nigel cheerfully, pulling out the chair next to him. "Have a seat. We were just taking stock of our character, waiting in eager anticipation of what is sure to be a meal fit for The Queen herself."

Ernie was clean-shaven and wearing a freshly pressed tweed suit. He nodded, and with a smile, sat down next to Nigel. All three could sense his apprehension about their feelings toward him, especially after what he'd blurted out in the taxi.

It was a bit awkward at first, but Nigel soon opened the conversation, determined to put the issue at rest. He finished pouring wine into the two remaining glasses, handing one each to Lily and Ernie.

"I would like to propose a toast," he started, indicating to the other three to raise their glasses, "to this rather remarkable lot assembled here. We share the distinction of being the only group of lawbreakers ever to be chartered by The Crown. Patterson, for your brief incarceration in Istanbul; Lily, for your contemptuous act in New York; I, myself, will never forget the less than luxurious accommodations afforded me in that Cairo prison, and Bisquets, your brief, but I'm sure memorable, stay in Edmunds Hill. To us!"

"To us!" they all cheered, even Ernie, but a few seconds behind the others.

"If The Queen ever knew what a sorry lot we are..." Patterson finished, giving Ernie a wink.

Ernie was very much surprised by this. "I'm not sure I understand."

"You see, Ernie," Lily began, "at times our methods, or motives, have become suspect, and if wasn't for the government intervening on our behalf, Lord knows we might still be sitting in those jails."

"She's right, old man," Nigel agreed, refilling his glass. "So you see, it's judge not lest ye be judged. You're one of us...more so than you think."

Ernie looked from one to the other of them and smiled, very much relieved and even more thankful to be included in such a group as this. All at once they looked up toward the kitchen, sniffing the air. Moments later the door swung open and Mrs. Chapman emerged with her large silver tray in hand.

"And with all the trouble you're bound to get into," said Mrs. Chapman with a mischievous smile, putting the tray down on the sideboard, "you're lucky to have His Lordship lookin' after the three of you. No finer man walks this earth. Now, the steak and kidney pie is almost ready, but first, who wants soup?"

Twenty-Two

BACK TO BUSINESS

I T WAS INDEED a fine meal, common in substance but of uncommon flavor, made that much nicer because it was prepared especially in celebration of their safe return. Lily savored every spoonful of soup, but still poked about in Nigel's steak and kidney pie with her fork for a bite or two. This little habit had started in the dining hall at Oxford. In the beginning it had irritated Nigel to no end, but he'd long since given up trying to prevent it. Now he just pushed a small portion off to one side to make it easier for her.

No one was more thankful for the meal before them than Ernie, commenting quietly to himself more than once what a fine meal this was indeed. Patterson was a man of large appetite, enjoying two bowls of soup and a generous portion of the pie, but as usual Mrs. Chapman had anticipated that in her preparation.

They spent time between bites elaborating on the stories Nigel had alluded to in his toast and laughing at the utter stupidity that had landed them there. One antidote lead to another, with each one more fantastic than the one before. Ernie was absolutely amazed at the stories being related during their meal, despite Patterson's warning that each retelling of the tales seemed to be introducing additional embellishments. Trying desperately not to smile, but with little success, Lily and Nigel dismissed that notion and continued on with the harrowing details of their past adventures.

When they had finished the last spoonful of soup and the last morsel of pie, Lily and Ernie both helped clear the dishes to make way for the Yorkshire pudding, ignoring Mrs. Chapman's insistence they not bother.

With the pudding served and the last sips of sherry downed, they were once again ready to pick up the museum theft where they'd left off. Patterson gave them a brief overview of what had transpired during their captivity, noting specifically that the forgery had been quietly moved to London in anticipation of its use as bait. He also mentioned his surprise at Miller contacting Paine the way he had.

"I've got a few calls to make," Patterson said, rising from the table. "I suggest we convene by the fireplace around seven o'clock and decide what we intend to do next. Lily and Ernie, if you wouldn't mind, I would like to borrow Nigel for a while and go over some of the facts in my study?"

They all agreed and Nigel excused himself from the table.

"With your permission, sir," said Ernie, "I'd like to go out for a short walk and maybe get the paper?"

"There's certainly no need for permission," Patterson replied, patting Ernie on the shoulder. "You must consider this your home and, as such, you are free to come and go as you please. I will warn you though, Phynley Paine knows who you are and we've seen first hand what she's capable of. Keep this in mind and try to stay in public areas for the time being."

"No need to worry about that, Guv'nor," stated Ernie firmly, wiping his mouth. "I 'ave no intention of spending any more time with the likes of her."

"You know," Lily said, "I could use a little exercise myself. I'm still stiff from that damn boat. Let me get my jacket and I'll join you."

Nigel echoed his uncle's warning as he helped Lily on with her jacket and then adjourned to the study. Ernie and Lily asked Mrs. Chapman if there was anything she needed while they were out and soon found themselves walking up Conduit Street. It was late afternoon and the sun was just starting its decent behind the buildings, but they both agreed the crisp air felt good.

The lights on Regent Street were just starting to come on as they turned the corner. Lily looked in the window of one of the fashion shops while Ernie purchased a paper from the newsstand on the corner. With the paper tucked under one arm, and Lily holding the other, they continued their walk down Regent peering into the windows along the way. They blended right in among the other couples shopping or on their way to dinner, but still kept a cautious eye to the crowd.

While stopped in front of the window of a fashionable men's shop they felt the presence of someone close behind them. Lily was about to turn for a better look, but Ernie whispered for her not to. Instead, he began talking as if answering something she'd asked and continued on to the next shop window. As they walked, and taking what opportunities he could, he whispered to Lily that he knew who was behind them and suggested they continue as if nothing was wrong. She was reluctant at first, but felt safe enough for the time being with all the people around them. When they stopped in front of the next window the man who had been following behind walked past them, stopped and pulled out his mobile phone.

"I'm surprised to see you," Ernie said quietly, but gave no indication he was talking to the man. "You know you almost got us killed, you did."

"Rubbish," the man responded, talking into his mobile. "That's a fine how do you do. Saved your life, I did. I got her attention off you and here you are. It's your turn, now. I'm going to walk away and get a table in the back of that little Italian restaurant on Heddon Street. Take your time looking in the shops and meet me there."

When he'd finished what he had to say to them the man looked at his watch and hurried off down Regent Street. By the time they turned around he had disappeared into the crowd, so Lily never got a good look at him, but it didn't matter.

"Let me guess," she whispered as they walked along to the next shop. "Jackie Miller?"

"Right you are, Miss," replied Ernie. "I thought he might be lurkin' about. This painting is turning out to be more trouble than it's worth, so I'm sure he's ready to make a deal."

"Should we call Patterson?" Lily asked as they turned onto Heddon.

"I think it might scare him off." Ernie stopped to read a menu posted outside a French restaurant. "Let's see what he has to say."

Ernie took a casual, yet thorough, look up and down the street, as did Lily, before entering the Trattoria. They politely waved off the *maitre d'* and proceeded to a back table where they saw Miller peeking out from behind his menu.

"Not as cocky as you were last time, are you, Jackie?" Ernie asked sitting down across from him. "This is Lily Corbitt. She's with the—"

"Yes, I know," Miller replied nervously, "Nice to meet you." He shot a quick glance around the room then leaned in close to Ernie and said, "This business is getting out of hand. That woman's mental and you need to do something about it!"

"Where's the painting?" Lily interrupted. "You give us the painting and I'm sure we can make this whole thing go away."

"It ain't that easy, dearie," Miller replied smugly. He looked around again and continued in a lower tone. "You don't know her like I do. Don't you think I would have given back the painting if that were the case? The whole plan got buggered up. No, she's not about to let me walk away after being made the fool in front of her buyer."

"I'm curious," said Lily, "what *was* your plan?"

"If you must know"—Miller looked nervously around the restaurant once more—"Paine knew I had access to the museum so she approached me about stealing the Manet. It was her idea to replace the original with a forgery. She paid me well but I got greedy. I painted two forgeries, figuring to give her one and leave the other behind for the museum. That way I'd get to keep the money and the original."

"She must be pretty sharp, if she figured out you gave her a fake," Lily interjected.

"Oh, it wasn't her—it was her art expert. Apparently, I duplicated a label on the back of the frame incorrectly and he noticed it. Anyway, when I didn't show up at the museum gala with the real painting she sent her thugs to my flat. They arrived looking for me—I wasn't there, but Thomas Fournier was...he'd come for his share of the money. They found him and what they thought was the original. Under orders they killed Thomas, thinking he was me, and took the painting I had in the crate back to Paine. Seems it was the next morning when she realized it was a forgery, too. She put the word out she was looking for me and I've been hiding ever since."

"I'm sure if you turn yourself in the police will protect you," Lily offered, but Miller just shook his head and laughed.

"What do you want us to do?" asked Ernie.

The waitress came over with Miller's wine and asked if they wanted to see a menu, also. Lily smiled and explained they only stopped to say hello to their friend and weren't staying.

"I stuck my neck out just contacting her," Miller said, after the waitress walked away. "I've got things started for you. She knows I'm scared and ready to deal. I just need to name the place."

"You're not going to give her that painting!" Lily stated abruptly, and louder than she realized.

The three of them looked nervously around but there was enough noise going on that no one had really paid any attention to her outburst.

"No," answered Miller, growing a bit impatient with her. "You need to get the other forgery from the museum. I'll touch up that label on the frame and you can use that to lure her out in the open. All you have to do is be there when she shows up and arrest her."

"Don't you think she's too smart to fall for that?" Ernie asked, sitting back in his seat.

"Well, of course, she is," Miller replied coarsely. "That's why you and your little group need to think up a way she will. Like I said before, Bisquets, you get her and I'll give back the painting. I had a nice simple life before I mixed up with the likes of her."

"Just like that?" Lily asked suspiciously. "We capture Paine and you'll just give back the Manet? And what about you? You'll turn yourself in, right?"

"I didn't say nothin' about that, dearie," Miller sneered. "You don't want me, you want the painting. That should be enough. And don't worry, the painting is safe enough for the time being."

As Lily and Ernie stood up Miller took a piece of paper from his pocket.

"Here." He handed the note to Ernie. "That's my mobile number. I can put Paine off for now, but I have to tell her where and when by tomorrow night. If you want the painting back, you'll call me tomorrow afternoon with a plan."

Miller picked up Ernie's newspaper and opened it, indicating their meeting was over and his desire to obscure himself from view had returned. Without another word they left and hurried back to Regent Street where they had no trouble getting a taxi. Ernie was a bit annoyed at Miller's attitude, but Lily's excitement over the prospect of securing the painting far outweighed her irritation with the man.

Within minutes they were back at the flat on Conduit Street, where Lily bolted up the stairs with all the energy of a schoolgirl, calling out to Nigel and Patterson as she did so. Nigel came running out into the foyer to find out what all the commotion was about.

"You saw Miller?" Ernie heard Nigel exclaim as he gained the top of the stairs.

By the time he had his coat off Patterson and Mrs. Chapman had joined Nigel in the foyer to hear what Lily had to say. She recounted the meeting with Miller briefly, promising to relate the whole story after she caught her breath. Smiling at Ernie, she was very quick to point out it all came about because of a hunch he had.

"Just a bit of luck," Ernie said modestly, quickly changing the subject. "He's a bugger, he is. Expecting us to devise a plan to nab that Paine woman. She's a sharp one, and that's not going to be easy."

"Easy or not," Patterson said, "it's what has to be done. In your opinion, can he be trusted to return the painting if we succeed?"

"He's a forger, sir, and a good one at that" answered Ernie sincerely, "but I think he's also a man of his word."

"I don't think he's left us much of a choice," Nigel remarked. "Well, Mrs. Chapman, I think a pot of tea is in order. Do you have any of those scones left over?"

"I'll bring them out with the tea," she replied, hurrying off to the kitchen.

The phone in Patterson's study rang so he excused himself, indicating he would meet them in the lounge. They went in to wait and Nigel took the opportunity to stoke the fire and take the chill off the room. By the time he was done Patterson had returned.

"That was Marie," Patterson said, "She's at Waterloo Station and should be here momentarily."

"I'd best be turning down the bed in the guest room," called out Mrs. Chapman, as she crossed the room with her tray of tea and scones. "I'll just put these here on the table."

"Thank you, Annie," Patterson said. "Lily, I'm very eager to hear what Miller had to say, but why don't we wait for Marie. I'd like her to be here. I'm sure she'll find this of interest, too."

"I'm sure she will," Lily stated, pouring herself a cup of tea. "Miller also told us what happened to Thomas Fournier, so we'll have to contact Inspector Flannel."

"Did he mention the shoes?" Nigel asked.

"The shoes?" Lily repeated slowly, thinking for a moment. "Oh, that's right, someone changed Fournier's shoes. No. I forgot all about that."

As this light conversation continued Ernie sat back and smiled, sipping at his tea. He was very much at peace with everything that had happened to him over the past few days, and reflected on his good fortune and the people who now called him friend. He chose not to dwell on how close he'd come to death at the hands of evil, but instead on how kind the Fates were to extend to him this opportunity of redemption.

Here he sat with two people who accepted his background without bias and placed their trust in him fully, and without fear.

Their capacity for kindness and ability to think through a problem was impressive, but it was their genuineness that he admired most. He saw in Nigel and Lily a bond stronger than love. It was incredibly evident to everyone—save Nigel—and surely defied explanation.

Turning his attention to Patterson, he watched him pace back and forth in front of the fireplace. Here was a man of great wisdom and noble strength, capable of conquering any challenge thrown before him, yet the anticipated arrival of this woman had him as nervous as a schoolboy.

Suddenly, Ernie realized Nigel was speaking to him. There was an awkward pause followed by a slight laugh. "Are you all right, old man?" Nigel repeated.

"Sorry, squire," Ernie said, hesitating as he spoke. "I was thinking about these past few days."

"Don't let it bother you," Nigel said encouragingly, "you'll get used to it."

The front door buzzer sounded and all four of them turned and looked out to the foyer. Mrs. Chapman waved as she walked by the doorway. The familiar squeak of the front door was next, followed by an excited Mrs. Chapman's greeting and Marie's voice coming up the stairs.

"I'll just take these bags to the guest room," they heard Mrs. Chapman remark, as she walked by the doorway. "You go right in, dearie, they're all waiting for you."

Twenty-Three

A MEETING OF THE MINDS

I HOPE I'M NOT interrupting anything important?" Marie entered the room and walked over to where Patterson was standing. "*Bonjour*, Lily. *Bonjour*, Nigel."

Patterson met her halfway, explaining how excited he was to see her so soon, and even more so that she'd decided to stay with them while in London. The delight in seeing her washed across his face and had a calming effect on his outward nervousness, which had been evident prior to her arrival. They exchanged a quiet greeting and he escorted her to the sofa where Lily, Nigel and Ernie were standing. Nigel and Lily greeted her warmly with a hug and a kiss on the cheek. Ernie wasn't sure what to do so he smiled politely and made a slight bow. It was evident he was a bit uneasy, and this prompted a reassuring nod from Patterson.

"Please allow me to introduce Ernie Bisquets," Patterson said, with his hand extended.

Marie was a beautiful woman, whose soft voice and accent only enhanced her ability to captivate anyone she spoke with. Whatever nervous response this loveliness triggered in a new acquaintance the genuineness of her smile soon wiped away any apprehension a person might have about the level of her interest in what they were about to say.

"It's a pleasure, mum," said Ernie crisply, with a broad smile as he shook her hand.

"I hear wonderful things about you," answered Marie tenderly. "I'm delighted you are helping the museum retrieve the painting. It's one of my favorites and it would be terrible to lose such a treasure."

"Don't you worry, mum." Ernie nodded his head. "Jackie

Miller just told us he'll return that painting just as soon as we—"

"*Que voulez-vous dire?*" Marie exclaimed, looking to Patterson for some clarification.

Ernie was relatively sure he hadn't said anything offensive, but not being familiar with the French language, he, too, looked to Patterson for help understanding what he had said that had excited her that way.

"Why don't we all have a seat," Patterson said taking Marie's arm. "I was just as surprised as you are when they told me that. I suggested they wait until you arrived to explain their meeting with Mr. Miller, as I was certain you would be excited by this latest development. It appears I was correct, so let's hear what Lily and Ernie have to say."

During the conversation Mrs. Chapman had replaced the teapot with a fresh one and brought an additional cup and saucer for Marie. Patterson poured out the tea as they eagerly awaited the story. Ernie was still a bit nervous about his whole situation, especially with Patterson's return and their guest, so he asked Lily if she wouldn't mind explaining their meeting with Miller.

Lily wasted no time at all getting into their meeting, enhancing the intrigue a bit by starting with the sinister shadow that followed them down Regent Street. They all listened intently as she explained what Miller told them about Phynley Paine's plan and how he'd become greedy and double-crossed her. Knowing what they did now about this woman they had no trouble understanding why Miller was so scared and why he had no intention of showing his face until she was apprehended.

Marie was relieved to hear the painting was safe for the time being, but just as much concerned that its whereabouts were known only to Miller. The details of the unfortunate end of Thomas Fournier brought a tear to her eye, despite his suspected duplicity in the theft.

Ernie filled in a detail here and there, mostly about Miller's background, but Lily continued to recount the incident. All of them remarked at the ease at which Miller was able to casually circulate around London, especially with the ubiquitous Phynley Paine and the law looking for him. It was certainly a mystery in itself, but Ernie offered up the explanation that London was filled with backallies and underground passages that even they would have little knowledge of. He also suggested he wasn't convinced Maunder didn't have a hand in hiding Miller while he was in London.

Patterson sat quietly listening, pleased with how well Ernie was adapting to his new calling and the level of his contribution to the case at hand. There was still a lingering concern for his safety, thinking that others of his late profession may consider him a turncoat and treat him accordingly. It was something he would need to speak with Ernie about in greater detail if he fully committed to joining the East London Adventurers Club. Fortunately, the secretive nature of their work would help to shield him from public exposure of his decision, but certainly it still demanded consideration.

Lily finished up by relating Miller's willingness to help and return the painting even though it was obvious it was purely for his self-preservation. She explained that Miller said he'd contacted Paine in an attempt to aide in their escape and set the stage for her capture. It was also his suggestion to use the second forgery as bait to lure Paine out into the open, noting his offer to touch up the label on the back of the frame to help convince her it was the original. Ernie agreed with Lily completely in that Miller was scared and he had no intention of forfeiting his life for a painting. Lily then indicated they had his mobile number, which Ernie took out of his pocket and handed to Patterson. So, the only thing left to do was devise a plan to trap Paine.

"Remarquable!" said Marie, quietly to herself.

"Well, if that's all we need to do," boasted Nigel sarcastically, "she's as good as caught."

"Let's not be hasty," Patterson said, dismissing the remark. He stood up and started pacing in front of the fireplace. "We have more things in our favor than I believe she is aware of. Remember what started this investigation, and the one fact that has remained constant, though clouded by two murders and a kidnapping—everyone believes Miller has the original painting. Miller is correct in indicating this is the leverage we need to expose Phynley Paine, and if he is willing to participate we must take advantage of it."

"I'm still not convinced he can be trusted," Nigel said.

"Be that as it may," Patterson replied with conviction, "all hope of returning the Manet will be lost if Phynley Paine locates him first. No, I believe Ernie is correct in thinking Miller will return the painting in exchange for eliminating this threat to his life. He made the same mistake we did in underestimating who we were dealing with, so it's a small price to pay."

"He's right squire," Ernie agreed gently. "Old Jackie-boy can deal with the police—at least he knows they won't shoot 'im."

"I suppose you're right," Nigel said reluctantly. "So, what do we do next?"

"I don't think it's our place to suggest how to make the exchange," Lily advised.

"She's right," said Patterson, poking at the fire. "In order for this to work and be above suspicion, Paine must believe she is in complete control. So, our friend Miller will have to contact her and agree to whatever arrangements she makes for the exchange. We'll need to react then with a plan."

"How do you know she will not just kill him when she gets the Manet?" Marie asked.

"She won't make the same mistake twice," Lily said. "They killed Fournier thinking they had the painting. I don't mean to be insensitive, but it was only dumb luck on their part that they killed him instead of Miller. She may still kill him, but it won't be until after she has verified the authenticity of the painting."

"And how will she authenticate the Manet?" Marie asked slowly, pondering her own question as she looked up toward Patterson.

"I would imagine she has an art expert of some type in her employ," answered Patterson.

"That right," Lily added briskly. "Miller told us it was her art expert that identified the painting they took from his flat as a forgery by a label on the back that was incorrect—"

"I'm sorry," Patterson interrupted, putting the poker back with the other tools, "what was that last part?"

"There is apparently a label on the back of the painting," Lily repeated, "that Miller copied incorrectly, and her art expert noticed it."

Patterson and Marie looked at each other and together blurted out, "Emory!"

"Emory?" Ernie asked, very confused over the importance of the name.

Nigel and Lily were also confused, but for a different reason—they both knew who he was.

"But Emory can't be part of this," Marie said in earnest, though with some hesitation.

"How many people would know about the label?" Patterson asked gently.

"As much as I hope to deny it," Marie responded sadly, "it is not something anyone else would know. Emory has an intimate knowledge of every aspect of the impressionists' paintings hanging in the Musee d'Orsay, so it can only be him. He even supervised the work Jacques Millet did on the frames. I will call my brother and inform him of this." She opened her purse to search for her mobile.

"No!" Patterson, Lily and Nigel exclaimed all at once, startling her; surprising Ernie, too, but he knew why they were stopping her.

"We must not do anything to alert him to our suspicions," Patterson said, resuming a slow pace in front of the fire. "I'm sure he's employed in a similar capacity with Paine as he is with the museum, and I doubt very much that he had any part in the murder of those two men. He is, without argument, an accomplice, but I don't see him as a threat. I'm sure the authorities will agree, so we should update Inspector Flannel with this information. I will ask him to relay the facts to the *prefect,* suggesting that Emory only be observed for the time being. I can also inform him of Miller's explanation about the death of Fournier."

"And what about Miller?" Nigel asked, reaching for another scone.

"That's where you come in, Ernie," replied Patterson with a smile.

"Me, Guv'nor?" Ernie said slowly.

Patterson handed the paper with the number on it to Ernie and continued, "We need you to call Miller and ask him to contact Paine immediately and make the arrangements for the exchange of the painting. The important thing to remember is that the exchange cannot take place until tomorrow afternoon."

"Tomorrow, sir?" Ernie asked.

"This should give Miller enough time to make the correction to the label on the frame," Lily offered, earning a smile and a nod of approval from Patterson. "We also need the time to formulate what we are going to do after she gives him the drop point."

"Miller should understand," Patterson continued. "He can make the excuse that he has to get the painting to London. As for that, you can tell him we have the other forgery here and ask him where we should deliver it."

"He'll probably say Maunder's," Nigel interjected with some irritation. "His paints and brushes are there, but I would also assume Paine is having that place watched."

"Inspector Flannel may be able to help us there if it comes to that," said Patterson, sitting back down next to Marie. "For now let's just wait to hear what Miller has to say after he speaks to

Paine."

"Magnifique!" Marie clutched Patterson's hand. "This is very exciting and I want to hear more, but if you would not mind, I would like to freshen up."

"Of course," Patterson replied, rising to his feet. "You get settled in and I'll have Annie make you a plate. We'll make the calls we just discussed and when you get back we can turn our conversation to a more pleasant topic. If I'm not mistaken, I saw an apple pie cooling on the counter. We can make short work of that after you've had a proper dinner."

Marie kissed Patterson on the cheek, smiled at the others and excused herself. Lily offered to accompany her and Marie was very quick to accept. As they walked out into the foyer, Patterson handed Ernie his mobile phone.

"Do you think Jackie-boy will go for this, Guv'nor?" Ernie asked, taking the mobile from him.

"Yes." Patterson sat back down. "Our bigger concern is whether he can convince Phynley Paine he is acting on his own. That's why we need to leave as much of the planning to her as possible. When crated, this painting is a rather large object, so it limits the means of transporting it. She'll know that and have to tailor the arrangements accordingly. That will slant the odds more in our favor."

"What about Miller?" Nigel asked. "He can't possibly think he'll hand over the forgery and simply walk away. Even if we do capture Paine, the police will be right there nipping at his heels."

"He knows he's a very small fish in this rather murky pond, so he'll play that to his favor for as long as he can. Don't think for a moment he isn't making alternate plans to secure his continued freedom. He might be scared, but he's no fool. The original is still his best bargaining chip on both sides and he knows it."

"I must agree, squire," Ernie chimed in with a smile. "Old Jackie-boy's done many things in his time, but he ain't never been caught at any of them. No sir, not that one. He's as sharp as a tack, he is, and he's probably forgotten more tricks than you and I both knows. He'll convince 'er all right, he will, if just to save his own skin."

"I hope you're right, Ernie," Patterson said, rising to his feet. "If you two will excuse me, I'm going to call August and give him our preliminary plan. He'll need to make arrangements to move the forgery when called, so it's best we advise him as soon as possible. You should ring Miller now. Nigel will help with any questions he might have."

Ernie agreed and made the call after Patterson retired to his study. It was a brief conversation, with Miller reluctant at first to allow Paine that much freedom with the arrangements. Ernie relayed the information Patterson wanted him to know, emphasizing the importance of putting the delivery off until the afternoon of the next day. When he informed Miller the forgery was already in London, the forger didn't hesitate to request it be taken to Maunder's and placed in the lorry in the courtyard. Miller told him he was certain Maunder's was being watched, but Ernie assured him they would take care of that. At the end, Miller asked for the number where he could reach him, promising to call back after he spoke with Paine.

"What do you think?" Ernie asked, after putting the phone down on the table.

"As much as I can't stand that irritating little man," Nigel replied, "at least we know what we're dealing with at Maunder's. Will Miller contact him?"

"Yes," Ernie said, taking the last sip of tea from his cup, "and he wants us to make arrangements to move the painting as soon as possible. He'll tell us more when he calls back. Do you think we can get the painting there without alerting Phynley Paine?"

"Patterson's right in thinking Inspector Flannel can assist us there," replied Nigel. "I'm sure he has a few more questions for Maunder, and while he has him occupied his men can scare off any of her thugs long enough for us to slip the painting in."

Twenty–Four

BLACK AND WHITE AND BEIGE

A S EVENING SETTLED in over London, Ernie found himself alone in the lounge. Marie and Lily had not yet returned and Nigel had excused himself to join Patterson in his study to update him on their call to Miller. As Ernie poked about at the fire he could just make out fragments of the conversation in the study. He heard Patterson express how pleased he was that Miller had agreed to help, but suggested they remain cautious of his motives. At some point Mrs. Chapman had put out the pie and the room was filled with the aroma of freshly brewed coffee.

Ernie was just returning the poker to its stand when the mobile phone Patterson had given him rang. It was Jackie Miller.

Miller told him they needed to get the painting into the lorry in Maunder's courtyard as quickly as possible. Correcting the label would take less than an hour and he could attend to it in there, but they must make sure they got the painting there without anyone knowing...including Maunder. At noon the next day he would get the final delivery instructions from Paine, so it was important that the painting was in the lorry and ready to be moved. Miller said he would call back then, and reminded him once more that Paine had eyes everywhere.

Ernie started to thank him for his cooperation but Miller just abruptly hung up.

"Was that him?" a soft voice asked from behind him.

"Sorry?" Ernie turned to find Marie standing there.

"Was that Millet?" she repeated.

"Yes, mum." Ernie brushed his hands on his pants to remove some soot. "He's agreed to help, he has."

"That's wonderful," Marie replied. "Please come sit here with me and we'll wait for the others to return. May I call you Ernie?"

"By all means, mum," Ernie said, sitting down beside her. "Thank you."

"Patterson told me how he came to meet you," Marie said with a big smile.

"Well, I'm not at all proud of it, mum," replied Ernie repentantly, lowering his head and tugging at his jacket. After reflecting for a moment he cleared his throat and raised his head. "But it's grateful, I am, for what's happened on account of it. They've all been right kind to me, they have, especially His Lordship, and don't think I don't appreciate it. I'd still be sweatin' in that prison laundry if it weren't for him speakin' up for me like he did."

"I think it's Patterson who is grateful," Marie reminded him fondly. "He might have lost Lily and Nigel if it weren't for you and your commitment to them. Gratitude is an honor bestowed on the worthy for their actions, without prejudice to their past. You've earned your place here, so you should leave your past behind."

Ernie sat a bit straighter. "Thank you, mum."

Marie playfully raised an eyebrow in response to the statement.

"I mean, Marie," Ernie corrected himself, with a very broad smile. "Thank you, Marie."

"Thank you, *Marie*?" Nigel interjected, walking into the room. "You've been here three days and we've been threatened, kidnapped and almost reduced to flotsam together, and I can't even get you to call me Nigel! I don't know, Bisquets, we may need to rethink this whole arrangement."

Ernie started to stutter out a response but Nigel interrupted him, pointing toward the table and braking into a hardy laugh. "Just having a bit of sport, old man. Come on, we've got work to do."

Ernie smiled and jumped to his feet. Nigel took Marie's hand and the three walked over to the dining table. Patterson and Lily had just sat down. The coffee was poured, the pie cut and distributed, and the conversation remained light until they were finished.

"I spoke to Inspector Flannel," Patterson said, getting back to the issue at hand and resting back in his chair. "He and his men are going to Maunder's now. He'll keep Maunder occupied while his constables flush out Paine's men and chase them away long enough to place the painting in the back of the lorry. He'll also put two tracking devices in the lorry—one for them to find and one we hope they don't. It's up to Miller at that point to make the correction and get the final instructions from Paine."

"Old Derby Flannel is being incredibly accommodating," said Nigel.

"So you would think," Patterson agreed. "But this accommodation doesn't come without a cost. He is getting pressure from his superiors to make an arrest in the Fournier matter so he'll be coordinating this little charade of ours. We must remember, this is a police matter; our concern is the safe return of the Manet. It was only by happenstance that we stumbled across the murder of Fournier and although it is directly related to the stolen artwork, we cannot in any way hinder the efforts of the police to bring the parties responsible to justice. No one believes Miller killed that poor chap, but he is still an accomplice to the act and must be held accountable for his involvement."

"That's why I'm surprised at Miller's willingness to help," Nigel remarked, shaking his head. "He could just as easily disappear and keep the police busy for years looking for him and the Manet."

"Oh, he's not afraid of the police," Patterson said, tapping his spoon lightly on the table. "But Phynley Paine is another story. The only reason Miller is still alive is because she's allowing it to be so. I'm sure Miller's double-cross and running us about like this is as much amusing to her as it is irritating, but I think we've also witnessed the end of her patience, and more so, the patience of her buyer. I believe he's the real threat, and he's the one controlling the situation now."

"I'm not sure I understand," said Marie.

"This woman is ruthless." Patterson leaned forward to rest his clasped hands on the table in front of him. "She thought nothing of killing a museum guard and a French policeman, so why not this buyer? My guess is his power and his reach is equal to, or greater than, her own, so she will need to satisfy the situation one way or another. Killing him is not an option. It could only bring retaliation to her door. We know the buyer wants the painting or her life, not Miller. No, Miller knows just what he's doing. Eliminating Phynley Paine from the equation is our best chance of having the painting returned and Miller is the only one who can deliver her to us."

"We're depending an awful lot on someone we can't readily locate," said Lily.

"True," Patterson replied, picking at the crumbs on his plate, "but we've demonstrated we can be trusted and that's worth something in a situation like this."

"Right you are, Guv'nor," Ernie chimed in. "If old Jackie-boy thought otherwise he'd be long gone by now. I'm sure he's also thinking that giving up Paine will go a long way with the coppers when it's his turn in front of the magistrate."

Nigel smirked. "Not if Inspector Flannel has his way."

"We'll worry about that after we get the painting back," replied Patterson. "If he does, in fact, help in the capture of Paine, and returns the painting, I will certainly speak up on his behalf." Patterson checked his watch, stood up and addressed Marie. "If you would excuse me, I've got some correspondence to catch up on. Inspector Flannel should be here by nine o'clock and I'd like to finish before he arrives. Afterwards, maybe you would join me for a glass of wine before retiring?"

Marie smiled and nodded her head. As Patterson left the room Nigel suggested they all wait by the fire. He had twice expressed a desire to hear more about Ernie's colorful past and thought this would be a fine opportunity to do so. That suggestion prompted a sharp poke to the ribs from Lily but Ernie just smiled, flattered anyone would be so interested in such an old occupation.

Ernie modestly explained it was not as exciting as they would think, but agreed to relate a few tales if they so desired. Once he started, he more than made up for the bashfulness exhibited at his introduction to the group with detailed accounts of the more affluent pigeons that had crossed his path, complete with visual examples of how it was done. No one was more impressed than Marie, who admittedly was as far removed from any illegal activity than could possibly be imagined. Ernie was quick to give both women a few tips on protecting their purses in a crowd, while Nigel insisted on trying his hand at picking Ernie's pocket. It made for a very enjoyable way to pass the time, complete with Nigel inadvertently tossing his wallet in the fire as he attempted to remove it from Ernie's pocket.

The time went by quickly, terminating with the sobering arrival of Inspector Flannel. For obvious reasons, Nigel whispered to Marie, it would be best if the subject were changed for the time being. They heard Patterson greet him at the door, and after a brief conversation in the foyer the two men joined them in the lounge.

Marie's charms were not wasted on the austere inspector. As Patterson introduced her, the slightest hint of a smile could be seen on Flannel's face as he tipped his hat. Lily was greeted with a cordial handshake and a nod, and Nigel and Ernie with the usual raised eyebrow and grunt. The inspector expressed his regret over the death of Fournier and assured Marie he was working closely with the French authorities to bring the murderer to justice.

Patterson invited the inspector to join them, offering him a slice of pie, but he replied he was needed back at the Yard and had only stopped to give them the results of his visit to Maunder's flat.

He explained Maunder was less than happy about seeing him and had complained non-stop for the forty-five minutes he was there. While he and two constables questioned Maunder inside, another group of constables were outside securing the area. Flannel found out after he'd left that they'd run off a couple of Paine's thugs and had been able to place the painting in the lorry undetected. The tracking devices were also in place and being monitored from a vacant flat around the corner.

"Brilliant!" Nigel exclaimed.

"You'll not think so," the inspector replied, annoyed by the interruption, "if he pulls something funny overnight. I don't mind telling you I'm not at all happy about this Miller chap walking about free as a bird. I've stuck my neck out and, if he slips through our fingers, there'll be hell to pay. If I had my way, I'd have him sittin' in a cell at the Yard until we sorted this whole business out, but it seems Mr. Bisquets is the only one that's able to make him appear. I guess we'll just have to take his word, here, he's going to play it square with us."

"I have no reason to think he won't," Patterson said, "so for the time being I appreciate you giving us this bit of rope."

"Just don't hang yourself," Inspector Flannel replied, raising an eyebrow in contempt at Ernie. He took out his notepad and continued. "I also got the ballistic report back from the French police. It seems the officer and Fournier were killed with the same gun, a .38 caliber revolver. The boys in the lab are leaning towards a Walther P99."

"That's curious," Nigel said. "Those buggers that broke in here with Paine were carrying 9 millimeter Brownings. I wonder who has the Walther?"

"A good question," Patterson said. "I would be surprised if it's Paine. She doesn't seem the type to do the dirty work herself."

"She pointed a twenty-two at me," Lily remarked smugly, "but I'm sure it was just for show."

"How about this Miller?" asked Inspector Flannel.

"It ain't him. Jackie-boy wouldn't hurt a soul," declared Ernie confidently, but the severe look thrown his way by the inspector indicated he had no intention of discussing Miller's culpability with him.

"Desperate men do desperate things," replied the inspector slowly, further indicating his displeasure with the remark. "We'll just see where the evidence leads. For now, I've got a man watching the courtyard, so I guess we'll just wait and see who shows."

"I'll walk you out," Patterson said, very much annoyed by his friend and pointing towards the doorway. "Perhaps the events tomorrow will offer up an explanation. I'll ring you as soon as we hear something."

Inspector Flannel tipped his hat to the women and followed Patterson to the foyer. Ernie was a bit embarrassed by the remark directed at him by the inspector and it didn't go unnoticed by the others. He could see in their eyes all three of them wanted to say something supportive, but all three refrained until they heard the door close and Patterson returned.

"That man can be downright rude," Lily said.

"It's quite all right, Miss," Ernie replied, putting on a braver face.

"No, it's not," Patterson interrupted, taking an imposing stance in front of the fireplace. "His contempt towards you is a result of my actions, certainly not from something you've done. I just explained to him that you're as much a part of this organization now as Nigel and Lily and, as such, he will extend to you the same courtesies afforded them or he will not be welcome here. He has an insufferable habit of only seeing things in black and white, and refuses to entertain the thought that occasionally the world is beige."

"I did notice he was a bit more severe than usual," Nigel remarked, raising his eyebrow and snarling to mimic the inspector. "Whatever did you do to him Bisquets?"

"It's of no concern, now," Patterson replied, returning to a more cordial tone. "What does matter is that we must decide how we will proceed. Tomorrow should prove to be an exciting day and we must be ready for anything. It appears whatever happens, it's going to initiate from the courtyard at Maunder's."

"Taxis have worked in the past," suggested Lily, "and we can stay in contact via our mobiles."

"I agree," said Nigel. "If we take up positions on the streets emanating from St. Paul's, we should be able to cover all the escape routes. London is the worst possible place to make a run for it, so we'll use the traffic to our advantage."

"This is just so exciting," Marie remarked to Patterson. "Whom will I be with?"

"I think it best if you remain here away from any danger," Patterson said, displaying a genuine concern for her well being.

"I don't think so," she responded, jumping to her feet and placing her hands on her hips to emphasize her determination. She was serious, but in a playful way. "If I wanted to be safe, I would have stayed in Paris. I'm going with you or I'm going sightseeing at St. Paul's. The choice is yours."

"Marie can come along with me," Lily said through a slight laugh. "She can watch while I drive. You know how nervous I get driving in London."

Patterson just looked at the group and shook his head. "I'm sure I have no chance at all to dissuade you from this course of action, so I'll at least remind you how serious this business is. Two people have already been murdered because of this painting, and three others narrowly escaped the same fate. You keep your head down and do whatever Lily says."

Marie smiled, very pleased with the decision.

"Then I guess it's settled," Nigel said, ringing his hands. "We should take our positions early so we're ready when Miller calls with the final instructions."

"Let's not forget our place," Patterson cautioned. "We are there as an extra set of eyes for the police. They get Phynley Paine and we get the Manet. Now before this mutiny gets any worse, I'm going to steal Marie away for that glass of wine."

Marie took Patterson's extended arm and the two of them walked off to his study.

Nigel went to the sideboard and poured three glasses of wine, as well. He returned giving Lily and Ernie each a glass and placed his down on the table between the sofas. After tossing a few more logs on the fire he sat back down across from Ernie and Lily.

"Well, Bisquets," he said, raising his glass, "I commend you and your ability to irritate Inspector Flannel beyond the limits that even I thought possible. Like it or not, it looks like you're officially one of us. Are you ready to have a go at it?"

"You know, squire," Ernie said with a big smile, raising his glass, "I think I'm going to like being beige."

Twenty-Five

KNOWING WHERE TO PUT THE CHEESE

I F THE WEATHER Saturday morning was any indication of how the day was going to unfold, it was understood they were not going to have an easy time of it. The unexpected warmer air had caused a blanket of fog to settle over parts of the city, so visibility was limited. It was also the main topic of conversation as they enjoyed their breakfast, as a factor that couldn't be ignored. After a few pieces of toast and a slice of ham it was agreed they should not waste any time taking up their positions in the city, even though the idea of waiting in a taxi for hours was less than appealing. Miller was going to call sometime around noon with the final instructions, but they weren't about to be caught by surprise again by Phynley Paine if she decided to take advantage of this turn in the weather.

So, it was settled. After breakfast the table was cleared and Patterson brought out a large street map of the city. The map itself was no stranger to previous adventures, evident by the yellowed tape holding parts of it together and the burnt and frayed edges. At some point in time it had been adhered to a thin piece of canvas, surely due to the numerous repairs, and it was now rolled rather than folded. Standing around the table, they each held down a corner of the map and leaned in for a closer look.

Patterson placed the sugar container on top of the spot where Maunder's was. The saltshaker was to be Ernie and Nigel, and the pepper was Lily and Marie. Nigel suggested they use a discarded piece of toast as Inspector Flannel, which brought a smile to everyone's face except Patterson's. He just shook his head and continued. He moved the shakers here and there, with consideration of suggestions from the group, until finally settling on two spots. Nigel and Ernie would take a position on Black Friars Lane, covering any movement west or south of St. Paul's, while Lily and Marie were to wait on Cheapside across from Bread Street. This would give them a good vantage point to cover the roads leading east and north from St. Paul's.

"Where will you be?" Nigel asked Patterson, placing a plate on his corner of the map and sitting back down. Lily did the same with the other corners and they all settled back in their chairs.

"Inspector Flannel and his men"—Patterson adjusted the position of the piece of toast on the map with his finger—"are in a flat on St. Andrew's Hill. I'll stay there and monitor the movement of the painting and relay the information to you. I've made arrangements for three taxis for the day. They are scheduled to be here at eleven o'clock, but in light of the fog I'm going to call and get them here right away. I don't trust that woman."

While the others put their coats on in the foyer, Patterson called to revise his arrangements for the taxis. Their voices filled the foyer with anticipation as they busied themselves buttoning up for the weather, too excited to notice Mrs. Chapman's presence in the doorway to the kitchen.

She always worried for their safety any time they went off on a case, but this time the deep creases on her forehead showed an even greater concern. Mrs. Chapman had seen first hand what this evil woman was capable of and the thought of them setting out to capture her was beyond what she cared to think about.

Patterson came out of his study with two revolvers in belt holsters in his hand. Mrs. Chapman's concern didn't escape him and he was quick to address it.

"You know, Annie," he started, attaching one of the holsters to his belt under his jacket, "Phynley Paine will be thanking us for bringing her in. I would hate to think what would happen if you got your hands on her."

The remark brought a broad smile to her face, but she quickly returned to a more serious countenance. "I'll thank you to just look after those youngsters. She's ever so mean and I'll not have a bit of harm come to them again."

"Nor will I," said Patterson, with a slight laugh. He tossed the other holster to Nigel, then leaned down close to Mrs. Chapman to continue in a quiet tone, "I've asked a rather burly acquaintance of mine to keep an eye on the flat while we take care of this business. I'll not have a bit of harm come to you again, either."

Nigel walked over and handed Patterson his coat, indicating the taxis were out front. Lily and Marie were already heading down the stairs along with Ernie, who expressed a desire to see just how bad the weather was, but was actually more interested in seeing if anybody was loitering about the flat. It was only a few minutes later that Nigel and Patterson joined them. Nigel walked over to the taxi where Ernie was waiting while Patterson gave Lily and Marie a last bit of advice, along with a final reminder of the danger involved. It was nearly nine-thirty when the first group was on their way to their designated location, hours before they expected to hear from Miller but confident they were doing the right thing.

"Nigel and Lily have mobiles that will allow us to stay in constant contact," Patterson said, patting Ernie on the shoulder. "Call me the second you hear from Miller."

"Speaking of Miller," Nigel said, "do we know if he made the correction to the painting in the lorry?"

"I spoke with the inspector before breakfast," Patterson replied, opening the door to the taxi. "He had a man stationed in the building on the corner with a clear view of the courtyard. It appears that late last night he saw a dark figure enter the back of the lorry. He was there some time and then slipped out and disappeared around the corner. Flannel didn't pursue him because he didn't want to alert Paine's men to the surveillance. He apparently went back into Maunder's so at this point we can only assume it was Miller and he made the correction."

"I'll bet lettin' old Jackie-boy go got his knickers in a bunch," Ernie said through a grin.

"You're right about that," Patterson agreed with a grin of his own. "Let's just hope Miller lives up to his part of the bargain and delivers Paine. You two better get going. Let me know when you get to Black Friars Lane."

The two men climbed in the taxi and Nigel called out the address. The vehicle eased out into traffic and was quickly consumed by the fog.

Patterson took his mobile out as he climbed into the third taxi. After a quick call to Dragonetti to confirm their arrangement to watch the flat, he had the driver drop him off on Queen Victoria Street. It was close enough to the flat on St. Andrew's Hill where Inspector Flannel and his men were, but far enough away from Carter Lane to avoid being seen by Paine's men. For his walk up St. Andrew's Hill the fog was an unsuspecting ally, yet it also confirmed his fear that it afforded the same protection to Paine if she so desired and acted quickly enough to utilize it. The advantage they held was slowly diminishing, but if the fog lifted before she put a plan in motion it would swing the odds back in their favor.

Halfway up the street Nigel reported Miller had just contacted Ernie and said Paine was sending a man over to Maunder's to authenticate the painting. Miller was to accompany the man in the lorry for part of the trip. He had no idea of the final destination but they were to travel west and Miller was to get out at Trafalgar Square. At that point the other man was going to drive the rest of the way.

"Excellent," Patterson exclaimed softly, trying not to attract any attention as he walked. "That means they'll be heading down Ludgate Hill so you should be able to meet up with them at Pageantmaster, across from Old Bailey. The lorry has a white cab and a black cargo box. Inspector Flannel said the petrol tanks are painted blue so you should be able to spot it easily. Lily, did you get that?"

"Yes," she replied. "We'll go down to the Thames and wait just in case they head south over one of the bridges. If not, we'll be able to follow west along Victoria Embankment and shoot up Northumberland to Trafalgar Square. The fog is lifting a bit here, but visibility is poor and traffic is still moving slowly."

"I'm here now," Patterson said, arriving at the flat where Inspector Flannel had his men stationed. "Nigel, you and Ernie stay with the lorry. Lily, you and Marie follow Miller. Marie knows what he looks like, so if he does get out at Trafalgar we don't want to loose him in the crowd. I'll tell all of you once more—be careful."

As he turned to go up the stairs the door opened and the inspector came out. "They're moving," he said, motioning for Patterson to follow him.

The two men walked back down the street and around the corner to Wardrobe Terrace, where the inspector had a taxi waiting, or so it appeared. Climbing into the back Patterson noticed it was fitted with surveillance equipment. London is remarkable for the number of taxis on its streets, so it's the most inconspicuous vehicle you could want to travel in. This taxi was equipped with monitors capable of acquiring a direct feed from the control center for the city's surveillance cameras. There were two GPS monitors with flashing green lights, one each for the tracking devices.

"There's our boy," Inspector Flannel remarked, pointing to a vehicle on one of the monitors. "He's about to cross New Bridge Street so this monitor here will pick him up on Fleet Street."

Patterson watched as the lorry moved from one monitor to the next, as it crossed over each corner. He relayed the progress to his group, also commenting on their relation to the vehicle. The fog was dissipating quickly, now, so Patterson suggested they keep a little distance back from the lorry. Lily replied they were just pulling over on Northumberland, close to the corner at Trafalgar Square, and Patterson indicated their position to the inspector. Nigel and Ernie were about a kilometer behind the lorry, just crossing Wellington Street.

As they waited for Miller and the lorry to arrive at Trafalgar, Patterson mentioned to Inspector Flannel that he had instructed Lily and Marie to stay with Miller if he indeed did get out there. The inspector was reluctant at first about their involvement at that level, but realized that having someone who knew what Miller looked like was worth something.

"There!" Patterson exclaimed, pointing to a vehicle on one of the monitors. "That's them— Lily, they should be passing in front of you right...*now.*"

"I've got them," Lily replied. "Wait, the truck just stopped halfway around the square."

Flannel pointed to the lorry on one of the monitors and Patterson heard wheels screeching in his earpiece as they watched other vehicles swerve to avoid hitting it, including the taxi Lily and Marie were in. Then one of the flashing green lights went out on a GPS monitor.

"Someone just got out of the lorry," said Patterson. "Can you see who it is?"

Lily had the taxi pull over as it turned onto Cockspur. There was a short pause but then she exclaimed, "Yes, we see him... Marie said it isn't Miller...he's crossing over the street and heading towards Nelson's monument. We're going to follow him."

Patterson repeated Lily's statements aloud to convey the information to the inspector, who in turn informed the men he had stationed at the monument what was unfolding. As he did, he pointed to a monitor to indicate the lorry was moving again, and that was confirmed by the movement on the remaining flashing green light.

"Where are you now, Nigel?" Patterson demanded.

"We're just entering the square," he replied. "Which direction have they taken?"

"He's on Pall Mall," Patterson said, looking at the monitor Flannel was pointing to. "They must be heading towards Hyde Park. We're behind you, but not by much."

Patterson sat back and, along with Inspector Flannel, quietly monitored their progress as they watched the lorry cross each street and come into view of the cameras. At one point Flannel pointed out the missing flasher on the one GPS monitor, mentioning that he hoped the other one hadn't been found. They had caught up to the taxi Nigel and Ernie were in, but cautiously stayed behind them. The lorry went up St. James's Street and took the ramp onto Piccadilly. Park Lane was next and—by the time it reached Cumberland Gate—Lily had reported that they had lost the man in the crowds at Nelson's monument. Inspector Flannel wasn't at all happy about this turn of events, as was evident in the look he gave Patterson, but he was confident his men would locate him.

Bayswater Road was next, and the lorry traveled along at a steady pace with traffic, giving no indication of urgency or duplicity. It wasn't until it turned onto Craven Road that the two men realized Paddington Station was just ahead. Inspector Flannel called his men stationed there, alerting them to the suspected arrival of the lorry, but instructing them not to approach the vehicle.

The lorry crossed over Westbourne Terrace. The next monitor showed it approaching Eastbourne Terrace and then continuing on Praed Street, slowing down as it approached the traffic light at London Street. The lorry inched slowly towards the intersection, stopping in a blind spot between the surveillance cameras.

Nigel's taxi had just turned onto Craven, followed closely by the inspector and Patterson. They were only a few blocks behind, but losing sight of the lorry had them both on the edge of their seats. They waited anxiously for the light to change so the lorry would come back into view, but when it did, there was no sign of the lorry. The inspector made a frantic call to his men, hoping one of them would spot the vehicle. He tapped the driver on the shoulder and instructed him to speed up. The taxi raced ahead, dodging traffic and screeching to a halt in the center of the intersection where they'd lost the lorry.

"There it is!" Patterson heard Ernie faintly exclaim in his earpiece from the other taxi.

"Back up!" Nigel shouted.

Patterson and the inspector looked out the back window of the taxi and saw Nigel and Ernie jump out of their taxi and run down the access road to Paddington Station, just before London Street.

Patterson followed, along with the inspector who was calling in the location. Sirens from the approaching police vehicles filled the air. Uniformed constables running up from the lower entrance to the station quickly joined the four men. With revolvers drawn they approached the lorry.

The driver's door was open but the cab was empty. Ernie stepped back out of the way, but Nigel and Patterson followed the inspector to the back. The inspector took hold of the tarp, signaled his intention and threw it up over the top of the cargo box. Inside was the open crate the painting had been packed in, leaning against the side of the cargo box. The frame was still secured inside, but the painting had been cut from the frame and removed.

"Isn't this just great," the inspector grumbled, putting his gun away. "We've lost Miller and the forgery, and there's no sign of Paine. I'll thank you next time to stay out of police business."

Patterson was familiar with the inspector's temperament, and how quick he was to assign blame, so he just ignored the disparaging remarks. This unexpected turn had left him irritated, as well, but he had a far greater control of his emotions and chose to center his thoughts on an assessment of the resulting situation.

As the inspector called to have the lorry impounded, Patterson suggested to the constables they search the station, paying particular attention to anyone carrying a tube or a large case. Flannel grumbled his approval. They could tell by his voice he saw the effort as fruitless but it wasn't in his nature to just give up, especially when an explanation was going to be due his superiors when he got back to the station.

"Who are you calling?" Nigel asked Ernie, who was still standing off to one side.

"Miller, squire," replied Ernie. "I'm ringing back the number he called from. He's made me out a fool he has and I'll—"

Nigel raised his hand to interrupt Ernie and turned his head slowly, as if listening for something.

"Quiet! he shouted to the crowd of police, grabbing the attention of everyone standing around the lorry. "Listen! It's a mobile phone."

It was, and it was coming from inside the lorry. All the constables drew their weapons. Two of them jumped up into the back and moved the crate away from the far end of the box. The ringing had stopped, but Nigel told Ernie to call the number again. They could hear it ringing and it was coming from behind the bulkhead, close to the cab.

Inspector Flannel jumped up and shouted out, "You've no chance at all. Out with you or we'll come in after you."

The inspector and the two constables stepped back after hearing movement from behind the panels. The center panel fell forward revealing a shallow cavity, just large enough to conceal a person.

"Don't shoot," a voice snarled from behind the panels. A man dressed in black slowly emerged from the cavity, holding his hands up in front of himself. He struggled a bit as one of the constables helped him out of the lorry, while the other stepped inside from where he emerged. As the inspector put cuffs on him, the constable in the lorry held up a revolver, the mobile phone, and what appeared to be the tube containing the painting.

"So, who might you be?" asked Inspector Flannel smugly, turning the man back around. He was quite pleased with himself, now that he had someone in custody.

The man just sneered, refusing to answer. He was dressed very well and had an air of superiority. It was obvious he wasn't Miller, and just as obvious it wasn't Phynley Paine, but the inspector assured him within time he'd know everything there was to know about him.

Inspector Flannel gave a nod and the man was put in the back of one of the police cars. As the car drove away he walked over to where Nigel and Ernie were standing with Patterson.

Patterson was talking to Lily on her mobile, explaining what had happened and suggesting they meet back at Conduit Street. There was a pause on the phone and he could hear Marie talking in the background. Lily gave a hasty reply and abruptly hung up. Before he had time to think about Lily's reply he glanced up to see the inspector waiting patiently behind Nigel and Ernie. Patterson folded his arms behind his back, cleared his throat and gave a nod with his head in the direction of the inspector, prompting both Ernie and Nigel to turn around.

Inspector Flannel looked from one to the other of them, an act that had little affect on Nigel and Patterson but caused a very nervous reaction in Ernie. Then he gave an approving nod of his head. Without uttering a word he tugged at one end of his mustache, tipped his hat and turned and walked away.

"What was that?" Ernie asked after a long exhale, watching the inspector drive off in one of the other police cars.

"That, old man," replied Nigel, starting to grin, "was the closest thing to an apology I've ever witnessed by our dear Inspector Flannel. I'm not sure, but I think he's starting to like us."

"I knew when I saw him nothing good was going to come from this," Ernie said with a smirk, shaking his head.

"There could be more truth in those words than you think," Patterson remarked gravely. The three of them walked back over to one of the taxis. "I'm very curious about who this man is the inspector has in custody, and what role he played in this business, but I'm not at all sure we haven't hurt our chances of locating the Manet with what happened here this morning. All we can do now is hope Miller contacts us again, and wait to hear what the inspector finds out about the man in the back of the lorry."

"What about Lily and Marie?" Nigel asked Patterson, opening the door to the taxi. "Did they find the man that jumped out of the lorry?"

"I'm not sure," answered Patterson with a slight hesitation, giving the question careful thought. "She started to tell me something about Marie spotting him and then she abruptly hung up. I'll guess we'll know more when they get back to Conduit Street."

Twenty-Six

A FRIEND YOU CAN COUNT ON

PATTERSON HAD CALLED ahead to Mrs. Chapman with news of the capture of the man in the back of the lorry and their expected arrival back at Conduit Street, hoping to relieve the anxiety their morning departure had caused. She had tried dismissing his concern, explaining how she'd been too busy preparing the salmon and prawn fish cakes for lunch to bother about such things, but he could hear the delight in her voice upon hearing all were safe.

Lily had also called Patterson back, apologizing for the abrupt way she'd hung up earlier and had explained she had a remarkable development to share with them back at the flat. As exciting as their morning had been, the afternoon was promising to be that and more.

The three men climbed out of the taxi in front of the stationery shop on Conduit Street, still talking about the man in the back of the lorry and speculating on his involvement with this nasty business. Nigel continued his conversation with Ernie as he opened the door to their flat, but before following them in Patterson gave a quick look around. Across the street and down a few buildings he spied the familiar and unmistakable silhouette of Dragonetti, who gave him a nod that all was well and walked off towards Regent Street.

Patterson quickly caught up to Ernie and Nigel on the stairs and soon found himself in the foyer, greeted by a very animated Lily. What surprised him was that Marie didn't appear to share her enthusiasm. As he took off his topcoat he watched Lily reenact their chase through Trafalgar Square, her arms waving wildly to demonstrate the tourists being knocked about and culminating with the capture of the man who had jumped out of the lorry.

"You caught him?" Nigel asked eagerly, fumbling a bit to get his coat off. "That's brilliant! Who is he?"

Lily didn't answer; she just glanced over at Marie.

"Emory," Marie replied slowly, answering both the question and the heartrending look on her face that Patterson had noticed when he'd arrived.

"Emory?" he repeated. "From the museum? We suspected he was hired to authenticate the painting but I'm surprised to see his involvement may go even deeper."

It had upset Marie earlier when they'd suspected that Emory was mixed up in this business in even a small way. This new revelation just further confirmed their suspicions. Everything had happened so quickly in the square that she hadn't had time to think about it, but now the reality of the situation was settling in.

Seeing the tear on her cheek, Ernie pulled a handkerchief from his pocket and handed it to her. Marie smiled and thanked him. Patterson put his arm around her and together they walked into the lounge, followed by the others.

The silver tea service was on a tray on the table between the sofas, surrounded by cups and saucers. Ernie removed the cozy and poured tea for everyone, as Lily consoled Marie and Nigel poked a bit at the fire to take the chill off the room. Patterson wanted to give Marie time to digest what was happening so he excused himself; stating he was going to call the inspector to see what he could find out about Emory's involvement. Marie smiled and nodded her appreciation.

"I blame myself," she said, accepting a cup of tea from Lily. "I can't believe all this was going on while I was in charge. Surely the museum board will question my ability to ensure the continued safety of the treasures housed within the museum. I must confess, I don't blame them if they do. I hired Emory two years ago, so I am responsible for his actions."

Nigel shook his head. "I think you're being far too hard on yourself. You assume his intention in getting his situation with the museum was to assist in this robbery, but there's more evidence to indicate he was corrupted as a result of his position. Money is a powerful persuader in the hands of someone like Phynley Paine. Before we condemn this man we should hear what the police have to say."

He was replacing the poker in the brass rack on the hearth when Patterson returned wearing a very satisfied expression.

"It seems Nigel is correct in his line of thinking." Patterson sat down across from Marie and Lily. "I just spoke with Inspector Flannel and he tells me Emory is talking faster than they can take down the information."

"So, was he working for this Phynley Paine?" asked Marie cautiously.

Patterson hesitated for a moment, and then smiled. "Yes, but innocently it appears and in a round about way. It seems he was in the employ of a Dr. Montague Rhodes."

"Who the devil is Montague Rhodes?" Nigel shouted. He had returned to his duties at the fire, poking about as if the aforementioned gentleman was hiding beneath the coals.

"He's a high priced fence, he is," Ernie stated confidently, "and not the kind of bloke you want to cross. Usually deals in jewelry and the likes, he does."

"Brilliant!" exclaimed Patterson, slapping his knee. "I can add to that by saying Dr. Rhodes was also Phynley Paines' buyer. It seems the good doctor had the desire to expand his business."

"I can't believe Emory would associate with these monsters," Marie said softly.

"According to his story, he thought he'd been hired as a consultant to evaluate a private collection," Patterson explained. "It wasn't until he saw Miller and the painting at Maunder's that he realized what was going on, but by then it was too late. Miller managed to secretly tell him to authenticate the painting and he would help him. Emory was afraid and even more confused, but he did what Miller asked. Dr. Rhodes was well aware of the error in the label on the back of the frame so Emory used the corrected label to substantiate his claim. He did this at gunpoint and then was instructed to drive. Rhodes stayed in the back of the lorry and he and Miller climbed into the front."

"*Je suis stupéfié,*" Marie said, wide-eyed over what she was hearing.

"Why did he jump out and run?" asked Nigel suspiciously.

"He didn't jump out at all—Miller pushed him out," answered Patterson. "Emory wasn't running from the police, he was running to them."

"Now that you mention it," Lily added casually, "it wasn't much of a chase. He turned and ran when he noticed Marie walking towards him, embarrassed no doubt, and ran right up to the first constable he saw."

"Do you believe him?" Marie asked Patterson.

"I've only had a few conversations with Emory," he replied soothingly, "but I would be very surprised if he was a party to this from the beginning. I could go further by saying Miller probably saved his life. Who knows what was waiting for him at Paddington Station."

"Yes, Paddington Station," Nigel said, anxiously. "Why did they end up at Paddington?"

"According to Emory—and only Miller can confirm this—the plan was to have the painting authenticated, and then Rhodes was going to conceal himself in the secret cavity in the back of the lorry. This is only speculation on my part but it appears to be incredibly simple from there. Miller and Rhodes knew they were being followed, but they only needed a minute to turn down the access road at Paddington Station, jump out and disappear onto the crowded platform. The abandoned lorry would be spotted right away and it would attract all the attention of the police, further aiding his escape. The police would have the lorry removed and Rhodes would exit the cavity and jump off the lorry as it made its way to the Yard."

"Brilliant!" Nigel exclaimed, plopping down onto the sofa. "I guess old Rhodes didn't count on Bisquets, here, calling Miller's mobile."

"I'm sure you're right," Patterson said with a smile. He looked over at Ernie, hesitated, then said, "but I'm just as sure Miller was counting on Ernie doing just that."

Ernie looked from one to the other of them not knowing what to say, or even if a response was required. He had been paying attention to Patterson's narration along with the others, but this last statement caught him by surprise.

The expression on Ernie's face prompted Patterson to let out a hearty laugh. The others were just as confused, except for Lily, who seemed to take umbrage at the remark.

"You're not suggesting Ernie had anything to do with this?" she snapped, albeit with some restraint.

"Not at all," Patterson replied in a reassuring tone. "I'm sure Miller recognized in Ernie the same quality I admire in him—integrity. Based on information he gained privately from Miller, Ernie has made certain assurances to the police and all of us. By doing this he has willingly jeopardized his own credibility if Miller crossed him. Miller was counting on this and I'm sure he left the mobile behind purposely, knowing that Ernie would call him wanting to find out what was going on."

"You mean he intended for us to find that bloke in the back?" Ernie asked, quickly shifting the attention away from himself.

Patterson smiled. "As I said, only Miller can confirm that, I'm just speculating."

"Well, there's just no end to your ability to amaze me," a grinning Nigel said to a very embarrassed Ernie.

Ernie did his best to shy away from the attention, but the others were all smiling his way. Fortunately, Patterson's mobile rang drawing their immediate attention. Patterson stood up and excused himself to answer it, but when realizing who it was, he didn't walk away. Instead he motioned for the others that they should listen.

"Hello.........Well, I was wondering when I was going to hear from you.........I had it in my head that you might have orchestrated this business, but I hesitated to share that idea with the others......... You're quite welcome.........So, stealing the Manet was never the goal.........We're just about to sit down for a bit of lunch, why don't you join us.........I thought not—"

Patterson listened intently for a moment and then snapped his phone shut.

"Who was that?" Lily asked.

"That was our friend Phynley Paine," he replied, sitting back down. "It seems by drawing us into the pursuit of the missing painting we've fallen into her well devised plan and unwittingly facilitated the elimination of her competition. She was extremely grateful, to a point of wishing us well in our continued search for the Manet."

"And Miller?" asked Ernie.

"I'm not exactly sure about that," Patterson said pensively, "It appears Miller was part of *her* plan from the start, but he could just as well have been duped, much like Emory. I say that because Paine did mention the second forgery came as quite a surprise to her. If Miller got wise to what was going on he may have used the situation to his own gain. Paine may not have wanted the painting, but it appears Miller did."

"What will you do now?" Marie asked Patterson, trying to mask her disappointment.

Patterson got up and walked over to the windows overlooking Conduit Street. "I doubt Miller loitered about at Paddington Station, so he should be very curious about the fate of Dr. Rhodes. I would wager he's still in London. In any case, we have no choice but to enjoy our lunch and wait to hear from him."

As he spoke, Mrs. Chapman was busy at the other end of the room setting the places for lunch. From her tray, resting on the sideboard, she carefully placed a bed of lentils on each plate, topped with two salmon and prawn fish cakes. A fresh pot of coffee awaited them, along with a Louis Roederer Brut Rose—a favorite of Marie's that Patterson had brought in from the wine chiller earlier. The aroma had captured the attention of the group, so they needed little persuasion to come to the table.

"I wouldn't worry, Miss," Ernie said, pulling out the chair at the foot of the table for Marie. "I'm sure His Lordship is right. Old Jackie-boy will call soon enough, he will. He may have been part of the plan, but he's afraid for his life just the same."

"And let's not forget the murders," Nigel joined in, pulling the chair out for Lily. "He may not have pulled the trigger, but the deaths of those two chaps is a direct result of his actions. That Manet is an excellent bargaining chip now, and I'm sure he knows it."

"There, it's settled." Patterson poured a glass of champagne for Marie. "We'll not spoil this fine meal by upsetting ourselves with worry. I have to believe Miller wants to cooperate, if only to walk away with the least amount of trouble the law has to offer for his involvement. It would be a greater crime if we allow these exceptional fish cakes to get cold."

"I couldn't agree more," Lily remarked, taking her glass from Patterson. She looked over at Mrs. Chapman, who had just tucked her tray under her arm. "And I have it on good authority when we've finished there's a Steamed Syrup Sponge that's been on the boil for the last hour and a half."

Mrs. Chapman smiled, slowly pushing the kitchen door open with her bum. "It's the perfect sweet for a chilly afternoon, it is, and just the thing to get your mind off your troubles."

Marie smiled and patted Nigel on the hand. She was comforted by their optimism and apologized for any doubt she may have exhibited. Patterson dismissed the idea and suggested she put aside the Manet for the time being and enjoy the remainder of her stay with them.

Their conversation drifted off into lighter channels, and with the exception of hearing the front doorbell ring, they had a very delightful and uninterrupted lunch. As they were enjoying their afters Mrs. Chapman brought in a letter that had been left at the door.

"Beggin' your pardon, sir," she said, handing the envelope to

Patterson. "This was left with the post."

Patterson took the letter from her and opened it. He read it quietly to himself, and then out loud to the group, who were very anxious to know its contents.

> Lord Coats,
>> Square me with the coppers and I'll return the painting.
>> Meet me in Paris at the museum tomorrow afternoon.
>> J.M.

"It seems Miller is quite content with the outcome of this morning's activities," said Patterson, handing the note to Ernie. "He must be very sure he can clear his name if he's willing to meet with us."

"That's his handwriting, all right," Ernie stated after carefully studying the note.

"*Magnifique!*" Marie exclaimed.

"Let's not get too excited just yet," Patterson warned, sitting forward in his chair. "I'll have to speak with Inspector Flannel first, and then there's the French police. I'm sure your brother will want a say in Miller's future." Patterson stood up and continued. "I'll make the travel arrangements now and call August down at Scotland Yard. I suggest we get an early start in the morning and take the first train to Paris. Miller's willingness to return the Manet seems innocent enough but I think it best to be prepared."

"Can I do anything?" asked Marie.

"You should call your brother," Patterson answered, putting his hand on her shoulder as he walked past. "He'll want to be there, I'm sure, when Miller arrives." Patterson continued to the doorway, paused and turned around. "After we make these calls why don't you and I go down and meet Inspector Flannel at the Yard. We'll get the full story on this Dr. Rhodes and see if they intend to release Emory."

"I would like that," Marie replied. "If he was tricked by those wretched people he must know we will help him any way we can."

"As for you three," Patterson continued with a playful look, "before we got derailed I believe you were pondering the question of exactly how Miller got the original painting out of the Musee d'Orsay in the first place and replaced it with the forgery. It might not be a bad idea to pick up that scent again and see where it leads you."

Twenty-Seven

THE LIGHT AT THE END OF THE TUNNEL

"GET UP!" PATTERSON shouted, standing by the side of Nigel's bed and waking him from a sound sleep. "Hurry, I'll wake the others."

"What's going on?" Nigel stammered, rubbing his eyes as he sat up.

"No time for that now," Patterson answered, pausing at the door to his room. "I'll explain on the way to Paris."

"Paris?" Nigel called out, picking his watch up from the nightstand next to his bed. "It's four in the morning!"

Before Nigel finished his statement Patterson was already down the hall, meeting Marie coming out of Lily's room. She had given Lily the same instructions, and after Patterson stopped to wake Ernie, the two proceeded to the foyer to wait for them to come down.

The excitement had started about three forty-five in the morning, when Marie was awakened by her mobile phone. The head of security at the Musee d'Orsay had called with an urgent message. She had him repeat it three times because she couldn't believe what she was hearing. Then she immediately got dressed and went down the hall to awaken Patterson, explaining the call she had just received. By five o'clock all five were hastily putting on coats in the foyer, with three of them still wondering what was going on. Mrs. Chapman, tireless in her efforts to tend to their needs, had prepared a thermos bottle of coffee and tucked a small travel mug in each of their pockets.

"Are we all set?" Patterson asked, giving his scarf one last loop around his neck.

"Are we all set for what?" Nigel grumbled, still rubbing the sleep from his eyes.

"The Musee d'Orsay, of course," Patterson replied, giving Marie a wink. "I've a car waiting out front to take us to Heathrow; I've chartered a plane to get us to Paris."

Patterson tucked Marie's arm under his own and started off down the stairs, not giving Nigel a chance to ask any more questions. There was a black limousine out front waiting for them, and they soon found themselves heading out of the city towards Heathrow.

"Whatever's going on," Lily remarked to Marie with a very large grin, "it appears to meet with your approval."

"I couldn't be happier," Marie replied briskly, loosening her coat as she settled back into her seat. "The Manet has been returned!"

Lily and Ernie looked at her in utter surprise. Nigel, however, remarked in a voice higher than usual, "The Manet was returned?"

"I said the same thing," Patterson laughed. "Marie will explain."

"About two this morning," Marie excitedly began to relate the details of her early morning call, "the motion sensors attached to the paintings in the Impressionists' Gallery started going off randomly. The police were called and the museum was checked, but nothing appeared out of place. It happened again at two-thirty, with the same result, and again at three, but that time the police only called asking the guards to check the museum and call back if anything was out of the ordinary. I can only imagine their surprise when they walked into the Impressionists' Gallery and found the Manet hanging on the wall as if nothing had happened!"

Nigel cleared his throat, bringing his voice back to its normal tone and repeated, "The Manet was returned?"

"Not only returned," Patterson remarked, "but even the velvet ropes used to cordon off the area had been removed. It's as if it never happened."

"He's a bit of a showman, that Jackie, ain't he?" Ernie said with a smile.

"Are we sure it's the real Manet?" Lily asked.

"That's why we're going to Paris," replied Patterson. "Marie called the curator of the Louvre, explained our situation, and she is sending over an expert to authenticate the painting. We should know something by the time we arrive."

The remainder of their trip to Heathrow was filled with speculation about how Miller managed to get the painting back on the wall and that, in turn, directed the conversation once again to the original question of how he had removed it in the first place.

Lily detailed their findings about the history of the museum, further fueling the speculation that there might be more to the museum than met the eye, but a closer examination would be required to substantiate their theories.

A small business jet was waiting for them at Heathrow, and by six o'clock they could see the channel below, glimmering from the sun just breaking the horizon. The early morning excitement had overshadowed their questions regarding Dr. Rhodes, but the conversation in the air had come 'round to what Patterson and Marie had found out from Inspector Flannel. They hadn't had a chance to present their findings the previous evening, as it was late when they'd returned from the Yard and the others had already turned in for the night.

"It appears Dr. Montague Rhodes is a right proper villain," Patterson remarked casually, pouring himself coffee and offering the thermos to the others. "They can place him at Maunder's when Fournier was murdered and the gun they found in the back of the lorry was the same gun used in both murders. Rhodes vehemently denies shooting Fournier, claiming it was one of Paine's thugs who were there with him, but Maunder insists he only saw Rhodes enter the building. Paid off, no doubt. It's all very tidy; his fingerprints were on the gun, the clip and on the cabinet in Miller's flat. Putting Miller's museum coat on the body was a nice touch."

"It's almost too tidy," said Nigel.

"Inspector Flannel agreed," replied Patterson, "but he must act upon the evidence before him. He hasn't dismissed Paine's contribution to this mess, but only time will tell if he can substantiate a solid link between the two."

"So Phynley Paine just walks away?" Lily demanded hotly.

"I'm afraid so, despite the matter of assault, kidnapping and blowing up that boat. She has long been wanted by the police—under numerous names—so our charges will just be added to the pile. As it stands now, the prospect of bringing her before a magistrate for anything is not very likely."

"At least we now know of her," Nigel remarked, "and what she is capable of. I'm sure we haven't seen the last of Phynley Paine."

Patterson agreed, although Lily found little comfort in that. He went on to explain their visit to Inspector Flannel the previous evening, and how the inspector intended to release Emory that morning. Despite Miller's suspected reputation as a forger, he was also a respected art restorer in some circles. Finding the hidden room in his flat may have seemed incriminating but would amount to nothing more than an art supply closet without sufficient evidence to link Miller directly to the forgeries, or a witness who could place him at the museum the night the painting was discovered missing. The ironic twist was Miller would be credited with assisting in the apprehension of Dr. Rhodes, along with saving Emory's life. He could accept this accolade while denying any knowledge of the forgeries or how they came to be. Unless the police could build a separate case against him he would, for the time being, only be a material witness against Dr. Rhodes. Patterson planned on presenting this information to Miller at the museum *if* he showed up and he could convince him to come forward.

As the plane began its final approach, Patterson finished up by noting how Dr. Rhodes had become quite popular since being brought in. It seemed his fingerprints also matched ones found at the scenes of a number of unsolved crimes throughout Great Britain. Rhodes, like Phynley Paine, was another villain whose existence was for years suspected but never verified. He had a long list of charges to answer for and his apprehension would be quite the feather in Inspector Flannel's derby.

Marie, although still saddened by the loss of life that had resulted from this business, was elated the painting had been returned and was anxious to return to the museum. Her brother, Jean-Paul, had a police car waiting for them when they landed and they were taken directly to the Musee d'Orsay, where they found him waiting at the main entrance.

The *Prefect de Police* was uncharacteristically pleasant to the group as they entered the museum, especially for the hour. He was, of course, happy to see his sister, greeting her with a kiss on the cheek, but he also expressed his congratulations to Patterson for his efforts, and those of his group, in effecting the return of the painting. Patterson cordially dismissed the compliment, stating only that any credit due should be directed to Lily, Nigel and Ernie for risking their lives in pursuit of the Manet

"Of course," Jean-Paul acknowledged, ushering them down the hall toward the Impressionists' Gallery, "Inspector Flannel told me about the incident on the boat and I join with him in saying how fortunate you are in escaping unharmed. I will be going to London tomorrow to speak with Dr. Rhodes about the murder of Officer Delavau. Am I to understand this Jacques Millet is still missing?"

"That's correct," Lily, who was examining each of the sculptures they passed in the central alley, said. "But he has indicated he will meet us here this afternoon."

"Well, that's something," replied the *prefect*. "I have a few questions for him, also. Here we are. I'm sure you all want to see what all this fuss is about."

The group entered the gallery, once again under the watchful eye of Émile Zola, and stood absolutely amazed to see the Manet back in place on the wall. It was truly a magnificent work of art and commanded all their attention. One of the security guards was there, too, but he stood quietly off to the side.

It was a few moments before anyone spoke. Nigel was the first, moving forward to take a closer look at the brushwork. "Has it been authenticated?" he asked.

"Oui," said Jean-Paul. "A more extensive examination will be made later this afternoon, but tentatively this is believed to be the original. The man just left, moments before your arrival."

Nigel continued to examine the painting. He didn't pay any attention to the gasps he heard when he slipped his hand behind the frame, slowly pulling the alarm tether out. After a moment he tucked it back in, satisfied it was attached. While this was happening no one noticed Ernie had walked over to the Pissarro. He looked at it for a moment and then, seeing it was crooked, he began to straighten it out.

When Marie and Lily realized what he was about to do they both gasped, anticipating the alarm, but nothing happened. This piqued Nigel's interest. He walked over, and much to Ernie's surprise, gave the painting a good shake. Still nothing.

"I don't understand," Marie finally said. "I had all these alarms checked after your last visit, especially that one. I can't believe it's not working again."

"Puzzling indeed," Nigel muttered to himself. He walked back over to the Manet, took a firm grip of the frame and gave it a quick shake. Immediately, the alarm sounded. He proceeded to the huge portrait of Émile Zola and repeated the action. Once again the alarm sounded at once.

Jean-Paul understood what he was doing. He took out his mobile and called into the station, alerting them to their presence in the museum and indicating that alarms were being tripped deliberately as part of an investigation.

The guard standing with them gave Nigel a perturbed look,

walked over to the entranceway and opened a concealed panel on the column. Inserting a small round key in the lock below one of the flashing red lights he reset the alarm, doing the same for the other. Before he could close the small door, however, Nigel and Ernie had come up behind him and were peering over his shoulder to get a closer look at the panel.

"What do all those green lights mean?" Nigel asked.

"There is one light for each painting in this gallery," the guard replied hesitantly in broken English. He glanced over at Marie, uneasy about the two men asking him questions and unsure whether he should continue.

Marie smiled and nodded her head to indicate it was all right. Then she walked over, offering her assistance in further explaining the security system.

"This panel controls the motion sensor alarms for the paintings in this room of the museum. There is a red, green and yellow light for each painting," she explained, pointing out the lights on the panel. "Each alarm is set individually each evening. If an alarm goes off, the light goes from green to flashing red on this panel, indicating where the trouble is. It is also relayed to the police station. If an alarm is disconnected for any reason the alarm will not set, but instead the light flashes yellow."

"But all these lights are green," Ernie pointed out. "Shouldn't one be yellow?"

"I suppose it should," she answered curiously.

Nigel had already anticipated the question and had begun to slowly pace back and forth, looking from the panel to the Pissarro and mumbling to himself. "Why would someone bypass the motion sensor on that painting?"

Lily, in the meantime, had been examining the panel the Pissarro was hanging on. Along that wall were three panels. Each recessed two inches back from the pillars that divided them. A painting hung on each, with the Manet being in the middle and the Pissarro on the panel to its left.

"Where is the Seine in relation to that wall?" Lily asked, stepping back and pointing at the wall she was just examining.

Marie thought for a moment, and then replied, "If you were to walk through that wall and turn to your left the Seine would be about twenty meters ahead of you."

"What are you getting at Lily?" asked Patterson.

"As I mentioned on the plane, this was originally the Gare d'Orsay," Lily began, "a train station built in the late 1890's. I believe we're standing directly above where the tracks were. It only lasted thirty years as a station and soon fell into decay. Eventually the track and platform areas were filled in and in the 1970's the transformation into the museum it is today began."

"*Absolument!*" Marie cheered, very much impressed with Lily's knowledge of the museum.

"I believe one of the forgotten features of that once grand station," added Nigel, motioning for Ernie to join him at the panel where the Pissarro was hanging, "was the access tunnel for transferring baggage from the Seine to the train platform. If Lily's research is correct, it would certainly explain why someone might want to disable the motion detector on this particular painting."

Ernie and Nigel put their shoulders into it and the panel slowly and silently swung open, revealing a dark hallway, which did in fact curve around to the left.

"Brilliant!" exclaimed Patterson. "Brilliant."

Everyone else was speechless, including the *prefect*. Nigel and Ernie stepped back, allowing the others to peer inside. The smooth marble walls reflected the light in the gallery, revealing the grandeur of a long forgotten, inlaid marble floor. Just inside the opening they could make out the handle of an old baggage trolley.

"What do you think of that, Bisquets?" Nigel slapped him lightly on the back.

"I'd say Jackie-boy is a right clever git!" Ernie replied, glancing back inside for a second look.

Marie was stunned, trying her best to speak but she looked over at Patterson and nothing came out. Jean-Paul smiled and shook his head in amazement. After a few moments he asked the guard to locate torches for them.

Discovering the hallway was exciting enough but they could hardly contain themselves over the prospect of following it into the past...especially Lily. She had no intention of waiting any longer than she had to and strolled right in, pulling Ernie along as she walked by.

"Don't you want to wait for the torches?" asked Nigel, watching as they disappeared around the corner.

There was silence as they all waited for her response. Nigel stepped closer to the opening and was surprised by Ernie, who reappeared, very animated, indicating he should follow him directly.

"What is it, Bisquets?" Nigel asked softly, being cautious of whether he needed to be quiet but motioning for the others to follow along as he spoke.

"We found something, squire!" Ernie whispered in a coarse low voice. "It's Miller, and he's asleep!"

Twenty-Eight

TOO MUCH SLEEP IS NOT A GOOD THING

FOR A MOMENT all was silent as Patterson, Marie, Jean-Paul and Nigel stood staring at Ernie, and then at each other, trying to validate what they'd just heard. Ernie saw the confusion on their faces, but before he could repeat the statement Nigel blurted it out for him, much louder than he should have.

"Miller's asleep in there?" he cried, then slapped both hands over his mouth in an effort to keep any other cries from escaping.

Ernie just nodded his head with a big smile and disappeared once more down the hallway, waving for them to follow. The hallway was dark, but only up to where it turned to the left and then sloped downwards. As the group passed the baggage trolley and rounded the corner they could see a dimly lit room ahead with the silhouette of Lily standing in the opening. In their excitement they wasted no time at all catching up to Ernie, who had been following along the wall of the corridor. When they reached Lily, and stood there looking into the room before them, it was hard to say who was more surprised and at what.

The room was remarkably dry and comfortable for being below ground, and one could just make out the drone of the cars on the Rue de Bellechasse above. It was dimly lit, with only half of what were apparently the original wall sconces alight. Despite its utilitarian purpose this one time baggage staging area had matching cast iron pillars and the same decorative stucco appointments of the adjoining platform, though the ceiling was much lower.

At the far end of the room was an ornate set of cast iron doors; about four feet high and shaped like an elongated, gothic arch.

They were recessed into the thick stone wall and secured at the top and bottom with heavy slide bolts. These doors were visible from the Seine, but they'd long been believed to be sealed shut and the cavity behind filled in during the station's transformation into a museum. If they were noticed at all from the river it was for their decorative aesthetics and not for any purpose related to the museum.

As astonished as they were with the room itself, what was on the walls all but dropped their chins the remainder of the way to the marble floor they stood on. There, hanging in the quiet solitude of this forgotten room along the wall to the left were a complete set of paintings from the Impressionist's Gallery at the other end of the hallway; save for a blank spot were Manet's *Le Fifre* had apparently hung. Among those represented were Monet, Pissarro, Sisley and Boudin. Manet commanded the space with no fewer than three of his finest works, including the portrait of Émile Zola who was curiously looking over his visitors.

"What can this be?" Marie whispered.

"It would appear," said Patterson, leaning down close to Marie, "our friend *Monsieur* Miller has been a very busy little man these past years."

"You mean these are all forgeries?" she asked.

"If I knows old Jackie-boy," Ernie said, leaning close to Marie's other ear, "I'd put a hundred quid on these being the originals."

Marie was speechless. She looked up at Patterson, who smiled and nodded his head in agreement. The others were also captivated by the paintings...so much so that if it hadn't been for the raspy wheeze of his breathing, they all could have easily overlooked the other occupant of the room.

Over in the far corner on a small settee, just to the right of a set of access doors, was Jackie Miller, fast asleep with his arms folded over his chest and a faded patchwork cover over his legs. He had a very content look on his face as his chest heaved up and down from the cadence of his breathing. Whatever he was dreaming, he seemed most pleased with it.

They approached and Nigel gave the leg of the settee a few light taps, but Miller didn't stir. Nigel did it again slightly harder, and this time it prompted a response.

Miller smacked his lips a few times and slowly opened one eye. With only a squint, and without reaction, he gazed up at the five people standing over him. He stared at them for a moment and then just as slowly closed his eye again.

As Nigel prepared to give the settee a more forceful kick, Miller's breathing abruptly stopped and his look of contentment turned to one of confusion. This time one eyebrow slowly rose, pulling the eye open with it—giving the appearance that if he peeked maybe what he thought he saw would be nothing more than an apparition worthy of a Dickens' novel. But it wasn't to be. With a sorrowful cringe on his face he slowly opened both eyes and exhaled.

"All right," Nigel said, pulling the cover off his legs, "up with you, now."

Miller was so surprised to see them that it appeared he all but forgot where they were. He sat up, cleared his throat and began to brush out the wrinkles from his shirt. Jean-Paul was tapping his foot, irritated over Miller's nonchalant attitude, but the rest waited patiently for him to speak. Marie finally sat down on the settee next to him.

"I don't understand, Jacques," she said, stopping his grooming by taking his hand.

"I just wanted them for myself," he replied with a sad smile.

"But how did you find this room?" she hesitated as she spoke, looking around the room. "How long have you been here?"

Miller sat back, brushed at the last of his wrinkles and began. "Thomas Fournier told me about this room years ago. It was when I first started restoring frames for the museum." He looked at her thoughtfully and continued. "You would have been a schoolgirl at the time. I had already established myself as a restorer, and a respected one at that."

"Restorer or forger?" Lily asked smugly, reminding Miller that they were there and this wasn't a social visit.

"Well, yes," he said, gazing up at the group with no sign of remorse, "there is that little sideline of mine. I had quite a go of it, too. At least until that damn woman showed up."

"I assume you're referring to Phynley Paine?" asked Patterson.

"Yeah, that's right," Miller replied, nodding his head. "She's an evil one, that one, and I wasn't about to let her nick that Manet and sell it off to that bloke of hers. He owes me from another job I did—"

He stopped suddenly, realizing he was probably saying a little more than he should to this mixed crowd.

Jean-Paul had been on his mobile, but quickly snapped it shut and said to Miller, "Please, continue. It will be a few minutes before my officers arrive and I certainly don't want to interrupt your story."

"Like I was saying..." Miller slowly turned back toward Marie. "Thomas Fournier told me about the room. He was part of the construction crew that worked on the remodel of this building. He said this was going to be a reception room. Those iron doors were going to be replaced with windows overlooking the Seine; all very posh, I think. After they started work on the room one of the directors of the project got his knickers in a knot about it being a security risk, and all that, and work stopped. Fournier and a few others were instructed to seal the iron doors and put up a temporary wall until they could change that bloke's mind. Once the museum was open, the other directors lost interest in the idea and no one pursued it any further. Eventually, the only person who remembered anything about the room was Fournier, but he stopped talking about it because people just laughed at him, saying it was an old man's ghost story."

"Everyone except you?" Nigel asked through a very wide grin.

"That's right," Miller snapped back. He glared for a moment at Nigel, but turned once again to Marie and finished. "I thought about what he had said and I decided to check it out for myself. Going through the museum was out of the question so I went down to the landing on the Seine. I was surprised at how easily the doors pried open and within minutes I was inside. I found it much the way you see it now, except I did clean it up a bit and add a chair or two. I'm sure you understand, Bisquets."

"I understand you almost got us killed," Ernie said sternly, wagging his finger at Miller as if he was a petulant child.

"And I would of felt bad about that," replied Miller quietly, looking down and brushing at his shirt once more.

Marie shook her head and stood up. She began pacing, stopping on occasion to look over at the paintings hanging on the wall. She was upset, but it was difficult to say over what. Finally, she walked back over to Miller, who was still brushing at the wrinkles on his shirt.

"Are . these . the . originals?" she demanded in an official tone, pausing between each word so as to be perfectly clear about the question.

Miller just nodded his head, never looking up at her.

"But why put the Fifer back on the wall in the middle of the night?" Ernie asked, sitting down next to Miller and pointing at the blank space on the wall across the room. "You should have just walked it right in the front door."

"I suppose you're right," Miller said with a slight laugh. "A bit of theatrics, really. I wanted to get your attention away from the other paintings so I thought if it just reappeared if would keep you guessing for weeks over how I did it. Once you got tired of trying to figure it out I'd just paint another copy and complete my set."

Nigel cleared his throat. "It would appear you seriously underestimated our deductive abilities."

"So it would," replied Miller, glancing up at the group with more of a sneer than a smile. "But no harm done. You've got your painting back," Miller said, pointing at Marie—"and the police got Rhodes," he continued, pointing at Jean-Paul—"and I would be more than happy to fill in the details of his dastardly career for you...for a price, that is."

"Aren't you forgetting something?" Nigel pointed over his shoulder at the wall of paintings behind him.

"A bit of bad luck, that," Miller said thoughtfully. He stood up and walked over to the paintings, stopping at each of them as if saying goodbye.

Footsteps could be heard coming down the corridor from the museum. The museum guard from earlier appeared with five French policemen in tow. He stopped suddenly at the entrance to the room, looked around and scratched his head in amazement. Jean-Paul gave a nod and pointed at Miller. Two of the officers walked over and took him by the arms. A third officer took Miller's coat from a chair and handed it to him. Miller took one last look at the row of paintings and smiled at the group as he was quietly led out of the room.

"Brilliant, everyone, brilliant!" said Patterson, patting Ernie softly on the shoulder. "I commend you all on a job well done. I would say the alarm problems the museum has been experiencing have been solved, also. Genius, really. Set an alarm off once and everybody comes running. Set it off again and the response is the same but with less enthusiasm. Set it off a third time and you can do whatever you need to do. What better way to replace a painting with a forgery than getting the museum to ignore the alarms you set off."

"I am forever in your debt," Marie joined in, not sure who to hug first. She walked from one to the other, kissing them on both cheeks, but stopped before kissing Ernie. "I especially wish to thank you, Ernie. You've done a very noble thing, and at great risk to your own life. I almost lost something more valuable to me than any painting—my friends. I told Patterson you were a lucky man to have someone like him watching over you, but I was wrong. It is he who is the lucky one to have you."

After a kiss on each cheek, Marie stepped back and gave her head a confirming nod.

"Well, you will stay?" Marie asked, turning to Patterson. "I'm sure the directors will have many questions."

"Yes," he replied with a wink, and then looked over at Nigel.

"As exciting as that sounds," said Nigel, looking back at Lily and Ernie with raised eyebrows, "I believe I can speak for the three of us by saying five is a crowd. If you don't mind, we'll just find a spot for a bit of breakfast and then get the first train back to London."

"Of course," Marie agreed with a smile.

And with that said, Lily, Nigel and Ernie had a very enjoyable breakfast just down the street from the Musée d'Orsay, and soon found themselves on a train heading back to London. Ernie was noticeably quiet during the return trip, but Nigel and Lily understood and didn't disturb him.

At one point Nigel remarked about Phynley Paine taking his book, but Lily answered saying it was just a book and that it just as easily could have been his life. Nigel thought about it for a moment and finally agreed.

"So, this is what you do every day?" Ernie asked abruptly.

Lily and Nigel were surprised by the question. They looked at each other and broke into a hearty laugh.

"Not at all, old man," Nigel said, slapping Ernie on the knee. "Most weeks we're trudging through a jungle or digging about in a dusty old tomb. You just happened to catch us on a week where a few people were trying to kill us. It doesn't happen often, but it does break up the monotony."

"Well, squire," Ernie started, giving his head a good scratch, "if the offer still stands, I accept. I don't know why you'd want a bloke like me, but I accept."

"Excellent!" Nigel replied. "You've made a wise choice, my boy. Allow me to be the first to officially welcome you to our little club. Now, first thing tomorrow we'll get you heavily insured."

Ernie's eyes opened wide and his mouth dropped. Lily did what she could to keep a straight face, but she couldn't help but laugh, then smacked Nigel on the arm.

"He's just kidding, Ernie," Lily said with a reassuring wink. "Marie was right, you know. *We* are the lucky ones. Welcome Ernie Bisquets. Welcome to the East London Adventurers Club!"

The End

Look for Ernie Bisquets and the East London Adventurers Club to return soon in

"Rook, Rhyme and Sinker"

R. MICHAEL PHILLIPS

R. Michael Phillips is a classically trained artist who has been painting for over 30 years. He has done numerous commissions, illustrations for national products and co-authored and illustrated a children's book. Writing was always something he enjoyed doing, but never had the opportunity to pursue seriously until now. By combining his creative talents with his passion for art and antiquities, he conceived the fictional world of the East London Adventurers Club. His first mystery, *ALONG CAME A FIFER*, is the result of these efforts. Michael lives in a historic community in southeastern Pennsylvania with his wife Janice and son Christopher.

New Releases by Tsylett Press...

DAYS OF SMOKE
Historical Fiction - WWII
Mark Ozeroff

DAYS OF SMOKE offers a compelling, mold-shattering view of World War II and the Holocaust from the unique perspective of German Luftwaffe pilot Hans Udet. Across aerial battlefields ranging over much of Europe, Hans progresses from a naïve young Messerschmidt pilot to an ace of increasing rank and responsibility. But unfolding events pit Hans' love of the Fatherland against his natural compassion for humanity.

ISBN 1-934337-44-7

AS THE WIND WALKS
Historical Fiction - Civil War
Harvey Tate

This is a story of two men, their wars and loves in two different eras. David Werner is a ninety-four year old veteran of the American Civl War. His great grandson, Edmund, faces maturity in 1940s Baltimore. While his great grandfather recounts his time in the Union Army, after enlisting at the age of fourteen, Edmund wonders about his own future, standing, as he does,on the brink of another crucial time in America's history... World War II. The candle burns low for David, but Edmund's flame and passion are just igniting—not only for war, but for a remarkable girl...

ISBN 1-934337-53-6

AARYN OF THE HIGH ISLANDS
Fantasy
Glenn Swetman

There is treachery afoot in Randast. An evil plot to harm the Pantocrator, Alan the Just, is being hatched and Aaryn is summoned from the High Islands to thwart those involved. Using his various magical talents and powers, he must ferret out the conspirators and bring them to justice.

Before he reaches the City, however, he finds himself rescuing a mysterious young woman, Jordana, and a dubious thief named Zompre from a band of vengeful gypsies. Together the trio enter the imperial city on the eve of the Banquet of the Gathering and Aaryn enlists the help of Zompre to gather the information he requires. But he soon learns the evil he pursues is more dangerous than he imagined.

ISBN: 1-934337-53-6

GOTHIC SPRING
Gothic
Caroline Miller

Victorine Ellsworth knows something about the death of the vicar's wife... but what? Is she the killer? Or the next victim?

Victorine is a young woman poised at the edge of sexual awakening, and cursed with more talent and imagination than society will tolerate. The conflict between her desire, and the restrictions that rule her life, lead to tragic circumstances.

ISBN: 1-934337-67-6

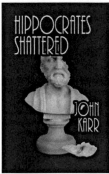

HIPPOCRATES SHATTERED
Medical Thriller
John Karr

Andrew Raynorr M.D. was forced from his practice by a managed care corporation. When he loses his family, his vengeance turns deadly. He creates a virus, one that causes the body's own genes to unleash an explosive leukemia, and targets managed care executives.

Bridget Devereaux, a young intern at Chambers Hospital, suspects something strange about the strain of leukemia in recent admissions...the patient dies within days. Though she finds no support within the upper echelons of hospital management, she researches the blood cancer and traces the catalyst back to Raynorr.

But Raynorr is aware Bridget has found him out. Now, not only her career, but her very life is in jeopardy.

ISBN: 1-934337-39-0

CROSSROADS
Suspense/Thriller
Steven Nedelton

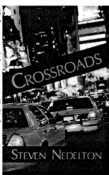

Tallman's received a new assignment. He's not certain he believes in this new secret technology, but he's only the handler. It's the men under his command who have to perform. But he wonders about the Russian, Mikhail. They say he's the best in the field. They say he's defected...

She knows her supervisor Sokolov doesn't trust Mikhail. He believes Mikhail has defected and is revealing Soviet secrets to the Americans. She knows he will destroy Mikhail if he can find him. But Tatiana will keep him safe. Sokolov doesn't realize the power she possesses...

ISBN: 1-934337-55-2

LADY LUCK
Western/Historical Fiction
Julie Lence

Lucas Weston isn't too pleased when he's roped into escorting Missy Morgan back to her home in San Francisco. Fate has dealt Missy more losing hands than she cares to remember. Against her will, she's drawn to Lucas' blue eyes and honesty. Would it be so bad to put her trust in him? The odds say yes...

ISBN 1-934337-57-9

BRIDGED BY LOVE
Historical Fiction
Patricia Lieb

"Bridged by Love," by Patricia Lieb - Spring Hill resident Lieb has written a historical adventure set in the late 1880s in Texarkana, a city that straddles the Texas-Arkansas line. Lieb draws on a bounty of historical knowledge to craft a tale of two women - one native American, the other white - linked together in a fight against injustice. ~ *Tampa Tribune*

ISBN 1-934337-41-2 (Print)

Other Recent Releases...

DEMON LORD
Dark Fantasy
Jason Jeffery

Talbot McCreary is dead...gone... reborn as a half-demon named Heretix. And the demon world now has complete access to our world. Alongside his friends and ex-wife, Heretix must find a way to close the gateway and prevent the Demon Lord from crossing over with his massive army to enslave the human race.

ISBN 1-934337-59-5

FORTUNE'S PRIDE
Historical Romance - Americana
Michele Stegman

As long as no one knows who Irish really is, she will be safe. But Tyrus Fortune seems determined to uncover all her secrets. Can she fully love him without revealing her true self to him? And if she does, will it also put him and his family in danger?

ISBN 1-934337-24-2

MURDERS IN THE SWAMPLAND
True Crime
Patricia Lieb

A collection of true murder cases and crimes that took place in the swamplands of Central Florida from the late 1970's to early 1990's. Reported by Patricia Lieb for The Daily Sun-Journal, Ms. Lieb includes personal notes from her own journals as well as 2007 updates on many of the convicted felons.

ISBN 1-934337-46-3

GEE-WHIZ MEETS S.H.A.F.T.
Romantic Spy Thriller
Valerie J. Patterson

Milton Gee is investigating the death of his partner, Chaz Whiz. He never could have guessed the investigation would lead to his recruitment by the UU to fight the worldwide evil organization The S.H.A.F.T. Or that he would come to face to face with The S.H.A.F.T's powerful leader...SHE.

ISBN 1-934337-49-8

𝔗sylett 𝔓ress titles
- ebook and trade-sized paperbacks -
can be purchased
wholesale
through our secure online catalog:

www. 𝔗sylett𝔓ress.com

Asylett ebook titles can also be found online at:
Coffee Time Romance
www.coffeetimeromance.com
Fictionwise
www.Fictionwise.com

Asylett trade-sized paperback titles are listed with
Ingram, Baker & Taylor and Bowkers
and can be ordered through:

Amazon
Barnes & Noble
Books A Million
Powells
Target
Walmart